SEE YOU at the STATION

SEE YOU at the STATION

L.M. O'NEAL

urlink
PRINT & MEDIA

See You at The Station

1603 Capitol Ave., Suite 310 Cheyenne, Wyoming USA 82001
1-888-980-6523 | admin@urlinkpublishing.com

URLink Print and Media is committed to excellence in the publishing industry.

Published in the United States of America

Library of Congress Control Number: 2021925360
ISBN 978-1-68486-061-6 (Paperback)
ISBN 978-1-68486-062-3 (Digital)

22.10.21

To my mother, Katherine O'Neal, and my late father, James O'Neal.

To all people handed a lemon in life who tried to make lemonade.

All of you and more kept me going.
Thank you.

ACKNOWLEDGMENT

In writing most works of fiction, truth is often its basis. This can be said for *See You at the Station* as well. The work and tolerance endured by persons other than the author were essential in the creation of this novel. I give all thanks to God, his earthly followers, and particularly to the following:

- ❖ My brother and sister-in-law, Thomas and René O'Neal, for repeatedly telling me it was good, but it could be better;

- ❖ Roni Freels for her endless listening and patience to what seemed to be endless rewrites and her encouragement to push on;

- ❖ Rosy Holcomb for being a perfect sounding-board and friend, and

- ❖ My mother, Katherine O'Neal, for giving me permission and encouragement to keep working toward my dream.

To all mentioned and unmentioned, I say, *thank you.*

WARNING

DO NOT ATTEMPT TO READ THIS BOOK OR ANY WRITINGS BY L. M. O'NEAL WHILE OPERATING MACHINERY, COOKING, OR CARING FOR SMALL CHILDREN. THIS BOOK IS A COMPLETE WORK OF FICTION. ANY SIMILARITIES IN LOCATIONS, CHARACTERS, OR EVENTS ARE PURELY COINCIDENTAL.

FOREWORD

Gloved Hands

How dark is the darkness,
When nothing can be seen.
How bright is the brightness?
When evil cast its beam.

The mind is held prisoner,
Encased in its fear.
The guidance is misleading,
The voice is not clear.

The touch is not tender.
Neither soft nor sweet.
The words from the dragon,
Are filled with deceit.

—L. M. O'Neal

CHAPTER
1

> "How far away is the past if it returns to warn us of the future?"
>
> —L. M. O'Neal

"Michael, you're not going to believe this."

"Ricky, you're the mayor. I believe everything politicians say."

"Sure, you do, but this time you really do have to listen to me."

Michael Stone knew Mayor Richard Lloyd could spin a good tale, but today was not the day for time-wasting chats or telephone calls. He had details to round up for the story he was writing. With a deadline drawing near, the wasting of time was something he could not allow, especially today. However, the tone in Mayor Lloyd's voice got his attention. He really wanted to avoid all telephone calls until he'd finished the article, but something in Mayor Lloyd's voice made him delay. Knowing, if he terminated the call now, Mayor Lloyd would call back until he said what was on his mind, Michael decided to let him continue.

"All right, I'm listening. Go ahead."

Mayor Lloyd, having captured Michael's ear, continued, "As you know, I eat breakfast most mornings down here at the café, and I did the same this morning. Well, Sheriff Long and I placed our orders, and we were sitting here waiting, then in walks this fellow. He stops inside the door and just looks around."

Michael, beginning to feel he'd made a mistake, said, "I hope you are going somewhere with this. I do have other things to do."

"Yes, I am. Just listen," replied Mayor Lloyd a little too quickly.

"Long and I both noticed he appeared to be looking for someone. Well, he finally comes in, takes a seat only three tables from us, and orders coffee. Then he just sits there staring out the window."

Michael, now becoming annoyed, made it known to Mayor Lloyd his patience was running out by first clearing his throat. "Get to the point, Ricky."

"Okay, the point is, he's carrying an old fishing rod."

The mention of the fishing rod was enough to convince Michael this telephone call needed to be over quickly and in such a way Mayor Lloyd would not call back today with another fish story.

"Ricky, this is Lake City. We are a town on the edge of a lake. Sooner or later, someone is bound to show up at the café with a fishing rod."

Michaels' annoyance came through loud and clear. Now it was Mayor Lloyd's turn to be annoyed.

"The fishing rod is not the point. The point is he looked identical to Bill Rayller. He didn't just look like him, he walked like him, and he even wore the same kind of hat. I'm telling you, I could swear it was Bill Rayller."

Michael's annoyance suddenly evaporated at the mention of Bill Rayller. It caused a shiver to run his spine.

"Did you or the sheriff ask who he was?"

"No. The sheriff had to go, and I didn't know what kind of person this was that would make himself up to look like Bill. For all I know, he could have been some escapee or something. Oh, one more thing, when he left, he did what Bill always did, he left a fish for a tip.

"Look, Mike, I have to go. Sheriff Long just walked in, and I need to talk to him about this. Michael, I thought you might want to know, so let me know if you can make sense of all this. Call me later, okay, buddy?"

Before Michael could ask more questions, Mayor Lloyd disconnected, leaving Michael Stone holding the telephone.

Michael forgot his small local newspaper, *The Republic*, purchased by him and his wife, Kathryn. When they purchased the newspaper, their daughter Michelle was only five years old. He did not comprehend his office, where he had written stacks of articles over the years. Michael sat behind the desk inherited from the previous owner, engulfed in his thoughts. He did not acknowledge the terminated call until the off-hook signal shrieked. The annoying sound quickly brought him back to reality.

Staring at the receiver, Michael wondered why he held it.

Absentmindedly, he returned the receiver to its cradle. With eyes focused on nothing of present, Michael remained captured in thought.

Mayor Lloyd could not have seen Mr. Rayller. He's been dead several years. However, if Mayor Lloyd says he saw who he thinks he saw, that would contradict Mr. Rayller's death. On the other hand, would it? The entire Rayller family is dead: two by car accident, one by a heart attack, and Mr. Rayller's granddaughter was murdered.

Stirred by the telephone call from Mayor Lloyd, the memory of the Rayller family stood prominent in his mind. Michael, years earlier, had learned to listen and trust his gut feelings. His gut now told him this was happening for a particular reason.

The memory of Mr. Rayller's granddaughter, Shelia Rayller, again reasserted itself. The nagging questions, once forced to the rear of his mind, burst forward from the slight crack in the door of memory caused by Mayor Lloyd. Its return came like a tidal wave, sweeping aside everything in his mind as the memories tore through his conscious thought. The sense of urgency increased with such intensity that it was frightening. Forcing himself to calm down, he struggled to organize his thoughts.

All of this is abnormal. I have to think logically if I'm going to make sense of what Lloyd said.

Feeling the increasing tension in his body, Michael walked to the bank of file cabinets along the far wall in his office. The files contained all the hard copies of articles written since his purchase of the newspaper. Within the files were not only articles, but also notes, photos, and correspondences.

Duplicated files were stored out of town for safety reasons. The second location offered a level of protection to the paper in the event of fire or some other disaster. It offered no such protection for Michael's mind.

The horrific stories were always there, just below the surface, waiting to remind him. No newspaper morgue or file cabinets could lock away the most horrific events that lingered in Michael's memory.

Each file cabinet contained three to five years of articles. The filing system of Michael's own design served to confuse uninvited eyes. Using the year his daughter graduated from high school as a reference date, Michael knew where to find what he wanted. He quickly drew out the index sheet, scanned for the dates and coded numbers, and reinserted the index sheet to its proper place. He then removed the desired coded files.

The selected files contained the gruesome discovery of the body, the police investigation notes, follow-up, and the cold-trail stories, all concerning Shelia Rayller.

After placing the files on his desk, Michael took his seat and began refreshing his memory with the details. Within the files of articles, notes, and the pictures resided his torment. Within these folders was hidden every parent's greatest fear. Michael thanked God his child had been spared, and then prepared his mind to face the results of a demon. With a heavy heart, he opened a file.

First was an article he had constructed from his notes at the crime scene. He glanced at it, and then laid it aside face down. This particular folder contained interviews with the sheriff and deputy at the scene. He scanned the interview notes he had made while talking with Shelia's neighbors, classmates, and her grandfather. Shelia had no surviving parents, having lost them in an auto accident years earlier. Michael then saw the pictures.

He himself, the photographer, had time enough to take only four shots before the deputy stopped him. When the camera clicked and flashed on the fourth frame, the picture was of the tall grasses to the right of Shelia's body. When Michael recognized the victim, he saw through the eye of the camera, his mind could no longer function as a photographer or reporter. This victim was not just another story.

Having had many years of experience covering crime scenes, he thought he was hardened to any effect of seeing the dead. He failed to consider the impact of seeing the body of someone he had known, murdered. The reality of who this young girl had been caused him to let the camera drop from his eye as it snapped the fourth and final frame. The crime scene caused him to see not a story but rather, a dead child. This was a teenager but still a child.

The body that lay before him was a girl near his daughter's age. She was someone he had known. She had been an acquaintance to his daughter and the family. She, at one time, had been pretty, petite, and very lively, with large curious eyes, chestnut hair, and a big smile. Now, she lay dead in a section of tall grass.

Her killer had left her hands tied behind her back, allowing her only avenue of escape to be through death's door. Her face beaten to the point she practically defied recognition. Her hair, once alive and bouncy with as much life as she, now hosted the color of dried blood.

One photo showed Shelia Rayller's picked, ripped, and torn tan skirt and matching short-sleeved blouse. At a glance, her clothes appeared to have been a new fad, featuring tattered clothing. This could have been assumed except for the blood. The hundreds of picks, small rips, and snags in her garments possessed bloodstains. The cuts and gashes in her skin appeared to have come from hundreds of small razor blades. Each nick and gash in her skin bled, causing the tan colored outfit to become a dull brownish-red color.

Her skirt lay high along her thighs with its top portion torn at the waistband. According to the county medical examiner's report, which Michael later saw, she had been sexually assaulted. The results of this gruesome act of evil had survived in his mind, refusing to be pushed away. Even without the aid of the pictures, he saw again the scene and was equally sickened.

He was not aware of the tears running down his face, the same as they had the morning Shelia was found. His tears were as much for her grandfather as they were for Shelia. Mr. Rayller, having been the one to discover Shelia's body, was not spared the sight or the impact. The finality of finding his only grandchild murdered, and in such a mutilated state, magnified her destroyed future.

It had taken twenty minutes of pleading with Mr. Rayller before he would release his granddaughter and reposition her the way she was found. It was clear to everyone that Mr. Rayller felt he had lost the last person in the world who was of any value to him.

As Michael reflected on the pain and loss, he did not hear Michelle come into his office. As she did every morning, Michelle brought her father coffee before the morning meeting. She now stood behind him, looking at the pictures.

The sight of the pictures gave her tremors. She spilled a small amount of hot coffee on her father's arm.

Michael watched the droplets run through the hair on his arm, then down in a jagged direction toward his elbow. He didn't feel the heat from the coffee and cared even less. Captured in the past, it was several seconds before Michael became aware of Michelle's presence.

Michael didn't know how long Michelle viewed the photographs from over his shoulder. He did know, he had promised himself, that she would never have to relive that period in her life again. But at this moment, she was seeing it all. Michelle, following her morning routine, happened to be at the right place at the wrong time. Her intense stare at the photos and her trembles were easy to explain. Shelia had been an acquaintance and a classmate to her. The fact that the murderer—the monster—had never been caught, forced Michelle to live with a different reality. She was unable to save Shelia from this heinous crime.

Michael hated the pain Michelle endured daily, and he was well aware pain was not limited to his household alone.

CHAPTER 2

Near the northwest side of the county, a hot air mass began its collision with a cold front coming from the north. Enough difference existed in temperature to create thunderstorms. The clashing of the two air masses fed the building thunderclouds into dangerous levels. As a result, a tornado was being born. Twelve miles away, thunder was unmistakable.

In a small weed infested vegetable garden, a young boy worked feverishly to finish another of his chores before the rain started. He worked quickly but awkwardly with a weeding hoe. In his haste, barely missing the delicate stems of vegetable plants, his focus drifted between what he was doing and what could happen if he did not complete his chores. When finished, he knew there would be no praise. He knew the words, "Well done," would never come from his parents. Life had already taught him early to expect only condemnation and ridicule.

He was certain if the gardening was not finished before it rained, his mother would do bad and painful things to him again. The sting of being called stupid and lazy regularly drilled its way into his mind. If she felt so inclined, she would grind him into the dirt while telling him how ugly he was. She often screamed at the top of her lungs, "What a mistake it was to have you!" In her desire to inflict severe emotional pain, she would tell him, "I should have killed you before you were born."

He learned about abortion in school. Now, he believed she would have preferred an abortion rather than having him live. Hearing those words and understanding the meaning was pain, as if someone extinguished a lit cigarette directly on his heart. Without exception, every time he heard or thought the words, he felt the pain anew.

His mother's cruel words were not her only tool for inflicting pain and injury. She often struck him with whatever she had in her hand or could reach. Timmy had felt the sting of a hot fry pan, wire clothes hangers, pieces of wood, and many other objects. Her weapon of choice, however, was a loop of stiff wire wrapped around a wooden handle, in the shape of a tennis racquet but larger. It had been made for beating dirt out of floor rugs in the old days, but now it had a different use.

When he was beaten with it, the bite was painful even through his clothes. He would do anything she wanted to keep her from reaching for "the wire" as she called it.

His father offered no emotional support or protection. As Timmy's lot in life would have it, his father often returned home drunk and in a particularly evil mood. He would do all the things his mother did to him. At times, he hurt him even more.

Usually after his father and mother fought regarding his father's drinking, his father would beat his mother with the wire or his fist, and then bring the anger to their son. Two years earlier, just such an event had occurred with the beating, concluding with a back injury to their child. One blow to the back of the eight-year-old caused him to be unable to sit up for two days. He still felt occasional back pains.

When his parents decided he had been bad and they wanted to have their idea of fun, Timmy would be thrown into the storm cellar. Once inside, the doors would be locked behind him from the outside. His confinement had no predetermined time limit. It could be for a few hours or for as long as a whole day.

In the cellar, Timmy had no light, seldom food or water. By the age of seven, he had learned to hide meager provisions for his stay in the storm cellar. These few provisions helped stave off the pains of hunger. He was confined to the cellar on a regular basis for minor and major offenses.

The storm cellar was equipped with double doors and possessed handles on both sides. To lock Timmy in, they only needed a piece of wood or something inserted through the outside handles. This place of darkness and isolation soon became Timmy's dungeon of nightmares.

Timmy's bed and bedroom were usually dirty. His mother often said housework was for the maid. The maid never arrived, and Timmy did not attempt cleaning the room himself. His bed, ignored for weeks at a time, seldom offered the comfort of clean sheets. To Timmy, the dirt floor of the storm cellar was only slightly less comfortable than his bedroom inside the house.

In the storm cellar, he had no bed, no blankets, and no pillow, only a dirt floor. When the door closed, the place built for food storage and taking shelter from severe storms became his prison. When used for that purpose, Timmy often cried himself to sleep on the dirt floor.

When he wasn't crying or sleeping, he watched the shadows created in the darkness. Shadows and sounds combined with the smell of rotting fruits and vegetables shaped the world in Timmy's dungeon. He knew when he got old enough it would be his job to clear out the rot. Therefore, he suffered quietly and waited.

Just the thought of the storm cellar put fear in his heart and a tremble in his hands. He didn't notice the grapefruit-sized rock lying in the row behind him. Stepping back quickly, his bare heel struck the rock, tumbling him backward.

As a result, a jarring crash to the ground was not painful and would have been fun if not for the damage caused by his fall. Timmy had fallen on the row of corn he'd just finished weeding. Feeling the roughness of the leaves through his worn shirt, he lay on his back, giving a sideward stare at the cornstalk nearest his head. Beneath him lay three broken stalks.

Getting to his feet, Timmy turned to look down, inspecting the damage. The cornstalks were cleanly broken off at their bases. He knew there was no saving them. Knowing the likelihood the broken corn would be noticed, Timmy quickly saw the makings of another beating.

If Mom or Dad see this, I'm going to get killed, he shouted in his mind.

On hands and knees, he gathered the broken stalks in his arms with the intention of throwing them into the nearby woods, but when he stood to his feet, he saw her.

His mother stood statue-still, holding the screen door open with her body, watching him. Having been caught in the middle of the act was bad enough, but his mother had the wire in one hand, bouncing its loop off her other hand. From ten yards away, Timmy clearly saw the look on her face. His young eyes focused on her frown and the up-twist at one corner of her mouth. Then she spoke. She did not say words of encouragement but instead, she spat out words he'd heard repeatedly in his young life.

"You stupid, lazy sack of dog crap. Don't move an inch."

With that said, she stormed out the doorway, charging across the yard and into the garden.

Grabbing Timmy by his hair, she began striking him on any part of his body the wire could land. Timmy dropped the cornstalks and attempted to avoid the striking wire, but with no success.

He tried not to cry, but the pain was too severe. Then a thought occurred to him: if he cried, she would stop the beatings. He soon discovered this was also a bad idea. Her angry strikes to his body continued. Timmy did not understand why his mother enjoyed inflicting pain on him.

He soon realized he was being rough-handled all the way to the storm cellar. In sight of the cellar doors, he began to cry and beg more vigorously. Hoping against hope he would not be put into the place he feared most. His pleas were ignored.

With one door already open, she shoved him in with a hard strike to his back. He stumbled down the three steps into the darkness. Slamming the door closed, Phyllis smiled an evil smile without remorse or regret. Timmy's mother slid the wooden lock into place in the outside handles. Pleased with herself and Timmy's pleas for mercy, she returned to the house. She had made plans to go out for the evening.

In the dark, caged like an animal, he cried, not only from the pain of the wire but also from wanting to feel the love other kids had. He had no idea what love really felt like—he'd only heard about it. He could not remember experiencing a warm embrace from his mother. Sitting on the dirt floor in the dark, the only light Timmy had came from a crack between the two doors. In the darkness of the storm cellar, his dungeon, Timmy cried.

Locked away like a prisoner in a faraway land, he was alone, scared, and hungry. Isolated from the outside world, Timmy made his apology.

"Mom, I didn't mean to break the corn. Mom, I didn't mean to break the corn."

Getting to his feet, he walked the few feet across the dirt floor and stood on the bottom step to the exit. With his head nearly touching the doors, he took his small hands and gripped the two inside handles of the doors. He wanted to push the doors open but he knew if they opened and his mother was waiting, she would beat him again and throw him back in. With tears running down his dirty face, leaving clean trails, he repeated his apology.

"Mom, I didn't mean to break the corn. Mom, I didn't mean to break the corn." Then finally, he spoke in a whisper. "Mommy, I didn't mean to break the corn."

Holding the door handles, looking out through the crack at a sliver of freedom, his apology and weeping went unheard. He wanted to get out of his prison, but he was too afraid to push the door. Fear of another beating stopped him. He was tired, hurting, and felt the welts caused by the wire loop start to rise on his skin. The pain of the welts slowly gave way to soreness. Timmy was only ten years old, just a little boy.

Looking through the crack, as he had done many times before, he heard a whispering, raspy voice say his name.

"Timmy."

Timmy not sure his name had been spoken, held his breath between ragged inhalations, listening. The whispering raspy voice again called his name.

"Timmy."

Timmy turned, looking around in the darkness. He thought he was alone.

After staring through the crack at the outside light, his eyes had to again adjust to the gloom. Looking intently into the darkness, searching for the source of the voice, he could see no one and nothing out of the ordinary.

Timmy felt around for the old wooden bucket he knew would be in the storm cellar. When his hands made the discovery, he grasped it firmly, turning it upside down to use as his stool. Crossing his skinny arms over his knees, he placed his forehead on his arms.

The voice again spoke.

"Timmy, can I be your friend? I need a friend too. Will you be my friend?"

Timmy lifted his head, looking around again and saw he was alone. Through sobbing sniffles, he reminded himself of his mother's words.

"I'm crazy, just like Mom said."

The voice in the darkness seized the opportunity to offer comfort.

"No, you're not crazy. Your parents are just big people. They are being mean to you, and you didn't do anything wrong. You didn't mean to fall over the rock. You didn't mean to break the corn. They're just big people, you know, grown-ups. They treat us kids like that."

Timmy stopped crying. He was considering what he thought to be his imagination. The voice, a bit louder now, spoke again in a hypnotic and rhythmic tone, quieting Timmy's fears and isolation.

"Timmy, I can tell you how to feel better if you want me to. Do you want to feel better?"

"Yeah, I do," Timmy replied.

The voice, having captured his undivided attention, continued.

"I know a game that will make you feel better. Do you want to try it?"

In Timmy's young mind, he could see no danger in talking to a voice in the darkness. He reasoned a friend in the darkness was better than having no friend at all.

"What's the game called?" Timmy asked.

"I call it safe place. You want to play? It's not going to hurt, but it will always make you feel better. Come on, let's play."

Timmy had never heard of such a game. He felt no danger, no threat, and no reason not to go along.

"All right, I'll play."

"Okay. This is how it works," said the voice, continuing on. "What was the most fun place you ever visited in your life?"

Timmy sat quietly trying to recall if he had ever been to a fun place. His young life had not seen very much to call fun and enjoyment. The voice in the darkness probed further. "Did you ever go fishing, or to a playground, or any place that was fun?"

The suggestions were enough to remind Timmy of a short trip he thought he had enjoyed but was not sure. Not able to recall anything better, he settled on that particular occasion.

"I went to the county fair with Mom. She gave me ten dollars and told me to be back at the gate by seven o'clock, but I couldn't tell time, so I was late, and she was real mad."

"Yeah, but did you have fun?"

"Well, yeah, I think so. I liked all the rides, the food, and the games I got to play. I never had so much fun."

"Okay! I want you to first take a deep breath and let it out slowly. Do that three times."

Timmy, happy to have someone to talk with, did as instructed. The voice seemed pleased with what he'd said, and he was eager to receive praise from wherever he could get it. He was surprised to discover he began to feel better. His new friend continued, "Now, take another deep breath, let it out slowly, and remember all the fun you had at the county fair. You should keep doing that for a while."

Timmy, having someone to talk with, continued his breathing exercise, and talked about the fair. They talked for quite a while past sundown and into the night. Timmy, feeling he now had a friend, enjoyed the openness of conversation in the free-flowing easiness of kids.

Hours passed before he heard the wooden block slide from the outside door handles. He watched with relief mingled with fear as a single door opened.

Since the darkness outside was not as severe as the darkness inside, he could see who opened the door.

From the storm cellars dark interior, Timmy looked up at the open doorway. His exit from the darkness was blocked by a giant, his father. Those who knew him couldn't really call him Timmy's dad. The man didn't treat Timmy like a child he wanted but rather like something he enjoyed hurting.

"Come out of there, boy," ordered his father.

Timmy got to his feet and slowly climbed the steps. His father, towering above, looked down at him. Timmy couldn't see his eyes, but he could feel the stare. With eyes of hate and disgust shrouded in the smell of beer and darkness, his father slurred his words.

"I'll teach you to tear up stuff."

Without warning, he struck Timmy with the back of his hand. Timmy fell to the ground in renewed pain. He curled up into the fetal position, trying to protect himself, but there was little protection. He heard the sound of his father's belt slapping as it passed through the belt loops of his jeans. Knowing what was to come next, Timmy tried to curl into an even tighter ball, protecting his head and midsection with his knees and elbows. It took three long seconds before the belt struck. Timmy felt three stinging blows through his clothing.

It did not matter to his father where he struck Timmy, only that he struck him. He didn't care about the pain he caused, he simply enjoyed delivering a beating. The fact that he was drunk aided in his lack of caring.

Timmy's drunken father reached down, grabbed him by his arm, jerked him to his feet, and continued beating him with his belt. Shoving him toward the house, he yelled in an angry drunken slur, "Get in the house."

Timmy, crying from the pain of the belt, the backhand, and the wire hoop he received earlier from his mother, scrambled toward the house. When he reached the screen door to the back porch, he opened it and dashed across the porch. The door that stood before him entered into the kitchen. He rushed in immediately.

His mother, sitting at the kitchen table, turned to look at him when he entered. With no love in her eyes or voice, she said, "Look at yourself. You're a mess."

She ignored the fact that she had helped make him what he was. His father staggered in behind Timmy with the belt still in hand. He slashed Timmy again across his back.

"I will teach you to kill my stuff," he said with even more anger.

With a shout, his father ordered Timmy to his room. This order was not one Timmy would question or even want to. He ran into his own bedroom with his father close at his heels. Once in his bedroom, his father slammed the door behind him. Again, Timmy was in darkness, crying, waiting for more punishment.

Seeing his father had not followed him in, Timmy sat on the floor beside the bed. He was afraid to sit on the bed; if he did, he would get beaten for being dirty and on the bed. Remaining on the floor with his knees pulled up to his chest, he wrapped his arms around his knees. With his forehead lying on his arms, he listened. What he heard was what he nearly always heard when his father came home drunk: another fight.

They shouted angry words at one another, followed by

a dish crashing against the wall. Hearing this added to the ache in his young heart. Timmy then heard his father striking his mother with the belt. Their fighting scared him, causing more tears. Between the soft sobs, Timmy whispered, "Mom, Dad, please stop fighting. Please stop fighting. I didn't mean to break the corn." In his heart, he believed it was his fault they were fighting again.

Finally, quieted in the kitchen, the bedroom door opened, and his father issued another order as the heavy odor of beer gushed in.

"Come out here, boy."

Timmy stood from the floor and nervously went to the door. He was afraid of being hit again but when he entered the kitchen, his father was not to be seen. His mother, Phyllis, sat at the kitchen table with a tear-streaked face. Seeing her with bruises and tears hurt Timmy.

He walked toward her, watching closely. She looked up at him with eyes filled with hate and anger. He did not know why she hated him, but he knew she did. He wanted to comfort her, but the fear of what she may do stopped him.

Unable to think of anything to say that would make her feel better, he said instead, "Mom, I'm hungry."

Eyes unchanged and devoid of compassion, she spat out her reply, "Look in the pot."

Timmy turned away with the intent of reaching for the pot then he remembered his hands were dirty. He looked at his mom, afraid to speak but felt he must.

"Can I wash my hands?"

His mother gave him a look that screamed, "Don't ask me a stupid question. Of course you can wash your hands."

Timmy, afraid to do anything without first getting permission, went into the bathroom.

The bathroom was not the picture of cleanliness. Timmy did not compare the relative cleanliness of the restrooms at school to the conditions at home. He opened the door, partly blocked by dirty clothes, and stepped into the small room. He did not notice its general condition. The cluttered floor and dirty fixtures have long been ignored. Pictures on the wall, intended for decoration, were covered with layers of dust and moisture stains. A plastic shower curtain sporting a layer of soap scum and dirt hung half open along the tub. The large, comfortable white bathtub had lost its luster due to many layers of dirt never removed. A gray ring started five inches from the top and steadily darkened as it went farther down the tub. On its bottom, brownish black streaks and splatters were prominent from years of a dripping faucet.

The toilet, also once white, maintained its own ring around the inner bowl, and a layer of dirt and dust covered the entire unit. It had not been cleaned or even wiped for many months.

Bathroom sinks were usually one of the main stops for anyone preparing themselves for an appearance in public. The sink and countertop showed evidence of many preparations using makeup of all kinds and few attempts at cleaning. The sink stood streaked and dirty on its own cabinet. The cabinet, looking no better than the sink, also lacked a door to hide its overflowing contents.

Above the sink, a mirrored medicine cabinet displayed a single crack running diagonally across its plan. The broken glass surface hosted a few water-splattered stains, showing evidence it had been recently cleaned. The bathroom fixtures, accented by walls painted drab yellow, also possessed yellow paint peeling from the ceiling. The entire room was bathed in light by two seventy-five-watt bulbs.

Timmy turned on the water at the sink, soaped his hands with a perfumed flowery-smelling soap he did not like, and washed his hands. After rinsing, he soaped his hands again and started to wash his face. Seconds after touching his face with soapy hands, he felt the sting of soap.

Standing on an old stool, he peered into the mirror. The child's reflection showed clearly the bruise on the side of his face where he had been struck. He needed no other reminder to wash his face gently.

Drying his hands on the dirty hand towel, he could see clearly the remnants of his father's visit to the bathroom. His father Roger left more dirt on the towel than he put down the drain.

With clean hands and face, Timmy returned to the kitchen. His mother still sat in the chair, still angry. Taking great care not to cause any mishaps, Timmy took a plate from the cabinet. Setting his plate in the only clear spot on the counter, Timmy stood on his toes, tipping the pot in his direction. For his effort, he was rewarded with two small pieces of potato, a small piece of meat, and a meager amount of corn. Far short of a plateful, Timmy spooned the cold scraps onto his plate. He knew what he had would not be sufficient to silence his hungry stomach, but he did not dare complain.

Being careful not to spill a drop, he carried the plate with its meager rations to the kitchen table. Taking a seat, Timmy picked up his spoon as quietly as possible and began to eat.

His mother, looking at him with disgust and resentment, got up and walked out of the kitchen. Timmy watched his mother leave and listened to her steps as she moved along the hall. Relieved he now had the kitchen to himself, Timmy ate with the dedication of a starved man.

As quietly as possible, he carried his empty plate to the sink, placing it atop the stack of dirty dishes. Silently praying he would attract no attention, he returned to his room and, as quiet as a mouse, closed the door.

Timmy felt better after eating, but he still hurt from today's beatings and those from days past. The welts and bruises were painful, but nothing compared to the pain in his heart.

Returning to the spot he'd sat before, Timmy again sat with arms wrapped around his knees. A silent tear ran down his face, announcing to the outside world the pain he felt inside. Inside his bedroom, the outside world did not exist. There was no one in his bedroom to soothe his pains and reassure him things would improve. Feeling the wear of another day, Timmy soon lay down on the floor to sleep.

CHAPTER 3

Michael looked up into Michelle's eyes. Seeing the pictures rekindled the pain in her as well. His daughter, now a fully grown woman, made little progress recovering from the murder of Shelia Rayller. Yet, his heart saw Michelle as his little girl with the pain and problems perched on her shoulders.

His day had started like most workdays. The alarm sounded at 5:30 a.m. This was its usual time. Opening his eyes and reaching to silence the alarm, he looked around the bedroom, appreciating the beautiful job Kathryn had done making their home warm and comfortable.

In the early years of their marriage, she often arose first and was off about the house doing the things she must do. Sometimes, she would sit quietly with her thoughts. She called this her quiet time, and she made use of it. Other times, he listened to her in the kitchen preparing the breakfast she thought he needed to start the day. Today, wide awake and still lying in bed, Michael thought of how he first met Kathryn.

He was in college walking across campus to class, when a goddess of a girl crossed his path. She was so breathtaking that he thought his eyes had deceived him. He followed her to the administration building but did not have the nerve to approach her. Two days later, he saw her again near the same area.

After inquiring from his friends, he learned her name, Kathryn. Some of his friends, having encountered her before, advised him to stay clear. In their words, "She likes tearing guys apart, just for the fun of it."

Michael tried taking the advice, but on every chance encounter, the advice he received lost ground. He had no desire to be humiliated but felt powerless to erase her from his mind. Michael made the decision to wait. He knew the right time for his approach would arrive.

Time came some months later at the lecture hall. After the lecture on a topic he no longer remembered, he noticed Kathryn exiting to the hall a few steps ahead. Instead of approaching her, he chose to remain close behind. Having waited for months, he saw no mistake in waiting a little longer.

His patience had given Kathryn time to plan and practice tearing men apart, leaving them humiliated and confused. Kathryn attending the same lecture was more than a stroke of luck. She hated lectures and worse, the attention paid her by jocks. She stubbornly ignored the stare by yet another male jock student. Disregarding his stares, Kathryn mentally prepared herself for the mindless come-on.

After the lecture ended, she tried making a hasty exit but found herself trapped in the milling mass of students and cornered by the jock. Spinning on her toes like a ballerina, Kathryn came face-to-face with Michael, only a foot away.

Removing a hand from his pocket, holding a pack of breath mints, Michael made his move. Flawlessly planned, rehearsed, and now being delivered, Michael said, "Would you like to join me for a burger and shake sometime?"

He delivered his invitation while offering her a breath mint. So simple and clean was his invitation, Kathryn was completely caught off guard. Her deliberate and direct assault on any male's ego and manhood never had a chance to be launched once her eyes shifted from the hand holding the breath mints to Michael's eyes.

His eyes were soft, friendly, and intense. She was instantly disarmed to the extent she could only give a soft and agreeable yes. Forgotten was the sports jock she was trying to avoid. She wanted no part of him or any other man with an over-inflated ego. In Michael's eyes, she saw something stronger and more interesting than the iron muscles of a jock.

At that moment, the jock stepped up beside Kathryn, putting his arm around her waist, he said, "Little Miss Kathryn, I've been trying to catch up to you."

She turned her head and, looking him straight in the eye, took hold of his little finger, saying, "You just missed me again and always will."

She gave his little finger a slot-machine pull, bending it back at the knuckle, breaking his hold and stepping away from Mr. Jock at the same time.

The sudden pain of getting his pinky bent back caused him to announce the event loudly, attracting the attention of people nearby. This embarrassed him only slightly; however, not nearly as badly as realizing Kathryn had stepped out of his grip. He could not believe his eyes. She was walking away, arm in arm with a guy shorter than he and fifty pounds less his weight.

Mr. Jock, refusing to be blown off by Kathryn, stepped behind the two of them. Forcefully poking Michael in the back with his finger, he issued his first and only insult.

"Hey puke, I was talking to her."

In spite of Kathryn's protest, Michael stopped walking while unhooking his arm from hers. Fully aware a confrontation with a jock could likely result in his physical injury, Michael turned to face his challenge. Ready to fight if necessary, Michael chose the diplomatic approach. He hoped more forceful measures would not be required. To the jock he said, "It takes a big man to admit when he's wrong. Now is it going to take a little man to show you that?"

The words came from Michael's mouth but what the jock saw in his eyes made all the difference. He was willing to fight to protect Kathryn that was clear. The jock knew instantly this battle would have deep and long-lasting injuries that he wanted no part of. Being more aware than most of the willing girls on campus, the jock made a self-respecting retreat.

"Yeah, right," he said.

Michael's words and the look of determination in his eyes were a sufficient deterrent before he turned his back and retook Kathryn's arm. The jock, having looked into eyes more determined than any of his competitors, watched them walk away.

In Michael, Kathryn saw the kindness and strength similar to the attributes of her father. This was the first open display of Michael's determination witnessed by Kathryn. It would not be the last.

Michael remembered the first argument with Kathryn caused by his own brand of macho-ism. After the argument cooled, Kathryn made it clear she preferred a man who did not think he needed to act macho. The Michael she knew and loved was a man of kindness and strength. By the end of the cooling period, Michael knew his macho stunt nearly cost him everything.

After years of studying, laughing, and crying together, they grew into a loving and understanding couple. Their growth together did not go unrewarded.

Michael recalled the day of their wedding. Like a goddess, she portrayed all the virtues and values of a wonderful and well-balanced woman worthy of respect and admiration. For Michael, finding a woman with the values and virtues he desired proved to be a blessing and a visually pleasing reward. In Kathryn, he found all that could be desired and so much more. By the end of their formal education, a marriage proposal had been made and accepted. Thoughts of his completed degree were eclipsed only by the promise of Kathryn to become his wife. These thoughts were not exclusively his; Kathryn struggled with the completion of her studies, while making plans for a church wedding.

Kathryn always dreamed of being married in the church of her baptism. It only required making her wishes known for Michael to agree.

Standing at the edge of her hometown, the church appeared old but well-maintained. Majestic black oaks stood on each corner of the property, providing inviting shade.

With driveways on each side of the property, the congregations' vehicles could enter and exit with relative ease. Stone exterior walls demanded the structure be recognized for its strength. Its stained-glass windows, evenly placed along the walls, were inlayed with images of Christian teachings and events for all to see and learn from. Dark solid oak double doors stood centrally positioned below the bell tower and steeple pointing to the heavens. Past the exterior double doors was the atrium and the atrium hallways to the right and left led to the restrooms. The nursery located downstairs offered security and entertainment for the little ones during services.

Dividing the sanctuary from the atrium was another set of double doors.

Inside the sanctuary, an aisle in the middle divided the pews evenly with additional aisles along the walls. In the extreme front of the church, the pulpit stood steadfastly on an elevated platform, allowing the congregation an improved view of the minister from any pew. The choir loft was directly behind the pulpit. The pews, altar, and choir chairs were all covered in the same fabric, a striking shade of dark blue. The thick carpet covering the entire floor of the sanctuary was a medium gray.

In bright sunlight, the combination of the blue pews and gray carpet, along with polished wood accented by white walls and stained glass windows, gave the sanctuary an arrayed effect of elongated shapes and colors. This combination of colors and shapes served to accent any rousing sermon.

On the day of Michael and Kathryn's wedding, Kathryn's family and friends beautifully and tastefully decorated the church. They referred to themselves as The Committee.

The group, consisting of four women and two men, planned the decorations, flowers for the wedding, and the reception. They happily planned and arranged the entire event. They had, to their annoyance, no part in planning the honeymoon.

Michael remained extremely cooperative with Kathryn in all the planning and arrangements for the wedding. Even with the help of the committee, the to-do list seemed endless. Plans, arrangements, and decisions seemed never ending to Michael. For his own sanity, Michael's focus remained on Kathryn. He enjoyed imagining her being his wife. He did not care if the dogcatcher married them, just as long as they were married.

Both he and Kathryn soon discovered what their mothers would not tolerate. In view of the fact that each family had an only child, and those only children were getting married, their mothers were not interested in compromises. Michael, not being one to back down from a fight, knew very well when to remain silent with his mother and soon learned the same with his soon-to-be mother-in-law. Nonetheless, with the detailed planning, hurt feelings, bruised egos, giggles, and frayed nerves, the wedding day eventually arrived.

Michael stood at the front of the center aisle with his best man and the pastor. Nervously he listened to the organist playing the prelude to the wedding march. Kathryn, after a memorable dressing battle, was finally ready.

She had destroyed two pairs of pantyhose before she finally got the third pair to cooperate. Her bra refused to fit properly, requiring assistance from her mother. This task completed, her frustrations continued, until ordered by her mother to sit down and allow them both a minute of calm. Frustrated and near tears, Kathryn took a seat on the sofa in her dressing room.

In a calm and smooth voice, her mother spoke of Michael patiently waiting at the altar. Her mother also pointed out all Kathryn's strongest points. This short and direct discussion served to calm most of Kathryn's fears.

Now calmer and more confident, Kathryn finished dressing. She asked if her bridesmaids were ready, then checked her makeup in the mirror.

Kathryn's mother entered the reflection in the mirror beside her daughter. In her hands, she held a box, no larger than the type used to store a single shirt. Looking at the reflected eyes of her daughter in the mirror, she began her brief explanation.

"Something old, something new, something borrowed, something blue. When I prepared to marry your father, I found myself standing before a mirror much like this. I had a stomach full of angry bees. The butterflies left at sunrise."

Kathryn, sensing a long-drawn-out speech, attempted to speak but was silenced with a wave of her mother's hand.

"When I think about that day, I still feel a flutter in my stomach. He was so handsome and still is, for an old goat. My mother entered the room and stood beside me, as I am with you. She looked at me and said, 'God gave me you, and I gave you to him. Now the day has come for your father to give you to another man to be his wife. One day, I pray, you will be allowed the joy of giving this to your daughter.'

"She then opened this box and placed this wedding veil across my face, just as I am doing to you. If my life should end too soon, please pass this tradition on to my granddaughter when the time comes."

Kathryn looked into the mirror at her face now covered by a beautifully handmade veil. As her mother continued to speak, she learned she was now the fifth owner of this simple but beautifully made finishing touch. She felt the love of her family, the love of Michael, and the love of God. However, within all the love, a small doubt grew.

Was she worthy of the man she loved? This she needed to talk to her father about, if she had time.

The ring bearer, a handsome young boy of six, carried the satin pillow cradling two gold bands lying atop it. The flower girls were twins. They were then seven years old. The three were waiting in the atrium for their cue, each remembering what they had practiced the night before. Kathryn stood beside her father, a retired air force chief master sergeant.

She asked in a cracking voice, "Daddy, am I worthy to be his wife?"

Her father, knowing his daughter better than she knew herself, smiled while giving her a gentle hug.

"Yes, but my question would be, is he good enough for you?" He smiled. Holding his daughter's hand, he continued speaking softly.

"Kathryn, a marriage is what you make it. You two will have to decide what you are worth to each other as you go through life. Now, the old heads like your mother and I are good for giving advice, but you and your husband will make the final decisions. You are both diamonds in the rough. Together, the two of you present a beautiful glow but separate, the glow is less than half. You are my daughter. You are not perfect, and neither is he. You are worth your weight in gold, and Michael already knows that. Yes, you are worthy of him."

An usher gave the signal, and the matrimonial march music began. The pastor, Michael, and his best man stood in seized attention when the organist began to play the long-awaited wedding march.

Kathryn's dress was made with a high neckline that buttoned just under her chin with tiny pearl buttons. The bodice, sheer with delicate lace, tapered into a floor length dress of satin and lace. Her chapel train trailed behind her. The wedding dress had been her grandmother's, her veil now on the fifth generation, denoting the traditional "something old." Only the tips of her two-inch white satin pumps (something new) could be seen.

The guests turned to watch the bride make her entrance preceded by the bridesmaids, flower girls, and ring bearer. Michael could not believe the beauty of the woman coming toward him on her father's arm. In spite of the veil, he could see Kathryn's face. To him, she looked like a goddess ascending the aisle to the altar. She was incredibly beautiful. When she said yes, she would be his wife; he knew God truly loved him. However, with his knees weak, his stomach in the tightest knot he ever felt in his life, and perspiration building in his armpits, he asked God, "Do I deserve to have such a perfect woman?"

At the front of the sanctuary, the bridesmaids took their positions opposite the groom and best man. When they exchanged vows, Michael prayed silently for the wisdom and strength to be worthy of such a fine woman. Unknown to him, Kathryn was praying a similar prayer. She was not sure she deserved the high quality of man that stood beside her. Their parents cried and prayed this would only happen once to their children.

Before leaving the church, Kathryn threw her bridal bouquet, but she did not look back to see who caught it. Judging by the yaps and shouts, one of her bridesmaids had been the lucky one. She would later learn from her mother that the catcher was Jillian, her best friend.

After the reception, there was no honeymoon. Instead, Michael and Kathryn packed the Chevy wagon for a three-day drive cross-country to Michael's new job. He would start in his new position on Thursday of the following week.

With a small V-8 engine and automatic transmission, the poor Chevy wagon was heavy laden with the belongings of two college kids who were just married and starting a new life together. The old Chevy made the trip without a sputter of protest. It even continued to work beautifully until it was sold three years later. With its primer and white top and white wall tires, they still hated to see it go. It was replaced by a newer sedan.

For two years, Michael and Kathryn worked and planned their future. In the third year, Kathryn started having bouts of morning sickness, for the third time in three years. They both knew the cause and shared in the joy and apprehension. Considering they had suffered through two miscarriages in two years, they shared guarded optimism. Michael loved Kathryn so deeply. He hated to see the pain she went through with each loss. Michael tried always to keep a stiff upper lip. When it came to the love of his life in such pain, his stiff upper lip trembled, and he held her while they both shed tears.

This time was different. He guarded and fussed over her through the first trimester. She fussed and fretted over him through her second. However, nearing the middle of the third trimester, Kathryn began having odd pains.

Making an unscheduled visit to her doctor, she asked if she should be concerned. He paid close attention and told her to rest more. She did rest more, but the pain did not subside.

A month before her due date, she went to the doctor again, complaining of irregular abdominal pains. The doctor examined her then ran tests. The diagnosis determined she had an extremely swollen appendix. It would need to be removed before it ruptured. The doctor arranged for Kathryn's admission into the hospital and scheduled her for surgery immediately after admission. En route to the hospital, her appendix ruptured, sending poison through her and the baby. At the hospital, she was prepared for an emergency C-section.

Through all this, Michael refused to leave her side. He remained by her to the doors of the delivery room.

Their parents were en route; however, Kathryn went into surgery before they arrived. Two hours of surgery, with some unforeseen complications, and the baby was taken. The baby girl was underweight and struggling for her life. Kathryn was wheeled from the delivery room to an operating room while still under the anesthetics. The doctors started the appendectomy.

Michael, proud of being a new father, was equally terrified of losing his wife or his daughter. He paced the floor in the waiting room like a caged animal. His heart twisted with fear, and he did the only thing he knew to do: he prayed for a miracle.

When surgery was completed, Kathryn was taken to recovery. Their newborn baby had been placed in an incubator. When all had been completed, the doctor came out, sat Michael down, and explained to him the events that had taken place and the likely outcome. Kathryn had had a rough bout with a ruptured appendix, and this could have killed her if she had waited any longer to come in. He also explained the effect the rupture had on the baby. The result was that both Kathryn and baby were in ICU in critical condition. Michael listened intently. He understood little of the medical terminology, but what was clear to him was the fact his wife and baby were only inches away from death. If the heavens turned against him, he would lose them both forever.

After the doctor left, Michael went down to ICU. Not only did he want to see his wife, he needed to see her. On his way to ICU, Michael stopped by the post-partum unit to see his daughter. He reasoned by doing so, he would be able to give Kathryn a full report on their baby's condition.

She lay in her cradle, so small and so weak. Almost too small to cry, only lying there struggling to breathe. This was all heartbreaking for Michael. As he stood looking through the window at this tiny gift from God, the tears ran down his face. Feeling powerless and helpless, he prayed, not just for his daughter and wife, but for himself as well.

He asked God to spare his family, even if saving them meant taking him instead. Feeling himself not worthy before God, he prayed to be made worthy of keeping them as his family.

The doctor had also told him that another pregnancy could very likely kill Kathryn. All this he thought about as he prayed. Looking through the glass that separated him from his daughter, he knew there was nothing more he could do.

With a heavy heart, he turned away from the baby and went to his wife. Sitting beside Kathryn, he saw her face had lost its glowing color. He longed for her beautiful but now absent smile. All the joy was gone. In its place was the pain that showed in her furrowed brow. He sat beside her and, holding her hand, prayed the same prayer again. Kathryn was under heavy sedation and did not know he was there. While he prayed, her hands moved ever so gently and begin to rub and soothe his. With her eyes closed, she seemed to be sleeping, yet she still comforted him even as she suffered. In his heart of hearts, he knew he could never let her go.

She remained in the hospital for two weeks before being discharged. Very weak and recovering, she was restricted to bed rest. The bed rest worked for the first day, but on day two she was up and back at the hospital at nine in the morning. The post-partum ICU was empty but for a few worried parents and staff. She reached with gloved hands through ports in the incubator, watching their baby and hoping for a response.

At two thirty that afternoon, Michael arrived, having left work early. He had tried to concentrate, but it was difficult with the stress in his life. No one at the paper expected full output from him right now. It was all he could do to hold himself together. Michael and Kathryn stood together looking at their baby. Michael robed and gloved, inserted his left hand in one of the ports, and Kathryn had her right hand through the other. They both gently stroked the little hands and legs, because that was all they dared touch for fear of causing greater harm. Neither wanted to speak and held their silence until Michael spoke.

"Of all the names we picked, I think the one we should give her is Michelle."

This was a relief and a puzzle to Kathryn, considering he had been so determined to give their daughter his mother's name. She asked why.

Michael closely watching the baby, carefully considered his answer, and then he spoke.

"I prayed for a miracle for the both of you. For Michelle to survive, it looks like I will need to ask for another miracle."

Kathryn's finger stopped stroking the baby, and she looked at her husband. Her first impulse was demand he take it back. How dare he imply that their baby may not make it. She then stopped before speaking and looked at the situation.

Our poor little baby girl, which I carried nearly full term was now fighting for her life. Michael came face to face with nearly losing us both. If his prayer was for a miracle, he has received one so far. I am still alive, and he is as grateful for that as I am. Then his desire to name our baby Michelle will be mine also.

She looked her husband in the eye and said, "I've been granted two miracles in my life so far. The first was to have you as my husband, and the second is to see our daughter. I wholeheartedly agree her name shall be Michelle Faith Stone."

Settling on a name was satisfying and served to ease a small amount of the tension. At that very moment, little baby Michelle began to kick and cry, ever so softly. Her legs and arms movements were slight, but she was making her presence known. The monitors signaled the nurse who came over to see what was happening. She immediately paged the doctor with the news.

One month later, baby Michelle went home with her mommy and daddy. She was not in perfect health, but she was strong enough to leave the hospital.

Kathryn carried their baby out of the hospital with joy and care. Michael was the proud, attentive, and perhaps overly protective husband and father. He knew he had received his miracles, and he was forever grateful to God and the hospital staff.

Little baby Michelle had a rocky start but soon recovered and began growing and eating like most babies. She was crawling on time and even tried to start walking early, regularly landing on her bottom as her reward.

Near Michelle's fifth birthday, Michael and Kathryn heard of a small newspaper in another state for sale. They began to consider the possibilities of the investment. Kathryn had become a shrewd and hard-nosed negotiator. She could stretch a dollar farther than the most renowned miser.

Michael still worked for the same newspaper he had started with fresh out of college. Over the years, he had developed a reputation for writing a straight story, protecting his sources, and bucking the system. If the editorial staff wanted to change his story, they knew there would be repercussions. On occasions, the local cops gave him a little extra information and tips. Within the police department, it was a known fact Michael Stone would keep the lid on leads, if asked. However, not everyone loved his work.

He received hate mail in good quantity and, on occasions, threats by phone. He always informed his cop friends concerning the phone calls and mail.

One day a package measuring four by eight inches by three inches arrived at the paper for Michael. Wrapped in brown paper with no return address, the package drew little attention. The receptionist forwarded the package to the mailroom for later delivery.

Michael was out of the office on assignment when the package exploded. The two mail clerks were out distributing mail through the offices. The result of the explosion was only property damage. This was a great relief to Michael and the newspaper.

During the investigation, the cops pieced together enough information to track it back to the sender. A junior gang-banger, who did not like an article Michael had researched and written, sent the packaged explosive device. He liked it even less when two plainclothes detectives slammed him face down in the mud, read him his rights, showed him the search warrant, and proceeded to tear his already disastrous place apart.

For the officers' efforts, they found a couple of AK-47s, various handguns, a supply of angel dust, bomb-making materials, detailed descriptions and schedule movements and activities of Michael and two city officials.

News of the bomb maker's capture was initially pleasing to Michael, until he considered the long-term implications for himself and his family. He could no longer deny the words he wrote could endanger his family. Having come so close to losing both of them in childbirth, he did not want to put their lives in danger with anything he wrote.

When he told Kathryn about the events and the conclusion, she was considerably more concerned than he was. Her intense interest in creative financing methods for business purchases made it clear she wanted her family out of the city and soon.

CHAPTER 4

Sleeping on the floor in his bedroom, Timmy did not have to look at the reality of his life. Young age was his only protection from the knowledge of how things were as he learned how things should be. With the passing of each day, he became more aware of the wrongs done him at the hands of his parents, but that night he entered a different dream world. In this world, he left home, if only in his sleep.

Timmy found himself waiting at the train station. From his left, a faint light appeared and quickly grew larger. In seconds, he heard the fast approach of a train, and then it slowed and finally came to a stop. He watched as the conductor placed the stepstool below the first step then waited patiently for him to board.

The train was a sleek, fast-looking locomotive with only one car. As Timmy boarded, the conductor said, "Thank you for riding with us tonight."

Without another word, the conductor led Timmy along the aisle to join the other passenger. With whistle blowing, the train left the station continuing on its journey. Timmy left behind the pain and agony of being beaten and unloved. He felt no fear or dread; instead, he felt relieved to be getting away from home.

In his dream, he was wanted. He enjoyed the feeling of being accepted, welcomed, and not the sting of rejection. He was cared for and about. He felt a kind of comfort in the presence of the other passenger. Even the conductor shared in the relaxation when he brought Timmy and the other passenger candy and ice cream. Timmy, not being alone, enjoyed traveling with the other passenger, his imaginary friend.

He could see his friend's hands, feet, legs, chest, and neck, but not his face. The two of them dined in piggish fashion on the foods brought by the conductor, who waited to respond to their every request. His imaginary friend was visible to the conductor as well as to Timmy. In a lull in the childish pranks, feast, and conversation, Timmy silently wished he had no face also.

In their conversations, they talked about how good it was not to be around grown-ups and big folks, even though the conductor was a grown-up. In their mind, the conductor was a good grown-up. He was like Mr. Breeker, the old newspaperman. He was old and wrinkled, but he was a good guy.

Timmy listened as his imaginary friend talked. The face that should accompany the conversation was nothing more than a smudge, no features, no identity. Timmy did not mind this; he didn't want to see anyone's face, including his own.

For Timmy, sleeping through the night on the floor next to his bed was not unusual. In his sleep, he did not hear the thunderstorm for what it was. Rather than thunder, he heard a train ride in his dream. He felt the train rocking as it went along the tracks. When his travels ended, Timmy was sound asleep. No longer dreaming, he was at peace, for a short while.

At sunrise, Timmy was awakened by the sound of heavy footsteps outside his door. He knew the footsteps. Heavy and unsteady, he knew they belonged to his father. His father bumped Timmy's bedroom door with his shoulder. The door, having no latch, allowed his father, Roger, to push it open as he looked in.

Timmy was not asleep, only pretending to be. Awakened by the footsteps, the iron fingers of fear gripped his midsection while he forced himself to hold his breath. He was afraid of what his father might do if he appeared awake.

He heard his father say two words, "Stupid boy."

Timmy didn't know why his parents called him stupid, but they said it. So, he suspected he was because his mom and dad said he was. His father staggered from his bedroom door back along the hall to the bathroom.

Timmy thought his father may still be drunk, but he was not sure. A few minutes later, his father came out of the bathroom, then staggered into the bedroom he sometimes shared with his wife, Timmy's mother.

Sensing the danger had passed, he quietly got up. Dressing was a simple matter of putting on his old tennis shoes; he'd slept in his clothes. Quietly, he slipped out his bedroom door. After making sure no one heard him, he moved undetected through the kitchen and out the back door. The few sounds he made drew no response from his parents.

Outside, he felt safer. He believed if he was away from them, they couldn't beat him, until they found him. A thought crossed in his mind. *If I was gone for good, would they even look for me? Would they miss me or even care?*

This thought was like a pinprick to his heart. He did not know if they would or would not. Turning his back on his house, he entered the woods at a run.

When most boys his age were learning to ride bicycles and playing with toys in their backyard, Timmy chose the forest as his playground. It was away from his father and mother. He felt safer among the wild animals than he did in his own home.

After a quarter of a mile, the trail opened out near the home an old man who lived alone in a large two-story house. Sometimes Mr. Breeker, the owner of the house, talked to Timmy. On those occasions, Timmy liked the time the old man gave him for conversation. This morning he wanted to get away before his mom and dad started on him again. He felt a great desire to talk to the old man, to see him.

As he ran through the woods in the early morning sun, he noticed the trees were twisted and damaged. They were not as straight as they should be. Surprised, he stopped and looked farther ahead.

The forest as he knew it was no more. There were no trees where trees once stood. The tops of once-tall pines now lay on the ground with roots upturned to the sun. The huge oaks were torn and ripped apart. In the distance, he could see the old man's house or what has remained of it. Mr. Breeker's house, as he had known it, was gone.

What at one time was Timmy's safe haven was no longer.

Like a solo giant, a portion of the west wall stood alone, absent the second floor it once supported. There were no windows, no front or back door.

Timmy could not understand how something could destroy and scatter an entire house. What was once Mr. Breeker's house now resembled a salvage yard. Through Timmy's eyes, it looked as if a giant grabbed, crushed, and twisted everything, then scattered it to the winds.

Timmy stood, looking around at the destruction. His young eyes had never seen anything like it. In shock, he asked, "What happened?"

Confused, he took slow, cautious steps toward the wreckage of the house. He moved in slow motion, stunned by what he saw. Looking at the destruction, he had the feeling this was somehow his fault too.

CHAPTER 5

Two months before Michelle's fifth birthday, Michael and Kathryn closed the deal on a small out-of-town newspaper, *The Republic.*

On the day of Michelle's birthday, the moving van sat parked and loaded in front of the Stone's house with their household goods and belongings. In the driveway sat the family car loaded with suitcases, file boxes, and things they preferred to keep close. It would appear as if Michelle's birthday had been overlooked, but that was not the case.

Michelle was able to celebrate her birthday at the house of a friend. The birthday celebration was great for the kids; however, the adults saw it as a farewell. The clown heightened the laughter from the children among the floating balloons and backyard games. As much as the gathering appeared to be a party for the kids, the sad eyes could be seen, when anyone choose to look. The adults and kids alike knew "birthday party" was only a label; this was a farewell party. However sad the event, all put forth their best party faces for the benefit of Michelle.

Michelle, on the other hand, had decided days before not to allow her birthday party to be anything else. At five years of age, her mentality was well beyond her chronological age. This was not a fact missed by her parents. They were well aware of her more mature thinking. They often remarked, "She was four, going on forty." This often made parenting Michelle a tricky but rewarding task.

Michelle maintained the largest smile, the greatest of cheer, and was clearly the best at hiding her pain of goodbye.

After the gifts were opened, tears fell, and goodbyes could no longer be ignored. Soon among the many gifts, adults shared handshakes and goodbye kisses then quietly left for their cars. When all had departed, Michael and Kathryn helped the hosting family clean up. Then with a sadness of their own, they departed.

As they approached the interstate, Michael and Kathryn slipped into silence, each pondering memories and thoughts of the previous eight years.

They had arrived in this city, a newlywed couple and proud of having captured their college degrees. Michael secured his first job as a newspaper reporter in this city. They had arrived full of dreams and determined to accomplish their goals. Together, they endured hardships, planned and worked as a team, and were always concerned about the other yet stayed focused on their big picture and separate roles. Always putting their marriage first, they never allowed others to dictate to them the path they should take. Michael and Kathryn planned and executed their future together as husband and wife, striving to live up to the truest height of their marriage vows. They depended on their joint decisions to carry them forward and through all changes and challenges. Did they have regrets leaving?

Yes, they would miss their friends; however, they had set a new goal and traveled toward it. They left the city not broken, soiled, or worn down but rather more educated in the things of greater importance. Kathryn and Michael embraced a philosophy and attitude quite different from most they knew and prayed a simple prayer nightly.

"Lord, thank you for this day you have given us. Thank you for the challenges and changes you have used to strengthen us. Thank you for what tomorrow brings, for in your word, we find our strength. Amen."

These simple words of belief they taught their daughter also. These simple yet powerful words gave them the strength and courage to overcome many obstacles, all of which made them stronger.

They were not leaving as losers but going forward into a new business prospect in a new place, perusing a new goal. As a family, they were full of dreams and plans merging onto another of life's interstates. Confident they had made the right decision and standing on their belief in the Word of God, the Stone family left behind friends, jobs, and the stresses of the city.

While the two-day drive was uneventful, the transition was evident. They felt it not only in the change of scenery but also in the draining away of stress and old worries. Michael hoped this change would provide the safety and security he sought for his family. The occasional unobserved glance at his wife and daughter only served to reinforce the correctness of their move. Within his heart, mind, and soul, he was more than prepared to give up his life to protect his family. In the silence, he quietly prayed the day would never come when he would have to do so.

After traveling fifteen hundred miles of interstate highways, they turned onto U.S. highways. Later, they turned onto county roads and soon entered the city limits of Lake City.

For months, Kathryn had been in contact with a realtor. Prior to their departure from the city, Kathryn contacted the realtor, letting him know they were on their way. She, with Michael's agreement, had selected a new home from only photos.

They both knew it was risky to buy without seeing but meditated in prayer until one house in particular stood out. With all the details taken care of and nothing remaining except the closing, they felt they were prepared.

As they entered the edge of town, Kathryn navigated Michael with the directions she received from the realtor. Michelle was excited, commenting on all the new sights of her new town.

Entering town via the main street, they immediately noticed the absence of clutter. The shops and stores along the street appeared to be maintained by people who cared about their business's appearance. The streets were in good condition with no potholes or trash.

The edge of Lake City sported a feed and farm supply store with cars and pickup trucks parked in front and on a side dirt lot. After passing the farm store, they noticed antique shops, auto repair shops, and businesses of all sorts. There was no doubt it was a small town by city standards.

Lake City appeared clean and announced it had nearly as much to offer as larger towns or small cities. People stood on the sidewalks talking to one another. From time to time, they would see someone shout and wave hello to a passerby. Kids ran down sidewalks or side streets laughing and playing.

When Michael stopped at an intersection, Kathryn noticed an elderly couple standing on the sidewalk. It appeared they were window shopping for furniture. The grandmotherly-appearing woman was trying to interest the man with her, presumably her husband, in the furniture beyond the window. He was using a standard husbandly tactic, ignoring her while taking mental note of the piece of furniture she indicated. However, their comfortable ease with one another betrayed his attempts to ignore. Kathryn got the feeling the woman would at some point have her way.

Kathryn watched them and thought, *I wonder if Michael and I will be like that someday—old—and me talking and him ignoring me but not missing a thing.* As Kathryn pondered that thought, their car moved on.

Michael noticed the couple from the corner of his eye. It was clear they had been together many years. He suspected the man knew her taste and desires better than she thought. The older gentleman appeared to be a kind, straight-back individual, with a weathered face and hands. He wore a wide brimmed work hat and coveralls. His movements appeared younger than his obvious years.

The woman was shorter and a bit round. She had long gray hair, wearing it in a braid down her back. She was dressed in a high-collared short-sleeved print dress and casual shoes. Regardless of your acquaintance, this was a couple to be admired. Most likely, when they dressed in their Sunday best, they would be impressive in anyone's eye.

The middle of the town hosted a large town square. A city block in size, the town square hosted the courthouse, county buildings, and library with parking spaces around its outer perimeter. To the side, away from the buildings, a small park had been established. Many streets converged into the square, making it more or less the business center.

Passing the square, Michael saw the sign identifying Rogers Street. He turned right onto the street and was immediately struck by the scene. For a brief moment, he thought he'd just driven his family into a living Norman Rockwell painting.

The street offered a width sufficient for cars to be safely parked on each side and allow traffic to move in both directions without concern. Mature hardwood trees on both sides provided shaded sidewalks with well cared for flower gardens and lawns beyond. The houses looked well-kept and neat.

Six blocks down, he turned left into another well cared for street, Free Bird Road. This tree-lined street displayed houses not as large yet equally as nice and well-maintained.

A quarter of a mile farther, the street narrowed. Sidewalks no longer existed, instead replaced by grassy shoulders and a shallow ditch. Another mile and the shoulders were wide enough for a car to park and traffic to pass safely.

They passed through a gradual right-hand curve. As the road straightened, Kathryn said, "Oh my god." Michael saw it also.

Before them, beyond the curve and past the field of corn, they saw a single-family house with a real estate sign next to the road.

Kathryn looked at the house as they neared. Looking back at her directions, she again read the address on her paper work. It was clear 929 Free Bird Road matched the numbers before her eyes on the mailbox. It was unmistakable. They were at the right place.

The realtor's photos presented a brick ranch-style house, with a couple of trees in the front yard, a long covered porch, and shrubs along the front. The description said three bedrooms, two bathrooms, fourteen hundred square feet with an unheated attached two-car garage and acreage.

What they saw before them fit the description and so much more. The house sat on two and a half acres with one and a half in grazing pasture, plus outbuildings and a barn. Shrubs stretched across the front of the house and down the sides of the graveled driveway. The circular driveway was at the front of the house. A spur from the circular drive led to an attached double garage. Six large trees evenly spaced along the driveway provided a tall, shaded tunnel effect before the open lawn. The house itself sat positioned in the center of the acre lot that was not pasture. A fenced backyard also hosted an empty doghouse. A large old oak tree shaded much of the backyard and most of the rear of the house. An old tire swing hung suspended by a rope from one of the lowest limbs of the tree. Someone had kept the grass cut and the flowers watered. The flowers ran along the same pattern as the shrubs, presenting a burst of color starting at ground level.

Kathryn studied the picture she had removed from the envelope and then passed it to Michael. He looked the picture over before returning a glance to his wife. With laughter in his voice and eyes he said, "The picture doesn't do it justice."

Surprised by the beautiful house before them, Michael steered their car into the driveway. Rolling along the graveled drive, Michelle was overjoyed seeing the spots of sunlight breaking through the canopy of shade trees. On the circular driveway, Michael parked the car short of the front steps. In a state of awe, the threesome exited the car.

The windows had curtains, but signs of being vacant were apparent. On the front porch lay half a dozen issues of *The Republic*, the same newspaper business they had just purchased.

As Michael stood on the front porch with Kathryn, a car turned into the driveway. Michelle, seeing the car, immediately rejoined her parents. After the car rolled to a stop, a man of five feet five inches in height, a thick waistline, and double-chinned jolly face exited the car. The necktie, partially hidden by abundant flesh, did not appear painful even though it may have been. He introduced himself as Richard "Ricky" Lloyd, their realtor.

After the introductions, Kathryn and Michael felt at ease. The three of them had talked on the phone and exchanged correspondence for months and, in that course of time, had developed a respectful business relationship. It had only served to improve the relationship when Michael and Kathryn arrived in town on the date and time they said. Ricky Lloyd had also kept the appointment as promised. Producing a passkey from his jacket pocket, Ricky Lloyd unlocked the box and opened the house for their inspection.

The moment the solid wood door swung open and they stepped inside, Kathryn and Michael were hooked. The house was empty, but standing in the foyer, they knew this was their home.

It offered a layout of pure excitement to the Stone family.

The fireplace in the den immediately captured all of their hearts. One bedroom would be an office, another would become Michelle's bedroom.

The L-shaped kitchen was a focal point for Kathryn. She envisioned many great meals prepared for her family in this kitchen.

Michael admired the spacious backyard and outbuildings. He observed the abundant space for Kathryn to garden, if she chose, and appreciated the fenced backyard for Michelle to run and play in. Beyond that, he saw himself coming home and relaxing after a busy workday. This place offered everything that the city did not. The spacious countryside and peace and quiet were a welcomed setting.

Kathryn looked at Michael for an answer. Michael looked at Floyd, the realtor, for the question. Ricky, feeling confident, spoke in true sales agent fashion.

"Let's see. Your financing is already approved," he said, counting off on his fingers. Finger number two, "Your belongings are well on their way here, and unless I'm badly mistaken—" finger number three "—you love the house. Am I right so far?"

Michael looked back at Kathryn. She said yes, never taking her eyes off him. Michelle, not to be left out and making it known how much she really knew, asked her parent a question.

"Daddy, I feel safe here. Do you and Mommy?"

This question was such a surprise to both Michael and Kathryn. They both stared at Michelle for a long moment. Both her parents had gone to great pains to hide their stresses and concerns from her. Always presenting a solid, united front for her to see and take comfort in. Always making sure she knew she was loved, safe, and protected. Moreover, in a few words from their child, they learned not only had she seen through their efforts to protect, but she also loved them enough to keep quiet about it, until she felt it was necessary to speak.

Michael, recognizing this, knelt down beside his daughter looking into her clear and concerned young eyes. What he saw was all the promise and strength of Kathryn's eyes in his child. He said to his only child, "Yes, I feel safe here," then hugged her.

She wrapped her thin child arms around her daddy's neck as he picked her up. Turning, he faced Kathryn.

Before he could ask, she said, "Yes, I feel safe here too."

Michael then turned to face the patiently waiting realtor. The time had come to complete another step in their new venture.

"How soon can we get this finished?" Michael asked the realtor.

Kathryn stepped up to her husband's back. Looking over Michael's shoulder into Michelle's eyes, she said, "I love you."

Michelle replied, "I love you too, Mommy."

Signing the closing papers was done that day. Being a cash purchase, with the aid of their parents, red tape and delays were nonexistent. The house now belonged to them, and the moving truck was on the way.

The next morning, the moving van was parked in their new driveway, unloading their belongings. Having recently purchased the newspaper, they still had contracts to sign and vendor agreements to hammer out. They would need to meet with and contact suppliers, reporters, and news agencies. Printing companies that actually printed the paper and the mortgage company regarding the building that housed *The Republic* also had to be dealt with. When they bought the paper, they also bought the building.

While the moving company unloaded their belongings, Michael, Kathryn, and Michelle paid a visit to *The Republic*. The purchase of the paper had already been completed; however, taking physical possession would not happen for another two days.

Michael parked the family car in front of *The Republic*. With more than a little excitement and nervousness, the three exited the car and stood on the sidewalk, looking at the building. The building, newer than many already existing, stood on the corner with a vacant lot beside it. The empty lot served as an overflow parking lot for the shoppers in town. This allowed shoppers to park off the street and walk to the nearby businesses and shops. *The Republic*, a stand-alone two-story building, had a single door in front for street access and a rear door opening onto the vacant lot.

Michael thought to himself *This deal might have been a mistake.* He looked over at Kathryn and down at Michelle. Before he could say anything, Kathryn said, "No matter how we feel about it, we have to make it work."

Michael silently, again admired his wife. *This woman is just too optimistic, but I love the way she looks at life.*

Michael replied, "Let's go inside."

Opening the front door, he allowed Kathryn and Michelle to enter first.

The entrance had a small reception area with a young woman manning the desk. The three of them stood in the reception area taking in the office setup, when the receptionist spoke up and asked if she could help them. Michael looked at the young woman then said, "Yes, you can help us. We're the Stones. I am Michael. This is my wife, Kathryn and our daughter, Michelle."

Before he could say another word, the receptionist sprang to her feet and quickly began walking away, speaking to them over her shoulder, saying, "Please, wait here. I'll be right back."

Michael and Kathryn watched with surprise as the young woman knocked on the door of an unmarked office in the far right corner of the building.

After saying something to the occupant of the inner office, she stepped back and moved aside. From the doorway, stepped a small-framed, gray-haired old man. From the reception area,

Michael could see the stubble of a cigar hanging from his mouth. With reading glasses perched on the end of his nose, he looked at the Stone family for a long moment. Finally, with a wave of his hand, he motioned them over.

Michael Stone and his family walked across the open office area to where the old man stood. It was clear he was in charge.

The office door exhibited no name or other identifying markings. As they approached, the old man and the wide-eyed young receptionist stepped back and gave them ample room to enter. The old man said, "You folks come on inside."

He offered neither handshakes nor introductions. After the three of them had entered, the receptionist closed the door behind them, but she remained outside.

The office was a comfortable size with a leather couch along one wall. Worn from years of use, the old leather sofa presented itself as inviting and in good condition. The floor, recently carpeted, felt firm underfoot. The wood-paneled walls were decorated with clippings and photos of days gone by. Awards and mementos of various types each held their place of prominence. Near the window sat an old mahogany desk with a high-backed leather chair. A pair of comfortable wing chairs sat in front of the desk. It was clear the office furnishings had been together for many years.

After closing the door, the old man stood beside his desk as Michael, Kathryn, and Michelle took seats on the sofa. Michael and Kathryn sat close together with Michelle on her mother's lap. They sat silently waiting for the man to speak.

Michelle watched the old man, but she was watching something no one else could see. Having heard some of the conversations between her parents concerning the paper, she knew the old man's name, and now she knew more than she wanted. Leaning her head against her mother's shoulder, she watched the glow increase in intensity around the old man. The glow she decided to name, "The Goodbye Light." She'd observed this light around different people in different places. From as far back as she could remember, she had seen the light. The meaning of it was no longer a question. She knew what it was and what it meant.

The old man appeared tired, with the years showing in his face and hands. All the wrinkles and cracks of age, the hunch of his back, and the stare of his ice blue eyes said I'm-tired-but-ready-to-spring-into-action-at-anytime.

He looked as if all he needed would be a wide brim hat with a press pass stuck in the sweatband, a notepad in his shirt pocket, and a hot tip to become something other than an old and tired businessman.

The old man walked around behind his desk and took his seat. Looking at the Stones, he cleared his throat and began to speak.

"I am Charles Breeker Sr. I've been in the newspaper business for forty years. My wife and I started this paper from scratch, and it has served us well. *The Republic* has been our baby for those forty years. My wife and I lost our only child, my son, in the war, and the paper was all we had left. Years later, I lost my wife Grace to cancer, leaving me to run the paper alone. This newspaper is a very special part of me.

"Michael, I have read much of what you have written, and it's very good. I did some investigating and discovered you have a solid reputation with your former paper. Digging further, I discover the police also think highly of you.

"I didn't find much information on your business abilities. However, I did agree to stay on for a while and assist you in getting the hang of how things are done. This is what I agreed to, and that is what I will do.

"My late wife and I built this paper from the ground up, and from the information I have gathered and now meeting your family, I think you folks will do well. I think that with a little time you folks will make her yours, also.

"This paper, this business, has its secrets and surprises. This desk has secrets and surprises, this county has secrets and surprises, and this town has secrets and surprises. I have seen many secrets and a few surprises, myself."

Hearing this, Michael thought, *Am I hearing the I'm-turning-my-business-over-to-you speech or a eulogy?*

At this point, the old man focused his eyes on Michelle. Michael and Kathryn watched Michelle for some type of reaction. With her head leaning on her mother's breast, she stared directly at the old man.

Then Mr. Breeker said, "You folks will find many things around here to love and appreciate, and some things you will despise. Nevertheless, remember these are good people in this town, and there are a few bad apples to help keep things interesting. I am tired, old, and hope for few things now. But, for you folks, my hope is that you find lots of joy here."

Speaking directly to Michelle, he said, "Young lady, you are very fortunate to have such good parents."

Michelle, looking in his eyes, simply said, "Thank you."

Returning his attention to Michael, he said, "Michael, if you will be here at three tomorrow afternoon, I will turn her over to you."

Michael, having watched with a reporter's eye and ears, gave a simple reply designed to save time and effort. His intention was to wait for the details when the two men were alone.

"Yes, sir, that won't be a problem."

The old man then said, "Good that will do it for me. I know my child is in good hands, and I'll see you folks tomorrow."

He looked back down at his desk and began shuffling papers.

Kathryn looked at Michael with an expression of surprise. As if on cue, Michelle climbed off her mother's lap and stood on the floor looking at the old man. Michael and Kathryn stood and approached the door, ushering Michelle as they went. At the door, Michelle turned toward the desk and said, "Sir?"

He raised his head and looked at her.

She smiled, waved, and said, "Goodbye, Mr. Breeker." Then she turned to wait for her father to open the office door.

Leaving the corner office, Michael, Kathryn, and Michelle caught the side-glances and open stares of the others in the open office area. The three walked back through the offices, said goodbye to the receptionist, and left the building.

Michael opened the car door for Kathryn. Michelle scurried in over the console and into the backseat. Once seated, she locked her seatbelt. Kathryn took her place in the passenger seat and fastened her seatbelt. Michael walked around the car and opened his door after Kathryn had reached across and unlocked it. Seated behind the wheel, Michael looked up to see the old man standing in the door. Mr. Breeker caught Kathryn's and Michelle's attention as well. They could see the tear running down his face. Then, he dropped his head and closed the door.

Michael started the car, checked for traffic, and backed into the street. He then pointed the car in the direction of home.

The meeting had not been what he expected. In fact, he had not known what to expect. On the way home, they stopped at the grocery store and picked up a few things for dinner. They would enjoy their first meal at home, even if they ate on the floor.

Arriving at their new home, they noticed the moving people were gone, leaving no mess behind. Michael parked the car and was about to open the door when Michelle said, "Mom, Daddy, that old man at the paper is about to die."

Michael's movements froze, and Kathryn's eyes swelled with alarm. They both turned in their seats and looked at Michelle. As if this pronouncement came from God, Kathryn and Michael heard the roar of distant thunder.

CHAPTER 6

"Charles, is there anything else I can get for you before I leave?"

Janice, Mr. Breeker's personal assistant and assistant editor, stood in the doorway of Charles "Bill" Breeker Sr.'s office. She had kept a close eye on her boss from the minute he completed his meeting with the new owners. Now it was time for her to leave, and she felt uneasy leaving him alone. The stiffness and slowness of his steps made him appear to be much older than his seventy-six years. His stance, slumped shoulders, and the absence of his determined gait all said I'm finally done.

Breeker sat at his desk pondering his self-imposed upcoming retirement. For weeks, he tried to avoid thoughts about what he would do when the Stones arrived to take over. The thought had given him no joy, so he simply refused to think about it. Now that they were here, ignoring the future was no longer possible. Technically, they owned the newspaper; however, he had agreed to remain for sixty days as general manager. Now, Breeker pondered a question, *How am I going to tolerate two months as general manager when I can barely see beyond two days?*

Janice, asking if he needed anything, distracted him from his thoughts. She was such a great assistant editor. He dared not ignore her question.

"No, Janice, I have all I need. Thank you."

Janice, sensing his feeling of loss, turned to leave but was halted by Breeker's voice. The tone was not demanding but instead seeking.

"Janice?"

"Yes, Bill?" She seldom called him Mr. Breeker.

"Can you stay for a minute, please?"

"Yes, I can."

Janice stepped into the office, knowing this was completely out of character for her boss. Selecting one of the wing chairs, she took her seat and readied herself to be the listening friend.

After taking a seat, she crossed her denim-covered legs at the knee. Pushing her oval-shaped glasses up on her small button nose, she clasped her hands in her lap, making it clear she was ready to listen.

As Bill watched in silence, a thought came to mind.

She acts like a cross between a shrink and a gossip columnist getting ready for that once-in-a-lifetime interview.

She had, over the years, proven not to be a gossip, and on more than one occasion served as a patient and practiced sounding board. Relaxed in her presence and feeling confident with her silence, Breeker began to slowly speak.

"Janice, have you ever felt like what you have done you knew you had to do, but you did not want to face the why?" Janice pondered this twisted question for a minute. Weighing the question carefully before answering, she decided not to soft step. Janice reasoned her boss was hurting, and his talking would be the best medicine. He would likely continue with no further prompting.

"Bill, are you having regrets about your decision to sell the paper?"

Breeker's stare dropped to the desk blotter, revealing the shiny crown of his head. Holding that pose for a brief moment, he again looked up into Janice's eyes. His eyes showed the strain of the years and the pain of selling what he referred to as his baby, *The Republic*. In a voice that sounded on the verge of breaking, he resumed speaking.

"My son CJ was killed in the war thirty years ago. He left home and went off to college. Then he came from college with his degree and left for the army. That was his decision. Fifteen months later, we received a telegram from the United States Army. It was delivered to my house. I wish it had been delivered here.

"Grace called me here at the office and asked me to come home and open it. We both knew the army seldom sent out telegrams in times of war bearing good news. Well, I dropped everything and rushed home.

"When I walked into my house, Grace was sitting in the parlor on the sofa just staring at the envelope lying on the coffee table. Her face was washed out, and she clutched her arms across her midriff and sat there rocking back and forth. Now, looking back on it, I think she was trying to pray and will our son back into her womb where she could protect him.

"I walked over and picked up the envelope. I guess to her

it looked like I did all this effortlessly but in fact, it was the longest room I had ever crossed in my life. As I held the envelope in my shaking hands, I had a flashback of a young man jumping up and down like a kid when he read the letter of acceptance to college. On that day, I thought to myself, 'My boy is becoming a man.'

"I opened that telegram, and it did indeed say what no parent wants to hear. In simple words, it said, my son, Captain Charles William Breeker Jr., had died in combat while engaging the enemy. Those are the only words I remember. As I read the words aloud, the letter dropped from my hands. Grace screamed with a god-awful yell, and my knees went weak. I, weak-kneed, stepped around the coffee table and knelt down to hold Grace. Once again, all we had was each other. After CJ's funeral, Grace was never the same. How could she be? We had lost our only child.

"Then ten years ago, I lost Grace to cancer. One day, she started losing weight. She was a tall, solid woman, but in a matter of weeks, she started wasting away. Eventually she admitted she had not told me how terrible she felt. She'd kept it hidden, so not to worry me. She hid it too long. She lasted five months.

"The last day she was with me, she said, 'CJ was looking extremely good in his army uniform.' I assumed her to be hallucinating. I should have understood he was there for his mother. She passed away that night. The last thing she said to me was, 'I love you,' before she fell asleep.

"I often wondered, like an old fool, if I could have kept her awake, would she have seen the sunrise. I know now, that was complete selfishness."

Janice sat as still as a church mouse during revival. She didn't know what to say. Breeker paused and refocused his attention on a distant time outside his office window. His tired eyes stared into some faraway place as he continued.

"Grace and I started this paper forty years ago. Back then, Main Street was the only real street, and it was dirt. When it rained, it was a stinking, sticky, muddy mess. Now look at it.

"I wonder what she would say if she knew I had sold our baby. Janice, *The Republic* was the last thing I had to live for, and it looks like she will outlive me."

The ticking of the clock on Breeker's desk marked the silence in the room. Breeker listened to the ticking, then looked at Janice, smiled, and said, "You go on home, and I will too."

Janice, usually not at a shortage for words, had discovered what was missing in her own life. Listening to Charles Breeker Sr., her boss, Janice realized the value of telling someone you loved how much you really did. The story she had just heard magnified the pain of loss and the void that would be in her own life if she did not make immediate changes. Yes, she would go home and fan the embers of her now crumbling marriage. If there were any chance of its survival, she was determined to bring it back to a full flame.

Breeker, standing, came around his desk. Janice, determined to leave him with at least a grain of hope, stood and took a step closer to Breeker, leaned forward, and kissed him on his cheek. This came as a complete surprise to him. His face turned red, and he was left speechless.

At his office door, Janice turned and spoke to her boss once again. "Bill, there's a couple of things I want you to know. One, you're the best boss I have ever had, or that I will ever have. And two, you were a good man then, but you are a great man now. Goodnight, Bill." With that said, she was gone.

Breeker stood beside his desk recovering from the surprise invasion of his private space and receiving a kiss on his cheek. That was something he hadn't felt for quite a while. His pained heart felt relieved for a few seconds.

After Janice disappeared through the doorway, Breeker again felt the absence of Grace. Feeling a desire to talk with his departed wife, he stepped to his office window— his preferred spot when talking to his wife. He reasoned a passerby would think he was talking to someone in his office, and if anyone heard his mumbles, they would think he was talking about something outside. In this space near the window, he felt it safe to talk.

"Grace, we did well together, you and me. Together we started a family, and together we started a newspaper. But with you gone, I can't handle it anymore. I'm too tired. I'm too old, so I sold the paper. I sold our baby, and I don't feel as bad about it as I thought I would. Grace, I have gotten too old and too lonely to do this anymore. I know you probably already know all this, but I wouldn't feel right if I didn't tell you myself. I've said what I wanted. Now I'm ready to go home."

Breeker stood in his office window, watching a young boy riding his bicycle on the sidewalk across the street. Allowing his gaze to follow the boy as he rode, Breeker remembered CJ riding his bicycle into town, as a child, as a teenager, and finally as a young man. He watched as the young boy rode through the shadows and eventually out of his line of sight. Seeing the shadows had grown longer, he knew it was time to go home.

Turning from the window, Charles Breeker Sr. slowly surveyed his office. The office he had entered and exited thousands of times now seemed dull and empty. He sensed the fading of energy that was once so strong. Picking up his jacket and briefcase, he looked around again and surveyed his workplace. It was time to leave.

The drive home offered no surprise events or mysteries. Breeker watched the scenery as it passed uneventfully. The road was the same as it had always been. The sky was beginning to give a hint of clouds. As Breeker turned into his driveway, the air began to change. He suspected there might be a storm during the night.

Entering his home through the rear door, Breeker paused in the kitchen to read the note left by his housekeeper. She came twice a week to tend to the household chores. Like clockwork, she arrived on Tuesdays and Fridays, always before nine in the morning, completed her work, and departed before three in the afternoon. Never leaving behind a dirty dish or sock, and never touching his desk. After Breeker's past experiences with domestic help, he felt very fortunate to have this particular housekeeper.

Walking through the house, Breeker paused in the parlor. His mind replayed the awful day he read the telegram to Grace. With a tear in his eye, he spoke aloud.

"I'm sorry, Grace, CJ was a grown man making his own way, and I couldn't tell him he couldn't go in the army. He was doing what we taught him—to be proud, strong, and patriotic. We lost him, but I'm proud he stood up for our country, and I know you are too."

With tears sliding down his face, Breeker continued on to his study.

Breeker was not afraid of the dark. However, he was afraid of breaking another toe. To help prevent a reoccurrence, he left a freestanding shaded lamp turned on in the corner of his study. This lamp remained lit twenty-four hours a day, seven days a week. With the setting sun and thickening clouds, he hardly noticed the leather sofa and chair sitting near the fireplace as he approached his desk.

That evening, feeling defeated, he was also convinced he had let CJ and Grace down. Charles D. Breeker Sr. longed for the lost touch and presence of his wife. Having no appetite for food, he had not returned to the kitchen after reading the note. Living alone, he often slept the entire night on the leather sofa in his study. After the death of Grace, he seldom slept in the bed they had shared for so many years. He usually entered the master bedroom long enough to shower and change clothes. The memories in that room both refreshed and haunted him.

Feeling beaten and more tired than usual, Breeker mixed himself a tall scotch and soda before settling into the chair behind his desk. Even with the alcohol, he was unable to shake the defeated feeling that now engulfed him. Soon he resumed the conversation with his wife.

"Grace, I tried to be a good husband and father. I thought you were happy. You had your house and your job as a reporter with the paper. You were always so excited when you finished a story and couldn't wait to see it in print. The only thing I enjoyed more than watching you work on a story was watching you with our son. You were so sweet and gentle.

"CJ, you were the most inquisitive child ever made. I was so proud of the both of you. Why did the both of you have to leave me here alone?"

Another tear silently slipped down his face as he took another drink.

"Grace, why didn't you tell me you were sick? We could have gotten you help. But no! You decided in your usual stubborn way to keep silent and push on. I now know the doctors could not have done a thing, but we could have tried. You waited until you couldn't stand the pain any longer before you told me. How do you think that makes me feel? I was your husband. Taking care of you and protecting you was my job, but you wouldn't allow me to do it."

Draining the glass and picking up the framed picture of his wife and son, Breeker leaned back in his chair. The alcohol brought on a rush of fatigue. As he told Grace and CJ how much he missed them, Charles Breeker Sr. fell asleep.

His sleep was, neither restful nor relaxing, filled with troubling images and events. In his dream as in his earlier life, he and Grace attended a yearly ball, except this time he was alone. Breeker saw himself dressed in a tuxedo, made of beautiful fabric he could not identify, that fit him perfectly.

He stood among men of all ages and strangers to him, listening to a lively conversation about philosophy. The conversation was both interesting and entertaining. Positioned as he was with the small group of debating men, he had a clear line of sight to the raised entrance of the ballroom. From time to time, he would glance up at the carved double doors expectantly but unable to understand why.

The pleasant debate became more forceful, one man declaring the other a fool. This comment drew insults and accusations of being a communist. The changed tone did not sit well with Breeker. He looked about the ballroom and noticed that in different areas the conversations had become heated. He feared some of them would soon become shoving matches. The ballroom was awash with men arguing with men, women arguing with women, and even women openly arguing with men.

Suspecting things were going awry, Breeker started making his way across the ballroom to the entrance. If this collection of well-dressed and formerly well-mannered individuals continued to deteriorate, near the entrance was where Charles wanted to be.

Just beyond the half waypoint crossing the ballroom, the first slap echoed like rolling thunder through the room.

As Breeker slept, a cold air mass from the northwest collided with warm air from the south. The collision of the two air masses resulted in a battle in the clouds. The battling masses produced torrential rain from the heavens. With each strike of hot air upon cold or vice versa, lightning gave sight to the blow, and thunder gave sound to its delivery. Both opposing forces rode their own mighty winds that blew in disagreement and with great force.

Breeker, oblivious to the coming thunderstorm or the forceful winds, sat reclined, captured in his dream world. The events outside his home were no match for the turmoil erupting within his soul.

A second then a third slap quickly followed the first. Breeker found himself in the middle of a riving and battling sea of people. Breeker was confused. How it could go from a ballroom party to a ballroom brawl so quickly? He found himself ducking thrown chairs, evading thrown punches and kicks. For every three steps gained in advance toward the door, two were lost to the need for an evasive maneuver.

With only a quarter of the way remaining to reach the door, Breeker found himself facing more obstacles and more opponents. With a steadily increasing fear, he realized many of the people once fighting each other had turned their aggressions on him. He reasoned they were now determined to keep him from escaping the chaos. Among the chaos, he kept his eyes on his goal—the door.

He watched as the entrance's double doors flung open to the chaos. Barely inside the great hall stood his wife, Grace, flanked by their son, CJ, in full dress army uniform.

Feeling the energy of his youth returning, Breeker fought vigorously. He was determined to fight his way to Grace's side, even if it required him laying waste every soul that stood in his way. Over the ruckus and roar, Breeker could hear Grace and CJ calling his name.

CJ was not content to stand by and let his father fight this losing battle. With all the honor of a soldier seasoned by battle, he gracefully removed his hat and uniform jacket, placing them in the safe hands of his loving mother. Before entering the battle, Grace said proudly to their son words of encouragement and a command, "Go and help your father home."

The thunderstorm continued crossing the county, drawing nearer to Lake City. In the darkness, it delivered soothing satisfaction to those that sleep best during thunderstorms and trembles of dread to those that held a fear of storms. Hidden within the rolling and battling clouds, the winds had begun to turn.

CJ descended the stairs and waded into the fight. His sights were set on his father. Nothing could stand in his way. With deadly skill and precision, CJ progressed toward his father, leaving in his wake moaning and broken combatants that had once dared attempt to impede his progress.

Breeker, seeing his son had entered the fight, received and enjoyed a new surge of energy.

"If CJ will fight for me, I can certainly fight for myself," he proclaimed.

The beings in the ballroom, which had turned into a brawl, soon discovered they were no match for the two Breekers. Even though the attacks continued, the Breekers continued progressing toward a point where they would be able to merge forces. Charles and CJ's fight was so efficient and effective they resembled a gas-cutting torch burning its way through plate steel.

The thunderstorm descended into the county seat vigorously. In a matter of minutes, the streets and gutters were carrying their maximum capacity of runoff water. Combining the winds with the driving rain, the town was in the throes of a pressure wash. As it passed beyond the town, the winds in the clouds formed a tail that steadily grew downward with every passing mile.

When the two Breekers finally laid waste to enough opposition to join forces, Charles Breeker Sr. had only seconds to embrace his son. Wrapping his arms around the young man a half head taller than himself reminded him how proud he was of the young man that left his house a boy and returned a trained military officer before going off to war.

The embrace was short-lived as more assaults came from all directions. Both men focused their eyes on their goal of reaching the entrance beside Grace. They discovered the forces against them had formed to create a virtual barricade between them and the goal. This challenge, the two men took on with eagerness and determination. Working as a team, they slaughtered their opponents as they advanced. What were once well-dressed and well-mannered men and women had deteriorated into something inhuman, and their attacks were anything but gentle.

Charles "Bill" Breeker Sr., alongside his son, Charles William Breeker Jr., proved to be more than worthy opponents, exercising their superiority as they battled through their enemy.

Two miles out of town, the thunderstorm reached its most violent level. The tail of the wind, formed at the edge of town, now neared the ground. As the thunder and lightning grew more violent, the tail of the beast touched the ground, ripping trees out by their roots and splintering them like toothpicks.

The tornado set its course only a quarter of a mile from the home of Charles "Bill" Breeker Sr.

Side by side, father and son fought their way to the queen of their family. Grace stood atop the stairs and watched. It could not be said she showed concern for her husband and son, and she had no need to. She knew separately each was formidable in his own right. Together, fighting as one, they were unstoppable. Standing at the top of the steps, she sported more radiance in death than she could have outwardly shown in life. Nothing would stand in the way of her family reuniting, as the barricade of beings soon discovered. Her two men would rejoin her, and the beings would be damned if they dared stand in their way.

The tornado approached with what could only be called single-minded intent, its target Breeker's house. Its great spinning winds seized upon a line of barbed wire fencing, ripping the post from the ground. Taking the wire into its spinning grip, it would have consumed many thousands of yards of wire had it not been for the wires breaking under the intense stress. Still on the ground, the tornado shattered a wooden barn, where a cow had taken refuge for the night.

After shattering the barn, the tornado then swept up the cow as if it were a child's toy. The poor beast gave up its life when the barn shattered, sparing it the evil spinning and ripping of the tornado. The killing shredder winds seemed to be angry the cow was already dead.

As it approached Breeker's house, the cow was flung, much as an unruly child might sling a rock at a neighbor's plate glass window. The cow slammed against the exterior wall of Breeker's home.

As Breeker dreamed, the sound of the cow hitting his house registered as a punch thrown by one of the beings in the heat of battle. The punch glanced off his jaw.

Side by side, Junior and Senior fought as they advanced toward the stairway. Having no weapons of warfare, either current or ancient, they used their bare hands or whatever was convenient. This included, but was not limited to, chairs, tables, and severed body parts.

Grace, radiating pride for her men, stood atop the stairs, a beacon of light and hope. She also felt the pain for the injuries they were delivering to the beings as they progressed in the battle. She did not hate the beings her husband and son fought. She pitied them. She knew they had been trapped in a world of pain and torment and would remain there until the end of God's chosen time. She knew once her two men of valor reached the first step, Charles would near the end of his journey. When they reached the landing where she stood, no beast would have the will or the power to attack or pursue.

Charles Breeker Sr. never heard the approach of the tornado. The roar and battleground of the ballroom had wholly and fully captured all his attention. He never heard the tornado rip away the second floor of his house. He was totally unaware of his study shattering around him.

With dedication and determination, his heart and soul remained focused fully on Grace. He did not acknowledge the destruction of his home or the striking of the two-by-four stud through his back.

Charles Breeker Jr. fought with skill against a beast on the second step, clearing the way for his father. Charles Breeker Sr. fought equally as skillfully and approached the first step. From a direction unseen, Charles Sr. was struck on his back by a chair with such force it dropped him to his knees. Charles

Jr., seeing his father downed, returned to his side and fought beside him as he regained his footing. Side by side again, they battled their way up the steps. Climbing the steps, they lay waste one beast after another and grew stronger in the process. Nearing the top, the beast withdrew. The majority of them appeared to be too weak in spirit to continue the fight. The others had grown too fearful.

At the top of the stairs Grace remained like a lighthouse in a storm. Her presence showed the way for Charles Senior and Junior and, like an attentive and intelligent wife, she knew who and where to send help when it was needed.

Finally, Charles "Bill" Breeker Sr. held his wife once again and vowed to never ever let her go. With a radiant smile that lit the ballroom, Grace Ann Breeker made a statement her husband had longed to hear. "As we promised, we will be together forever."

CHAPTER 7

The sound of distant thunder, combined with Michelle's clear and precise statement, caused a chill to run down the spines of both Michael and Kathryn. Neither demanding nor gentle coaxing produced any results from Michelle. She had said all she was going to say about Mr. Breeker. With head bowed and lips pressed tightly together, she was determined to remain silent. When it was clear to Michael and Kathryn no more information would be given, the family finally left the car and entered the house.

Michelle, appearing to have dismissed the statement and light interrogation, entered her new home and immediately began searching boxes in her room. She thought it best to stay away from her parents for a while. Their wanting to know how she could say such a thing required far more explanation than she could put into words. The escape to her new bedroom was a wise move, but she was called to the kitchen in less than half an hour later.

Michael was grateful for the carefully marked packing boxes. With much of the kitchen to be unpacked, he knew life in their new house would be a search in progress for days or weeks to come. Still reeling from the impact of Michelle's statement in the car, he and Kathryn again tried separately and together to coax Michelle to say more, but she refused.

Kathryn noticed the movers had placed all the boxes marked kitchen in the kitchen. Richard Lloyd, their realtor, had personally vouched for the honestly and integrity of the moving company delivering their belongings.

"Don't give them any thought. They'll do a professional job. Just leave the door unlocked and a note concerning anything special you want done. They'll bring everything in and put it where you marked—that is, if you are not here."

Kathryn had marked where she wanted the larger pieces of furniture placed and left additional instructions on a legal pad in the kitchen. The movers had indeed followed her instructions, as far as she could tell. The care taken by the movers had truly proven to be professional. She had gone from room to room quickly inspecting the labels to ensure most had been placed in her desired locations. The quick survey became more difficult as clouds thickened outside.

Gradually, the clouds grew heavier and darker darkening the interior of the house. Michael found the boxes marked *Lamps* in a corner of the living room and quickly distributed them throughout the house. With lamps in position and working, the house took on a warm appearance, if you ignored the boxes. To Michael's surprise, the utilities were already on. He made a metal note to have the billing changed to him in a few days and to thank the realtor.

As Michael worked, he tried to recall if Michelle had ever before made such a profound and damning statement. He thought back to the first words he ever heard her say, and nothing came to mind. He made a mental note to ask Kathryn if she had ever heard anything.

As the day grew later, Michelle helped her mother prepare dinner. Being so young, she was not allowed to handle any of the adult preparations that might cause her injury. Standing at the sink, Kathryn chopped onions while Michelle inspected each leaf she removed from the lettuce head. She knew her daddy did not like lettuce with brown spots.

Kathryn, closely watching Michelle's progress, suspected her daughter knew a lot more than she was saying. This possibility troubled her, but she decided to wait. She knew that eventually it would all come out, probably all at once.

Glancing out the kitchen window, Kathryn was pleased to see the fenced-in backyard with a tire swing hanging from a low limb of the big oak tree. She looked skyward past the proud oak and was equally pleased the skies had darkened. In childhood, she had been able to sleep quite well during thunderstorms, and she still did. She felt the combination of unpacking boxes and being back in her own bed would quickly send her peacefully into a deep and restful night's sleep.

The Stone family enjoyed their first dinner in their new home. Michelle ignored the glances of concern that came from her father then from her mother. She knew what they wanted to ask, and she wasn't sure how to answer or explain. The only thing Michelle was certain of was that she had to say goodbye to the old man at the newspaper and inform her mom and dad that the man was going to die. Beyond those two things, Michelle knew she would make no sense if she started talking.

With dinner completed, like an organized team, the Stone family attacked the job of unpacking, Michelle helped her mother while Michael did the same and ferried empty boxes to the garage. At ten p.m. Michelle, unable to fight sleep any longer, surrendered to the comfort of her parents' bed. They would have preferred she slept in her own room; however in view of the task, they acquiesced. The chore of unpacking continued until shortly after midnight. Michael and Kathryn agreed sleeping through the thunderstorm was preferred to more than struggling with boxes.

At four a.m., the train stopped and let Timothy off. He waved goodbye and in seconds, the train was gone. At four thirty-five a.m. a different train picked up another passenger, Charles Breeker Sr. He boarded the train with his wife and son for the final journey. At four thirty-five a.m., a little girl had a dream—a little girl named Michelle.

Michelle saw the old man in the company of a very pretty young woman and a very handsome young man in uniform. As the train passed where she stood near the tracks, the old man waved goodbye. With each wave of his hand, he grew younger, until he was as young and handsome as the uniformed young man. Joy, happiness, and relief could be seen on all the faces of the passengers on the train. Even as the train disappeared, the glow from their joy could be seen fading in the distance. Michelle awoke frightened and confused. Lying quiet and still, she could hear the thundering of the storm far off in the distance. She continued to wait and listen. Michelle knew she was in bed between her mom and dad, but the dream had troubled her to the point she thought it wise to wake her father, just to make sure he was okay.

Shaking Michael's arm and calling him, Michael awakened the third time Michelle said daddy.

Michael opened his eyes and looked at her. Not focusing, but rather eyeing Michelle with a sleepy uncomprehending stare that quickly became aware and conscious. Focusing his eyes on his daughter, Michael asked if something was wrong.

Michelle smiled before speaking.

"No, Daddy. I just wanted to make sure you were alright."

Michael delayed speaking for a moment as he comprehended what had been said, and then he answered,

"I'm fine, sweetie. Now you go back to sleep."

Michelle did not know what the meaning of the dream was, but she knew speaking of it now would be a big mistake. Seeing her father awake and quickly return to his usual form, Michelle lay back next to her mother and quickly entered a sound sleep.

Michelle had awakened Michael for what appeared to be no reason at all, and then she had immediately gone back to sleep. Now, Michael lay in bed concerned and in deep thought.

Michelle seldom awakened in the middle of the night, but tonight, she did. Michael considered a question: could it be the new house or something else?

He noticed the storm had passed, allowing the quiet of night to quickly return. Unable to recapture sleep, he found himself thinking and pondering the possibilities.

Could my daughter be gifted, or did the events make it appear that way?

Soon his thoughts turned to the new business, and he decided it best to get up and make coffee. With it already being after five a.m., he saw no reason to try sleeping again. Moving into the new house had given Michael a sense of relief he had not expected. The hour spent with his thoughts and a cup of hot coffee would be great, except he could not find the coffee.

At six a.m. when Kathryn entered the kitchen, Michael stood puzzled and frustrated at being unable to find the coffee canister. Kathryn, in her usual manor, planted a kiss on Michael's lips. Michael had always enjoyed her good morning greeting. Not saying a word, Kathryn reached down, opened the flaps on the cardboard box beside Michael and removed the canister of ground coffee.

Michael looked at his wife then back to the packing box. Believing he had looked into all the boxes in the kitchen, he was having trouble understanding how he could have overlooked that one box. Kathryn eyed the look on his face for a second. Smiling, she again kissed him good morning, and then asked him to help her make breakfast. Michael did not refuse; however, he quietly continued to wonder how he had missed that particular box.

The smell of cooking bacon and the absence of two warm bodies brought a sleepy Michelle out of bed. Walking into the kitchen, Michelle stopped and giggled as she watched her mother and father kissing in the kitchen. This she had caught them doing on more than one occasion. Hearing the giggle, Michael and Kathryn, not expecting Michelle up so early, broke their embrace. Kathryn, embarrassed, informed their daughter she had not washed her face, and breakfast would not be served until she did. Michelle, still giggling, exchanged the kitchen for the bathroom to wash her face.

Kathryn, still slightly embarrassed, asked Michael to clear the table. Michael, having enjoyed the moment, issued a mischievous laugh while doing as she had requested. Recalling his mental note, Michael, in a low voice, asked Kathryn, "Can you remember Michelle ever saying anything before, like she said yesterday?"

"No, I haven't, and she's still not saying anything."

Michael remained silent. Michelle returned to the kitchen looking clean-faced and hungry. Taking a seat at the table, she waited for her breakfast. With full plates before them, the three sat at the kitchen table and enjoyed the meal together.

When breakfast was completed, Kathryn gathered the dishes and began washing them. Returning from the table for the glasses, she noticed the sheriff's car slowing to enter their driveway. With a surprised voice, she pointed this out to Michael.

Michael, dressed in jeans and a sweatshirt in preparation to help put things away for a few hours, did not hide his surprise at having a visitor so soon. Michelle had been finishing a bowl of cereal until her mother spoke. Now she sat staring at her mother. Kathryn noticed this sudden change. Addressing her daughter directly, she asked, "Michelle, what is it?"

Michelle, still staring at her mother, said, "I had a dream last night."

Kathryn would not normally give much weight to this statement, but it was something about the way she said it that made her concerned. The change had not gone unnoticed by Michael.

He asked, "Was there something special about this dream, honey?"

Michelle spoke quickly hoping to get it all out before the sheriff arrived. In a flurry of words, she said, "It was a dream about the old man at the newspaper, and he was on a train, and he was with another man and a real pretty woman, but the other man was a lot younger, and as the train passed by, he waved at me like he was saying goodbye, but every time he moved his hand he got younger until he looked as young as the other man. But they kept changing, and their clothes were old. The woman, she had on a big hat with flowers all over it, and then they disappeared."

After saying this, she dropped her head and said, "He's gone." Her tone did not imply he would be coming back.

By now, both Kathryn and Michael were trying to comfort and reassure Michelle that everything would be fine. That it was just a bad dream. She didn't want her parents worried, but she didn't tell them that she knew what kind of train it had been and the people it carried. A moment later, there came a knock on the door. Michael stood up, kissed Michelle on top of her head and then went to answer the door.

The man at the door was in his mid-twenties and dressed in a freshly pressed sheriff's uniform. He was strong jawed, wide shouldered, six feet two inches tall, and appeared to be fit. At first glance, Michael decided he would rather not be in a fistfight with him. He spoke to Michael in a strong but friendly tone, saying, "Good morning. Are you Mr. Michael Stone?"

Michael replied, "Yes, I am. How can I help you?"

"Mr. Stone, I'm Deputy Sheriff David Long."

Michael could think of no reason or event he had been engaged in that would bring the cops to his door. His training had taught him to be cooperative, but offer no information to a cop until you had an idea of the cost. Fortunately, the deputy continued.

"Mr. Stone, I understand from Mr. Breeker that you bought his paper."

"Yes, so what can I do for you?"

"Well, Mr. Breeker usually likes to ride along with one of us after an event like last night's storm to check the county and put together the story for the paper. When he told me he had sold the paper the other week, he asked me to give you the same opportunity. It's outside of department policy, but the sheriff approves, and the county folk don't mind. If you'd like to ride along, I'll wait for you in the car."

Michael, being a seasoned reporter, did not have to be asked twice.

"Thank you, Deputy Long. Let me grab a few things, and I'll be right out."

Deputy Long nodded and returned to his car.

Michael turned from the door to see Kathryn and Michelle standing in the kitchen doorway watching him.

Kathryn asked, "What's wrong?"

"Deputy Long wants me to ride with him to survey the damage, if there is any. I'll need my pad and probably the camera."

Michelle, watching him intently, said, "Daddy, don't forget to check on the old newspaper man."

After the way she had relayed her dream, he had no choice.

CHAPTER 8

As Timmy slowly made his way through the wreckage that was once the home of his neighbor, he could not fully comprehend the scope of the damage. He looked in all directions and still saw more of the same.

What had once been the backyard was now the resting place of an uprooted oak, and not just uprooted but split. Underneath it lay what appeared to have been the kitchen table at one time and beside it, the front door.

Turning to look in a different direction, he recognized something that was once a hot-water heater; now it resembled a twisted beer can. Next to the hot-water heater lay the sofa, broken in half with pieces of wood, wire, and other stuff sticking through it. He looked at the stubble of a tree nearby and noticed a pencil sticking out of it. Timmy made his way over to the stubble and tentatively touched the pencil. It was shoved into what was a green living tree, but the pencil was unbroken. However, half buried into the green wood, he knew it couldn't be removed intact.

Turning away from the pencil, he saw one half of a set of curtains that once hung in the old man's study. Recognizing the piece of fabric helped bring him back to reality.

Amongst the destruction, he began to look for his friend. Calling his name, he looked under shattered walls and shattered furniture. He even looked in the car, hoping Mr. Breeker had been trapped inside while trying to escape, but found no one there. Being careful where and how he stepped, he worked his way through the area that once was a house, but found no one.

Frightened and concerned for his friend, he looked around again. And again, his attention was drawn to the curtain hanging in what was left of a tree, but this time it seemed to be more of a flag than a curtain. And for a few seconds, he watched as the curtain furrowed and rolled in the wind. As if following some unknown direction, he looked down below the curtain flag. What he saw gave him motivation to move quickly through the debris.

The curtain was ten yards away from where the house had been and under it sat Mr. Breeker's roll-top desk. From Timmy's position, he couldn't see the front of the desk.

With some difficulty because of the debris, Timmy made his way within ten yards of the desk before being blocked by debris he could not identify. After taking a different route, he eventually came to the desk. For his efforts, the first thing he recognized was the foot of Mr. Breeker.

Timmy now approached much slower, calling Mr. Breeker's name as he neared. When he had a clear view of the front side of the desk five feet away, he knew there would never again be a response. Timmy saw the desk had come to rest upright, and Mr. Breeker, in his chair, lay on his side. Timmy would have had hope if it were not for the broken two-by-four wall stud and barbwire wrapped around Mr. Breeker and the chair.

Timmy saw, for the first time in his young life, the look of death after a few hours. The man that lay dead before him was not only a neighbor but also most of all his escape, protection, and friend.

Timmy stood looking at Mr. Breeker, wanting to help, but knowing there was no need. The tears began to flow down his swollen face, but this time the pain was in his heart. He had wished, even dreamed many times, Mr. Breeker was his father or even his grandfather. From the day six months ago when Mr. Breeker had found him sitting on a pile of wood behind his work shed crying, and had taken him inside for a glass of milk and treated his injuries from the wire beating, Timmy had known he was more than just an old man. In fact, he had not been just some strange old man that seemed to care about him, but indeed someone who did care, unlike his parents.

Timmy had seen dead animals before but never a person, and least of all someone he knew and cared for. He knew his world was bad, but now he felt it getting a lot worse.

CHAPTER 9

Michael gathered the tools he needed, kissed his two favorite girls goodbye, and dashed out the door. Kathryn and Michelle trailed as far as the front porch. Michelle clung to her mother, watching her father leave with the deputy. She knew she had said a lot in seconds but hoped her parents understood.

Once comfortably seated in the car, Deputy Long asked, "Any particular area you want to check out first?"

Michael, surprised by the question, said, "No, this is your county. I'm along for the ride. Besides, I don't know the county like you do."

With this, Deputy Long turned onto the highway in the direction of the countryside.

As in most rural counties, Deputy Long's radio was not very active. The quiet of the radio attracted Michael's attention. He even glanced at it a time or two just to make sure it was on. Deputy Long noticed his action and lifted an eyebrow in annoyance.

"Is something wrong?" Deputy Long asked.

Michael, embarrassed at being caught, said, "No, why do you ask?"

"You keep looking at the radio like something's wrong with it."

Michael realized he might need to explain himself and said, "In the more heavily populated areas, the patrol radios never stop. Your radio just seems awfully quiet."

For Deputy Long, this was his first law enforcement job out of the army and technical school. Having no experience in law enforcement in other places, he chose to simply agree and let it drop.

They came to an intersection of paved roads, and Deputy Long turned right. Michael had memorized the county map so he knew where it led. Five minutes later, they reached the main county road, which led into town. The deputy turned in the direction of the countryside again.

As the deputy drove, Michael looked out on green fields and forest. Not being a country boy, he didn't realize the work required to manage those fields. Nonetheless, he liked what he saw. After the overnight storm, the vegetation looked ready to grow faster and stronger.

The radio crackled alive with a gruff male voice.

"John."

The deputy picked up his microphone, saying, "Yeah, Sheriff."

"A call came in. Looks like a tornado set down over by 278 and Breeker Road. You want to go check it out?"

Deputy Long responded with, "10–4, Sheriff. I'm on my way."

A half-mile down the road they turned right on a narrow county road and traveled north. Two miles later, coming to an intersection, Michael spotted the sign for County Road 278. Deputy Long turned left. A couple of miles later, they came across an area that clearly had been struck by a tornado.

Assorted debris and trash were scattered one hundred yards before seeing the impact area. At the area of impact, the tornado had clearly cut a path of destruction. They stopped and looked around. Michael asked if anyone lived in this area.

Deputy Long replied, "Only a few people here, but they are farther down the road. There's another group over on Breeker Road."

This got Michael's attention. He asked Deputy Long, "Does Mr. Breeker live in this area?"

"Yes, on Breeker Road."

"Can we check on him?" Michael asked.

Deputy Long looked into the distant landscape to his left at the path that had been cut, knowing that only a mile and a half in that direction was Mr. Breeker and other people he felt might be in trouble. If his guess was right, Mr. Breeker's place was in the bull's eye.

At the next paved road, Deputy Long turned left onto Breeker Road. Not as wide as the county road, it was still wider than the other roadways.

A quick passing inspection revealed the house at the intersection looked undamaged, they drove on. Coming out of a curve in the road, they immediately saw the destruction.

The first to capture their attention was part of a rooftop lying beside the road. Looking farther down the highway, the view did not improve. As they drew closer to Mr. Breeker's house, they drove around yards of barbwire, chunks of brick, and concrete. Part of a grain silo lay crumpled on its side in the field. A complete half-mile of forest had been decimated on both sides of the road. The appearance could be compared to the damage a giant weed eater might do. Right in the middle of the strip that had been cut by the tornado sat what was left of Mr. Breeker and his home.

Timmy had not noticed the sheriff's car until it came into the driveway of Mr. Breeker's home. When he did see it, he ducked down and duck-walked in the direction of the largest pile of rubble he could see. It was too late. He had already been seen by Michael and Deputy Long.

Michael opened the door and stepped out while saying, "Oh my god." Deputy Long opened his door stepped out with the radio microphone in his hand. He radioed back to the sheriff, reporting the damage to the Breeker place. Michael, standing beside the car, looked around in surprise at the damage done by an act of nature. Being prepared to do his job, no matter the circumstances, Michael began taking pictures. He knew a couple of good pictures would carry well with his story.

The tornado had set down over a mile away and stayed down till it was approximately two hundred yards past where the house had been, destroying everything along the way.

Deputy Long walked in the direction of where he had seen the boy. He wanted to see what had captured the boy's attention so intently that he had not seen or heard them coming.

Michael, seeing the direction the deputy was walking,

stopped taking pictures and followed. They walked only thirty yards and came upon a clear view of the desk.

Mr. Breeker lay in the exact position he had been dropped by the tornado—on his side, nailed to the chair by a two-by-four through his back and wrapped in barbed wire. Deputy Long looked at Michael and said, "Don't touch anything. I'll be right back."

Michael, a seasoned and experienced reporter, knew better than to comment at the scene of a death. The backlash could be especially unpleasant when the officer personally knew the victim.

Michael had seen death and the dead before and on occasions a little too closely. With many years as a reporter, he had been to many crime scenes and battle zones. In forward fighting positions, Michael witnessed the deaths of writers, reporters, and soldiers alike. This time it was different. His daughter had warned him something was wrong.

He looked away from the body toward the pile of rubble that hid Timmy. Making eye contact, Timmy ducked his head.

Deputy Long returned with a blanket and was about to cover the body when Michael said, "Wait a minute."

He had changed to a different position, looking over Mr. Breeker's left shoulder. From this angle, he could see what the old man held in his hands. He motioned for the deputy to come closer. When Deputy Long was standing beside him, he saw it too.

Mr. Breeker had been holding a picture of his wife and son in his hands at the time of his death, and he still held it with a firm death grip.

Michael looked at the deputy, and Deputy Long looked back at Michael. With a shared sympathy, the two men said nothing.

After the body was concealed, Deputy Long finally spoke, "That was his wife and son. They've been dead for a long time.

Now they're all together again, like he always wanted."

The framed photograph Mr. Breeker held had no damage. Not even a crack in the glass.

This observation gave Michael a chill and a question: did Michelle see him die?

Michael looked at the pile of rubble that concealed Timmy, and then asked the deputy who the boy was. Deputy Long looked at him with an expression of regret. Speaking with a tone of despair, he said, "That's the kid from across the woods. He has a real nasty set of parents. Been trying to get the state to step in, but the daddy must know somebody because they won't do a thing."

Michael watched Timmy as he ran toward the woods then disappeared into the undergrowth. With a heavy heart, Michael began making notes for the stories that would run in the next edition. The first would be about the storm and damage. The second would be a contribution to Mr. Breeker.

CHAPTER 10

Timmy, motivated by fear, moved with speed along the deer trail. The trail meandered through the forest, eventually opening into the field near his home. He didn't really intend to go home, but with his presence having been discovered by the deputy and the unknown man, he felt he had no choice but to run. Being aware of the consequences of being blamed for things he had not done, running seemed to him his best option. He believed Mr. Breeker's death was his fault; however, he could not understand how. This thought heightened his fear and multiplied his efforts to run in hopes of finding someplace to hide. Timmy had not yet considered the magnitude of his loss. His main concern now was not to be caught and beaten by someone else.

Much sooner than he would have liked, Timmy emerged from the woods at the edge of the field near his home. Unfortunately for him, he was immediately seen by his father. The realization he had emerged in plain view of his father caused Timmy's heart to sink. This was an unpleasant reality only made worse when he heard the commanding voice of his father from across the field.

"Timmy, get over here."

Timmy knew by his father's tone he was in trouble. Considering the events of the morning, thinking of why was impossible. Knowing he had been seen by his father served to increase his level of fear. Wanting to return to the woods and avoid his father was his first desire. The fear of being caught later overrode his fear of a beating now. With a half-hearted effort, Timmy made his way across the field. Daily, Timmy expected to be hit when he neared his father. When he was within arm's reach, he was rewarded with his first slap of the day.

While Timmy lay on the ground, his father demanded to know where he'd been. Timmy, fearing more pain, blurted out his answer before considering the consequences. "At Mr. Breeker's place, Daddy." This infuriated his father.

"What the devil you doing with a newspaper man? You trying to tell something on me, boy? Don't you know I can beat you to death, and nobody will care or find your dead stinking butt?"

Timmy, lying in the dirt, curled and waited for the kick. The kick did come, but not from his father's foot, instead from his mouth.

"We'll tell them you went to live with family out of state. Everybody knows you're too stupid to live here for long. Remember boy, I own this house, and I run it. You don't talk to nobody 'less I say so. You understand me, boy?"

Too afraid to speak, Timmy nodded in agreement.

Finally, Timmy's father had had his say. This was not the end of it. Grabbing Timmy by the hair, Roger dragged him up from the ground. Still with a handful of hair, he practically lifted Timmy off the ground. Without concern for the pain he was causing, he both dragged and carried Timmy to the storm cellar.

Timmy began to cry and beg for mercy, but his pleas fell on deaf ears. Roger continued on his way to the cellar. Timmy promised to be good. He promised not to tell anyone about anything. He would have promised anything to stay out of the cellar, but it was not to be on this morning.

His father opened one cellar door and literally threw him in. Standing in the doorway, he said, "I'll teach you to go round shooting off your mouth."

The slamming of the cellar door rang in Timmy's ears. The sliding of the block, locking the door, sounded like the kiss of death to his young ears.

Timmy lay in the dirt crying as his father walked away. To complete the morning, Timmy heard his father's final words. "Shut up, you cry like a girl. Like a little sissy."

Timmy did not know why his father called him a sissy. He did not even know what a sissy was. All he knew was it hurt in his heart, his head, and his body. Again, he was locked away in the dark underground. Not having had breakfast, his stomach grumbled. The run back made him sweaty and caused his legs to ache. He was only ten, but was often mistaken to be older. He wondered if his size made his father and mother hate him.

Sitting on the floor, he thought about the loss of Mr. Breeker. The old man had helped and protected him. He had been his friend, and now he felt lonelier than ever before. He could no longer hide at Mr. Breeker's place, which now was all broken and never to be fixed.

Gradually the pain subsided, allowing him to feel more at ease in the dark. Not that he liked it at all, but he adjusted with the help of that little sliver of light through the door, preventing total darkness. Remembering how he had been taught to breathe in his dream, he tried duplicating the steps as best he could recall. Timmy was surprised by the effect his change of breathing had.

No longer crying, he sat on the wooden bucket in the dark. With a desire to find a place more pleasant than where he was, he began to remember last night's dream.

It comforted Timmy to remember the train ride. The fun he'd had was almost tangible. He began to remember and felt the rocking of the train. He could see the face of the conductor but not the face of his friend. Sitting on the bucket with his arms crossed over his knees and his forehead resting on his arms, he drifted off to sleep.

The rocking of the train relaxed him and made him feel safe. Timmy sat talking to his friend and finally realized it was not the same dream. This reality came to him as a bit of a shock. However, soon Timmy forgot it was a different dream and relaxed.

Feeling comfortable in this dream, Timmy asked his friend where they were going. The answer he received was, "To your safe place."

Timmy, even in his dreams, could remember the pain he felt when awake. Going to his safe place in his sleep was a pleasure. He gave his agreement with a simple okay.

As the train rocked and rattled, Timmy asked his second question.

"What's your name?"

As his friend ate what appeared to be chocolate-covered peanuts thrown into a void where a mouth should have been, the answer he received was, "Nats."

This was a name that Timmy thought he liked. Timmy looked around and noticed the train had more light and the seats were not as hard. He looked back at Nats, and he asked his third question. "Nats, this ain't the same train, is it?"

Nats, feeling pleased with himself, said, "Naw, this one is going somewhere else."

"Where's it going?" Timmy asked.

"To a fun place," Nats responded.

The only fun place Timmy had ever been was to the county fair. In what seemed like minutes, the train began to slow while blowing the whistle. When the train had completely stopped, the conductor announced in a loud voice, "Your stop, sir, the county fair."

With eyes wide in surprise, Timmy and Nats sprang to their feet and charged up the aisle, out the door, and off the train. Timmy looked around and saw all the things he liked and had enjoyed. He knew he was going to have fun here.

Timmy and Nats rode the rides, played games, won prizes, and ate cotton candy. Timmy had settled on a game throwing baseballs at a stack of tin milk jugs with the intent of knocking them down. The first ball missed the stack of ten completely. Nats laughed, saying, "You throw like a sissy."

The second ball he threw with more force, taking down six jugs. Nats continued to laugh and nudge him about his weak arms. This irritated Timmy.

Ball number three was thrown with all his might, impossibly wiping out the remaining four jugs. Having wiped out the jugs, the keeper of the game leaned over the counter with his arm extended to hand Timmy a teddy bear. His prized teddy bear was identical to the one that had disappeared from his room a few years earlier.

Timmy thought how cool it would be to have another one. He loved that stupid bear. Timmy, reaching for the teddy bear, nearly had it in his grasp when the entire county fair of his dream exploded in shattering light.

CHAPTER 11

The ambulance left the destruction that had once been Mr. Breeker's home quite different than it arrived. No sirens blared; only silent flashing lights announced the ambulance's presence. This time there was no need for the potentially lifesaving speed or blaring sirens declaring an emergency. Its only passenger was beyond pain, beyond help.

Michael watched with a heavy heart as the ambulance turned into the roadway in the direction of town. As he watched, he could not avoid thinking maybe Michelle had seen more than he thought in the office and in her dream.

Deputy Long was discussing something with the county sheriff and did not see the old pickup truck slow and turn into the driveway.

A few feet from the cars, the truck stopped. Two people emerged, an older man and woman. Michael recognized them from the storefront when he first came into town.

The sheriff, not having heard the truck before it stopped, turned to look. The couple obviously was upset, and the sheriff appeared to know them. The sheriff did not try to hide the news of Mr. Breeker's death. The three of them engaged in a clearly dreaded conversation. Michael, standing nearby, overheard him address them as Mr. and Mrs. Rayller. The sheriff proceeded to explain the obvious along with what they had not seen. The tornado had set down short of a mile away and cut right through old man Breeker's place and killed him in the process.

Mrs. Rayller, clearly attempting to comprehend the significance of the sheriff's words, responded with, "First he loses Junior in the war, then Grace to cancer. He spent all these years here alone with no one to take care of him."

This was a brief glimpse into the Breeker family for Michael. All he had known was the business side of Mr. Breeker; now, he knew the old newspaperman once had a family. Glancing around at the destruction, he now saw the area for what it truly represented—the end of this Breeker family line. He could only hope the old man was not an only child.

Mr. Rayller, speaking in a voice that betrayed his emotion, told the sheriff he and Mr. Breeker had been friends since childhood, and he would take care of cleaning the place up and the funeral.

The sheriff said, "I'll have the funeral home call you …" Mr. Rayller agreed.

To Michael's surprise, the sheriff called him by name and formally introduced him to the Rayllers.

Due to the occasion, there were no smiles, only handshakes and condolences. Mr. Rayller thanked him for buying the newspaper and turned away. Michael would have liked to have asked questions, but it was clear they had lost a friend and launching into an in-depth interview would be inappropriate at this time. Mr. Rayller returned to his pickup with Mrs. Rayller. With both wiping away tears, they left.

The sheriff instructed Deputy Long to finish up on the report, and then asked Michael if he would like a ride home.

Michael, having seen more than enough for his story, accepted the ride.

On the way home, the sheriff filled Michael in on the Rayllers and Mr. Breeker. Being careful not to give too much information to a newspaperman, he provided only enough known information to write a brief story.

Arriving home, Michael thanked the sheriff and left the car. Kathryn and Michelle waited for him on the front porch. Their expressions on their faces matched Michael's concern, stress, and quiet grief.

CHAPTER 12

After bidding the sheriff goodbye, Kathryn and Michelle returned to the kitchen, awaiting Michael's report. Experience had taught them he would be gathering what he needed before leaving again for the office. Even though it was to a new office, he would have time for them.

Michael entered the kitchen to a waiting cup of coffee and his two favorite ladies. The thought of the previous night's dream weighing heavy on their minds, the promise of a full report was most eagerly anticipated. Seating himself at the counter beside Michelle, Michael relayed the events of the morning. When he reached the part about the destruction of the Breeker house, Michael specifically addressed Michelle.

"Michelle, did you see anything odd when we were at Mr. Breeker's office yesterday?"

Michelle squirmed before answering. Kathryn would normally have objected to the directness of the question to their daughter, but she felt an increasing need to clear the air.

Michelle, coming to a quick decision, sat up straight and began to speak clearly and directly to both her parents. Absent were the actions of an overly energized child. In its place came a clear and unguarded response to her father's question. Before their eyes Michelle's mannerisms, tone, and quality of conversation became many more years mature.

"Mom, Dad, yesterday when we went to Mr. Breeker's office, everything was fine at the front door. However, Mr. Breeker was not alone. There were two others with him."

This revelation caused Michael and Kathryn to look at one another. They were certain there were only two people in the door, Mr. Breeker and the receptionist.

Michelle continued, "You remember the pretty woman and man in my dream? Well, they were the two, but they aren't really people.

When we went into his office, they just walked through the walls. Then they stood on each side of him listening the entire time we were there."

Michael held his coffee midway. It had not reached his lips from the moment Michelle started to speak. Kathryn leaned against the counter with arms folded under breast and made no attempt to hide the very worried look on her face. She said nothing, just listened.

Michelle continued, "In my dream, when he left on the train with them, it was like he could see me as well as I could see him. He waved goodbye to me."

Michelle looked down at her chocolate milk with a sad face.

Kathryn asked, "Honey, are you sure that is what you saw?" "Yes, Mother. I'm sure," Michelle replied.

Michael had been listening very carefully and now felt it was necessary to ask more questions.

"Did any of this make you nervous or scared?"

"No. They knew I could see them, but you couldn't."

Kathryn spoke, unable to contain her unease. "Have you seen anything like this in other places?"

"Yes," Michelle said.

"When, and where?" Kathryn was now unable to control her concern.

Seeing her mother was upset, Michelle said, "Sometimes I see other people or animals, but they do not want to harm us. We are what they call safe living, so they let me see them because they know I'm not afraid, and you two can't see them."

Michael asked, "Are there any ghosts around here?"

Michelle smiled and said, "Yes, Daddy, but they're not really ghosts. They are like spirits, and they're outside. They say they're here to keep us safe from the others, the bad ones. Can I go to my room now?"

Kathryn noticed Michelle had suddenly acquired the habit of retreating to her room when discussions like this developed, but no one objected.

When Michelle had left the kitchen, Kathryn took the stool beside Michael. Clearly shaken, she looked down at the counter for a moment before speaking.

"Michael, I had no idea this was going on."

Michael, equally stunned, replied slowly. "When did she become gifted?"

Not happy or comfortable with the term 'gifted', Kathryn's hard stare dug into her husband before speaking.

"Do you really think this is a gift for our daughter? It looks more like a curse."

Michael, having encountered people with such abilities before, was not at all uncomfortable with this being present in his daughter and set out to explain to his wife what he understood. Ten minutes into the discussion, the telephone rang.

The ringing of the telephone was a surprise. It was not supposed to be operational for another two days or so. The telephones, having already been plugged into their jacks, nonetheless gave them both a start when the call came in. Michael looked at Kathryn as he got to his feet and reached for the kitchen wall phone.

"Hello?"

The voice on the telephone was female and pleasant but nervous.

"Good morning, Mr. Stone. I'm Janice the office manager at the paper. I was wondering what time to expect you in this morning."

With the developments of the last half hour, he had forgotten all about the paper. His answer to Janice was that he would be there in half an hour. He thanked her for calling and hung up.

CHAPTER 13

One mile from the Breeker place, Mr. and Mrs. Rayller stood in their kitchen. Mrs. Rayller busied herself cleaning vegetables for the evening meal. Mr. Rayller watched her closely from across the kitchen. Knowing his wife did not often cry, he knew the events of the morning would surely push her to the breaking point.

Mrs. Rayller was not focused on getting the vegetables ready for cooking but instead was trying to keep Mr. Rayller from seeing the tears running down her cheeks. Mr. Rayller watched intently until her shoulders began to shudder.

He quickly walked across the kitchen, placed a hand on his wife's shoulder and gently turned her to face him. He could see she was indeed crying. Mrs. Rayller looked up at her husband to see he also had tears on his cheeks. The loss she felt was not exclusively hers. They had both lost the last of a good family and a dear friend. Taking her in his arms, they cried together, unable to put their pain into words.

The pain was shared and equally intense. There were no words of strength or promise, only the tears that came from a great loss. Minutes later, Mr. Rayller broke the embrace He could wait no longer.

Looking at his wife, he said, "I'm going back over there. There are some things I promised to do."

Knowing the long-standing friendship between the two men, Mrs. Rayller agreed.

Mr. Rayller drove his pickup back to the Breeker place. This was one of the darkest and longest drives he ever made. The two men had been friends since childhood, and he hated knowing he had lost another friend.

The occasional arguments now seemed so minor, so unimportant. He now saw himself and his duties differently, even more clearly, if that was possible. The questions:what would he do if he lost the misses? what would she do if she lost him? stood out once again in bold reality.

Pulling into Breeker's driveway, he again surveyed the damage. The two men had agreed years earlier if something happened to one of them and there were no family left, the other was to close out their affairs. Bill had instructed him to find his black strong box and force the lock open if necessary and but to follow the instructions inside. An agreement made beneath the large oak tree in Breeker's backyard now commanded it be carried out.

Walking through the debris, he searched for the black box, hoping it had not been picked up and thrown by the tornado. When he came upon the desk, he forced open the left side bottom drawer. Breeker had once told him the box was kept in the desk drawer. That seemed the logical place to start.

The left drawer contained files and records, but no box. Seconds later, he moved his attention to the right bottom drawer. In this drawer, he found the box and removed it. A quick glance revealed the box had remained locked through the disaster. Mr. Rayller made his way back to his pickup truck and returned home.

Walking in the back door, he put the box on the kitchen table. Not having a key, he asked Mrs. Rayller for her toolbox.

Opening the toolbox, he extracted a power drill and the proper sized drill bit. In no time, the box lay open on their kitchen table with Mrs. Rayller standing by the sink, showing an intense interest in its contents.

First out was Mr. Breeker's will with a lawyer's card. Next, he removed the insurance documents on Breeker's life, home, auto, and various properties. Lastly, he removed a thick manila envelope addressed to the Raylllers. Mr. Rayller forced himself to open the envelope. With a sigh and grimness, he poured the contents on the kitchen table.

Three different open letters tumbled out onto the kitchen table. The first, a letter addressed to Mr. and Mrs. William "Bill" Rayller. Second letter came from a hospital in St. Louis, Missouri. The third had only the name 'Charles Breeker' written in a woman's hand in red ink across its front.

The Raylllers looked at the letters, then at one another. The surprise was obvious. Mrs. Rayller nervously studied the three lying on her kitchen table. Using unnecessary caution, she selected one envelope. With just a slight shake of his head, she knew not to open it.

Mr. Rayller picked up the envelope addressed to them as if it weighed fifty pounds, then withdrew the folded sheets and began to read.

Dear Bill,

It must be assumed with your reading this that I have reached the end of my story. Before the final chapter is sealed with the dirt on my coffin, there are some matters of which I beg your assistance. There is not debt or threat available to me to hold over your head to force your assistance, so I must request your aide to the fullest extent of begging.

Years ago, I lost my beloved Grace of forty years. You know all too well she was everything to me. My burden was heavy enough with the loss of our son, but with her gone, I was completely empty. In my weakest time, I encountered, by chance, Mrs. Phyllis Scott. She was, at the time, in need of funds and asked if I was in need or desired a housekeeper.

You may remember this period of time because Mr. Roger Scott, her husband, had been incarcerated for over three years.

Well, I took her into my employ, and all was well for six months. I tried to keep things in a strictly business manner, but we became lovers. This lasted for three months. We were discreet, and no one knew; however, she abruptly quit my employ after the ninth month, saying her mother was ill in St. Louis. Months later, I learned by certified mail that she had become pregnant and had given birth to a boy. I have included the birth certificate as proof. She also included in a separate letter her demands that I must meet or lose my good name.

I made arrangements through a trust that Timmy L. Scott be taken care of, should I not live to see him an adult. Without your permission or knowledge, I appointed you as executor of the trust. For this I apologize, but I could not risk your refusal or my possible exposure. He is my son and all there is I have left. Please stand in on my behalf as best you see fit. This I have no right to ask, but there is no other choice. When my will is read, you will find more than ample compensation to carry out this task.

My attorney is aware of all this. My estate and worldly possessions will go to a trust for Timmy, under your care, as prescribed in my will. If you choose not to be involved, I will understand. Please forgive me for my weakness and forcing your involvement.

Sincerely,
Charles "Bill" Breeker Sr.

Bill Rayller reread the letter, wiped his face with the palm of his hand, and passed the letter to his wife. He then turned to stare out the kitchen window. Nothing was said until she finished reading.

Mrs. Rayller looked at her husband with shock and hurt on her face. She had liked and respected Charles Breeker, now she felt her respect and admiration had been wasted.

Unable to contain her disappointment, she said, "How could she do this to him? It is bad enough her husband was in jail back then for manslaughter, but she runs out and makes a baby with Charles. He was old enough to be her father, and he was a friend of ours. And he wants us to keep it quiet and continue on with this lie?"

Mr. Rayller looked at his wife but said nothing. He was thinking. He too was hurt but understood being lonely for the touch and feel of a woman, even if it was someone like Phyllis Scott.

To keep his wife from saying more than she could live with, he finally spoke. "Hold your tongue, and let Charles be buried before you crucify him."

With this said, he picked up the envelope from St. Louis. Opening it, he extracted a birth certificate for a nine-pound boy with the father being stated as Charles D. Breeker Sr. and certified. He handed this over to his wife for her examination also.

Finally, he opened the envelope addressed to Charles Breeker and removed another letter. This one was from Phyllis to Charles dated three months after the baby's birth. It read:

Billy,

By now you should have made arrangements for your son's well-being. You may think my only purpose for working for you was to get pregnant, but it was not. However, since it did happen, I demand you be a man and provide for him, since he is your only heir.

Proper care of him will require six hundred a month and a place to live. Considering you own the farm next door to you, I think our living there would be proper.

Living across the county is so inconvenient. Call me when it's arranged.

Phyllis

P.S. Roger might get parole.

Mr. Breeker finished the letter and handed it to his wife. This letter had soured his stomach, and he knew it would soon sour his wife's.

CHAPTER 14

Michael, standing in the kitchen, rested his hand on the receiver he'd replaced in its cradle. He was looking at Kathryn as a thought took shape in his mind. Kathryn, being familiar with his ways, knew he was heavy in thought and remained silent.

Michael, coming to a decision, said, "There is sure to be a funeral, and I think we should go."

This struck Kathryn as being a little premature and off the subject. This was a matter she would not let pass unchallenged.

"Do you think that would be appropriate? You know, with us being new in town and all?"

"No, not at all. We bought the paper and would probably be expected to be there," Michael replied.

Kathryn, not comfortable with attending funerals, questioned, "What about Michelle? She's much too young to be attending funerals."

Michael now half-smiling considered Kathryn's attempt to protect their daughter from the pain accompanying most funerals. However, he knew his wife had not considered the reality of what their daughter had already become accustommed to seeing.

"She's already seeing ghosts or spirits walk through walls. How is a body going to damage her psyche?" Michael asked.

Kathryn had no comment. The feeling she had entered the land of the unknown with no return took an uneasy hold within her. Unknown or not, she would stand by her family.

Michael saw the discomfort in her eyes and set out to put her at ease. "Look, she's already said she can see the dead, and she can obviously communicate with them to know the good ones are keeping an eye open for the bad ones. And she's a lot more grown up than either of us thought."

Kathryn considered this and had to admit, he did have a valid point. "Okay, she's much more gifted, as you call it, than we ever dreamed of, but she's our daughter, and I don't know how to keep her safe in light of this."

Michael's obvious concern was reflected in his reply.

"Neither do I."

Kathryn, resenting her own frustration, resolved to again push for answers from their daughter.

"There's not much we can do about it until we better understand what's happening with her. While you are at the paper, I'll try again to get her to talk about it."

Michael, seeing his wife's frustration matched his own, took Kathryn into his arms, kissed his wife on the forehead.

"I'll be back as soon as I can, okay?"

Kathryn mumbled okay, and then gently pushed Michael in the direction of his new study.

Going to the bedroom that would soon be his study, Michael quickly searched boxes and found what he thought he needed for the office. Standing at the door, he looked at his office cluttered with boxes and estimated the time he would need to organize it.

In the hall, he stopped at Michelle's door and looked in. Michelle looked up from her book, saying, "Daddy, Mr. Breeker is happy now."

Then she smiled, and so did Michael. A second later Michelle sprang to her feet in response to her mother's call from the kitchen. Taking Michael's hand, they both walked back into the kitchen.

Stuffing the items he'd selected into his briefcase, Michael said goodbye, kissed his family, and was off to the office. Kathryn and Michelle would spend the day unpacking boxes and arranging the house.

Finding the newspaper's office was easy. Parking his car on the side lot, Michael entered *The Republic* for his first day at work.

Michael's stepping through the door caused all activity to stop. His presence captured all eyes. Janice left her desk, meeting her new boss near the reception area. Janice, introducing and identifying herself as the person who called from the paper, was invited by Michael to join him in his new office. She instantly felt he was all business and followed him into what she knew would never again be Mr. Charles Breeker's office.

The entire newspaper company consisted of six people, including Michael. When Janice entered the office, she closed the door, an act of habit. Michael was standing by the sofa taking in again the room he'd seen a day earlier. The sound of the door closing served up a platter of possibilities for trouble. Glancing over his shoulder, Michael spotted Janice and the door closed behind her. Determined not to allow his first day at work to get any worse, Michael chose to start his open-door policy immediately.

"Janice, management will be operating under an open-door policy. I hope no one minds."

Michael did not need to say more. Janice opened the door, stood beside it, and made no comment. Hearing rather than seeing his request carried out, Michael made his second request.

"Janice, would you call everyone in for a quick meeting?"

Under other circumstances, Janice would have been upset being commanded in such a manner. However, in view of her last conversation with Mr. Breeker, and her decision to rejuvenate the embers of her marriage, quiet cooperation was her best course. Her attitude was also colored by a telephone call received from the sheriff's office an hour earlier informing her of Mr. Breeker's death.

"If this is about Mr. Breeker, everyone already knows."

Michael simply looked at her until she exited the office to gather the other employees. This took only a minute. Michael remained standing, but now by the desk. As the five employees filed in and took seats, Janice remained standing in the doorway to catch the incoming calls. She had been through such meetings in other places before and did not want to sit. When everyone was seated, Michael began.

"Hello and good morning. I am Michael Stone. My wife Kathryn and I bought *The Republic* from Mr. Breeker. For your information and to quell any concerns, there will be no changes at this time to the way Mr. Breeker ran the paper, but rest assured there will likely be changes as the need arises.

One at a time, I'd like for you to give me your names and your position here at the paper."

One by one the employees did as requested. This complete, Michael put faces with names and jobs, and then he continued.

"Last night we had a severe storm that produced at least one tornado. The tornado caused a considerable amount of damage in an area outside of town. The most severely damaged area was primarily at Mr. Breeker's home. I am fairly sure all of you have friends and family here, and have already heard Mr. Breeker did not survive. I know he was a friend and employer to you, and I'm sorry this has happened. I personally wish I could have had more time with him.

I have no other details for you right now, but I will keep everyone informed as I learn more, and I ask you to keep me informed as well.

Now, we have a paper to run, and I will need your help with the articles on Mr. Breeker.

That's all I have for now. Let's get back to work.

Janice, stick around please."

One by one they stood and left the office, each clearly carrying a new and painful burden. With everyone gone, Janice stepped into the office first business meeting with her new employer.

CHAPTER 15

The door of Timmy's prison swung open. At the top of the steps stood Phyllis, silhouetted by the backlight of the morning sun. Her elongated curvy shadow flooded through the doorway, disappearing into the darkness. The sudden light blinded Timmy for a bit; however, Phyllis seemed to be waiting for his eyes to adjust. After a minute or so, what he saw made him wish the door had remained closed.

His eyes focused on his mother's blood-covered right thigh. Seeing this, Timmy jumped to his feet with the intent of going to the aid of his mother, but what fell from his lap stopped them both. In the dirt lay an old dusty teddy bear.

Phyllis, standing in the doorway, held a plate of leftovers she'd prepared for Timmy. The surprise of seeing the long-forgotten teddy bear rekindled an anger usually kept just below the surface. Looking at the teddy bear and then at Timmy was all that was needed to give words to her true feelings.

"You and him ain't never done me no good, and now you made Roger cut me. For that, you can eat in the dirt with him."

With that said she threw the plate of food onto the floor of the storm cellar and slammed the door shut, barring it again.

Timmy knew now he would be in the storm cellar all day and maybe all night. He groped the floor in search of the teddy bear, not the food. He knew Mr. Breeker had given the teddy bear to him when he was a baby, but he didn't know why.

Timmy sat in the dark, squeezing his teddy bear like a drowning man clutching a life raft. The silence was interrupted with the sound of his father's pickup truck being started. As Timmy listened, he clearly heard the pickup leave. He hoped the driver was his father.

After hours of isolation, the door to Timmy's dungeon opened for the second time that day. Timmy, sitting on the ground, clutched his teddy bear. The food remained on the dirt floor, where it had landed. Phyllis, standing in the doorway, looked down at him.

"You gone eat?"

"I'm not hungry."

"Come out of there, then."

Timmy got to his feet. Cradling the teddy bear, Timmy approached the steps leading out of the cellar.

"Leave that in there. I don't want it in the house."

This was not a request. Phyllis offered no hint of concern for the security the stuffed animal offered Timmy. With reluctance, Timmy set the teddy bear on the bucket and left the cellar.

Inside the house, Phyllis resumed her insults and belittling.

"Why do you always look like dirt, huh? Can't you speak, boy?"

Timmy didn't know if she was questioning him or attacking him. So, he said nothing. Dishes were undone in the sink and bloodstains on the floor by the sink led down the hall to the bathroom.

The bathroom and the entire house showed pain and anger. Until the tornado that killed Mr. Breeker, Timmy knew he could escape for a short while. Now, even that was gone. The only person in his life that he felt treated him kindly was now dead.

Quietly, Timmy wished the tornado had hit his house and killed him, or at least his parents. He believed he could live alone, no fights, no screaming, and no more beatings. He felt that would be good. Saying this aloud would surely get him killed by his mother or father. Before he could fully think things out, he heard the pickup truck returning, and that meant his father was home. He did not know why, but his father hated Mr. Breeker, and he still remembered his most recent beating.

CHAPTER 16

With the dinner finished and dishes washed, Mrs. Rayller sat at the kitchen table thinking while drying her eyes. She not only felt the loss of an old and dear friend but also anger she could barely express.

"How could he have been stupid enough to lie down with her, not to mention make a baby?" she asked.

Mr. Rayller just looked at her. With an impassive facial expression, his mind worked through the problem as he remained silent. He understood how and why but chose to delay speaking. Whatever he said would offer little comfort for either of them.

He had accepted the fact an old friend was dead and had left him with a heavy responsibility, but he also knew it would take the both of them, working together, to see it through.

Choosing to defuse the discussion rather than allow his wife to a rant about the evils of loose women, he offered a more delicate response.

"He was lonely and afraid, like anyone else would be."

This response she seriously pondered. After being married to Bill Rayller for many years, she knew he would do as Breeker had asked, if at all possible. Sitting across the table, looking directly into Bill's eyes, she said, "Do you think you should call his lawyer and make an appointment about handling this?"

Indirectly, identifying the situation with Timmy was the only way she felt comfortable discussing it. With all their years together, she had always backed her husband and wasn't going to stop now. No matter the cost.

Mr. Rayller picked up the business card, read the number and name to himself, and then dialed the number.

After a short and uneventful wait, the attorney came on the line and indeed was familiar with the matter. The appointment was made for the day after the will was read. This seemed odd to Mr. Rayller, considering the death had just occurred, and he was two counties away. So he questioned the attorney.

"How is it that you can give me an appointment the day after the will is read when I don't know when that is?" he asked.

The lawyer said, "Two weeks ago, Mr. Breeker stopped by my office to say his time was short and to get his will and other matters in order. He also said your call would come after his death. That was how he had things arranged, and now that you have called, I will contact the necessary people so his wishes are carried out."

The lawyer seemed to have practiced this speech before and delivered it smoothly. This left Mr. Rayller a little uneasy. He asked, "Did he say he was feeling ill?"

"No, he said he had a gut feeling he should get things in order," the lawyer replied.

Mr. Rayller said, "Thank you for your time. I'll see you later."

With nothing else to say, he terminated the call. The one-sided conversation combined with the expression on her husband's face did not go unnoticed by his Mrs. Rayller.

Mrs. Rayller waited till he hung up the phone and then asked, "What was that all about?"

"Bill had a feeling he was going to die soon, so he went to this lawyer and told him to get everything in order, because I would be calling when he died," Mr. Rayller replied.

Under other circumstances, she would have said attorneys were only good for making up stories, but not this time. Especially since she had also experienced a troubling dream a week prior and had said nothing about it to her husband. Now with this, she decided to keep it to herself and pray it to be wrong. Bill picked up the phone again, this time to call their son, Bill Jr. He needed to come home and say goodbye to a family friend.

CHAPTER 17

With Janice's help, Michael only needed a few hours to gather the necessary information and construct the article about Mr. Charles D. Breeker Sr. He felt pretty good for doing so. This was his first story in the paper he now owned.

Janice put him in contact with the Reverend Andrew Burns, the minister at Breeker's church. A friendly and pleasant man, Reverend Burns provided good sound information about his character. A lawyer called the paper to give the obituary information and arranged for the burial. He said he represented Mr. Breeker's estate; however, in Michael's mind, all this was moving very fast.

Walking out of the office, he gave Janice the story and obituary to proofread and get to the printers. Checking his watch, he saw he still had two hours before deadline.

The funeral was set for three p.m. the next day. Michael told Janice to let everyone know they would be closing at two p.m. for the funeral and would remain closed the rest of the day. They would also be paid for the entire day.

Janice's expression indicated she was pleased about this, but she said nothing. Michael then left the office.

Outside, the sun was warm and the sky clear. The streets and sidewalks had dried. The grass and trees alike seemed to have appreciated the previous night's storm. The storm had been good for nature, but it had also taken a life and thrust him, prematurely, into his new role. He saw himself as the wearer of many hats, Newspaper owner, businessman, reporter, all this without the aid of the previous owner. Michael, walking along the sidewalk en route to the sheriff's office, encountered Deputy Long. Michael seized the opportunity to engage the deputy in conversation.

"Thanks for letting me ride along this morning."

"Not a problem. Mr. Breeker always did."

Deputy Long held a cup of coffee in one hand and paperwork in the other. He did not attempt to hide his mistrust of newspaper people or newcomers. He suspected this encounter was likely by chance but did not kid himself into thinking it would end with a simple, "Good morning, Deputy." Within seconds of the greeting, the first question came.

"Deputy Long, you said the boy we saw was from some nasty parents, right?"

"Yes."

"You indicated you knew where he lived."

Deputy Long eyed Michael with suspicion. The fact that he was the new owner of the newspaper did not help in the direction these questions could go. Coming to a quick decision, Deputy Long answered.

"Right next to Mr. Breeker. I think he found the body first, so this is going to be really hard on him."

Deputy Long, making a sorrowful sigh, knew all too well Timmy's parents. Wanting to give the new guy in town enough to work with or hang himself, Deputy Long continued. But not as hard as his daddy will be on him." "Why is that?" asked Michael.

"His daddy was pulling a prison stretch when he was born."

"And the problem is?" Michael asked this question while watching the passing traffic. He knew the deputy did not trust him, but why should he? He was new in town, and they didn't know each other.

"He had already been inside over a year when the kid was born," answered Deputy Long in a casual, matter-of- fact tone. Michael's surprise could not be hidden.

Deputy Long knew the numbers were all wrong for the man called Timmy's father to be his real father. The new newspaper owner's raised eyebrows pleased the deputy, but one more question had to be asked.

"If he's not the father then, who is?"

The moment the question left his lips, Michael knew he would not get an answer.

Deputy Long looked up at the tree they stood under as he thought, then back at Michael before he replied.

"This is a small town and a good-sized county. As you get to know the people, you will figure it out. Now you have a nice day, okay?"

CHAPTER 18

The rising sun did indeed announce the beginning of a new day. The sun chased away the night more efficiently than getting rid of an unwanted visitor. As the dark of night gave way to the sun, the light found Michael on his screened-in back patio sipping a cup of steaming coffee. Having not slept very well, he rose before sunrise to think. Being alone was not the issue, not waking the entire house was.

In seven days, he had moved his family, taken ownership of an existing newspaper, and discovered his only child may have access to the unknown and the unexplained on the other side. And, today they would attend the funeral of the former owner of *The Republic* newspaper.

Slowly sipping coffee, Michael admitted his family and life had not changed gradually but as quickly as the hands on a working clock. The past seven days had not only shifted them geographically but also mentally and physically.

From the sliding glass door, Kathryn spoke, disrupting Michael's solitude and isolated thought. He sat at the patio table, staring off into the early morning, holding a near empty cup of coffee. Her arrival surprised him.

"Is this private time, or can I join you?"

Standing in the open doorway, Kathryn held her empty coffee cup, a full coffee pot, and an electric hotplate. Sometime or another, she figured out he was on the patio and decided to bring what was needed to join him. She knew when Michael got up first and made coffee. It usually indicated something had not settled well in his mind.

"Yes, if you'll share the coffee," Michael commented.

Under Michael's watchful and lusting eye, Kathryn stepped out of the den onto the patio. Her simplest movement rekindled in him the reason why he loved seeing her in a dress. Her nightgown of conservative design always played a romantic melody in his mind as he watched her move.

She set the coffee pot on the patio table with her coffee cup. Michael plugged in the hotplate then placed the pot atop the hotplate to keep the coffee hot. Kathryn took her seat opposite him on a chaise lounge, leisurely stretching out her legs.

For a moment, Michael's thoughts toyed with the love in his heart and the desire of his flesh for his wife. He smiled and returned his thoughts to his previous subject.

Kathryn adjusted the backrest, picked up her coffee cup after filling it, and chose to recline and begin the wait. She knew Michael would talk when he was ready. Until then, she would enjoy her morning coffee, think, and wait.

For ten minutes, the only sounds made were the occasional distant passing of a vehicle on the highway and the morning birds singing. Finally, Michael spoke.

"Do you recall ever hearing of mystics or card readers in your family?"

Kathryn was not surprised or shocked by the question. She had also been wondering where Michelle got this new talent. It kind of made her uncomfortable. To see where her husband was going with his line of thought, she chose to be cautious.

"No, but as you know I'm only a third-generation American, so I don't know about Europe. What about your side?" she inquired.

Taking a sip of her coffee, she watched and studied him.

She knew there was more to come.

After a long pause, Michael replied.

"No, not even a hint, as I recall."

Michael refilled his cup and held it in both hands. Leaning forward with elbows on the table, he looked into the backyard several minutes before sharing his thoughts.

"Is Michelle's behavior and dream all that's bothering you?" Kathryn asked.

"Yes. Well, no. As a single matter, our daughter would be enough, but I'm looking or trying to look at the larger picture. Michelle dreaming of a train carrying Mr. Breeker away, then she says he's going to die.

That would be enough to ponder, but add to it the fact that, less than twelve hours later, Mr. Breeker is found dead. All of this coming together, at one time, can't be a coincidence. Besides, you said, there were no mystics on your side. And I am almost sure, none are on mine," Michael teased.

Kathryn fearing this conversation could get very intense concerning their daughter, sought to defuse it early.

"No, I said I didn't know of any mystics or card readers. That does not mean there were no gifted people in my family tree. And, maybe she really is gifted? That was your idea, wasn't it?" Kathryn said.

Kathryn smiled at their banter. She was pleased to see him taking a lighter approach. For Michelle's sake, she hoped he would continue to.

"I know of only one gifted person, and I'm married to her.

You refuse to let me worry in peace, don't you?" Michael replied smiling.

"Worry and peace cannot share the same space," she replied with a broad smile. He had surrendered his worry for a little pleasant conversation. She liked that.

"Do I get to choose?" Michael teased.

"Yes."

"Then I choose peace."

"Good, now would you like more coffee? Besides, I don't think we have enough information to be able to figure out which way this is going to go, yet," Kathryn commented.

Michael refilled both cups, handing one to his wife.

"We are talking about our daughter here. If she gets much more like you, we will never be able to figure it out." Michael teased.

Kathryn sipped her coffee, while concealing her thought*s*, *The man is as clever as a fox and still plays naïve very well.*

"So, what do we do now?"

"We wait and see." replied Michael.

As if on cue, they heard the distant train whistle blow as it passed through town. They looked at one another sharing the same thought. *How many more trains will she dream of?*

CHAPTER 19

Mrs. Rayller prepared a late breakfast. This was both a good and bad day for her. Her son and his family arrived during the early morning hours for the funeral. Their arrival home was a little too early for the time they were called. She suspected that Junior drove too fast, which was his habit.

While everyone slept, she felt it was her responsibility to have breakfast ready when they arose. Knowing her family was safely asleep under her roof made cooking breakfast not only a tradition, but a pleasure. She knew her labors would be appreciated and enjoyed by all.

Quiet as a mouse, a little girl walked over and leaned her body against Mrs. Rayller. She had not heard or seen the child walk in.

Little Shelia Rayller, eight years old, felt quite comfortable leaning against her grandmother, as she gave her a morning hug. Mrs. Rayller looked down at her granddaughter's eyes full of sleep and smiled at the sight of tangled hair covering the child's head. Suspecting Shelia would want to help make breakfast, she felt it wise to get her started toward the bathroom. All the while, her experienced hands continued to work the dough for fresh biscuits.

"Good morning, baby girl. Did you sleep well?"

Mrs. Rayller was always delighted to see her granddaughter had gotten her eyes and small nose from her father, but she had her mother's mouth and chin. Altogether, in her mind, there was not a more beautiful child.

"Yes Grandma, I slept good."

Shelia Rayller loved coming to her grandparents and felt she was growing up faster when she was allowed to help Grandma Rayller prepare meals. "Why are you up so early?"

"I had to go to the bathroom."

"And did you?

"Uh huh."

"That is 'yes, Grandma' to you."

"Yes, Grandma."

"Good, now go and wash your face and hands so you can give me a hand."

Shelia released her grandmother and returned to the hallway destined for the bathroom. Mrs. Rayller watched as Shelia left the room, only then did she return to her thoughts.

I wish Bill Jr. had stayed that size. I wouldn't have to worry about what might happen. Yes, what might happen? Dreams don't always come true. I certainly hope not that one.

Mrs. Rayller dreamed of Shelia standing in her doorway, bloody, and carrying a suitcase. Mrs. Rayller's son and daughter-in-law stood behind Shelia, but only in two-dimensional form, appearing as a photograph. Without warning, they quickly began to fade until they were gone, leaving Shelia alone in the doorway.

Mrs. Rayller was not a person that gave into superstition, but this dream shook her. It seemed to her for Shelia to remain alone, and then her parents to fade into nothingness might indicate she was subject to lose her parents long before she grew up. This made her hands shake. This meant she could possibly lose her son.

In a very low voice, she said, “I can’t tell Bill about this one. It would scare him to death. No, I can’t do that.”

“Can’t do what?” said the voice of her husband from across the room.

His voice gave her a start. She jumped, nearly tipping the tin of freshly rolled biscuits. Catching them in time, she shot Mr. Rayller an irritated glance.

“Sorry, didn’t mean to scare you. Now, what is it you can’t do?”

Quickly deciding to stick to her decision, she lied.

“I can’t get a cake made before the funeral, so I’m not even going to try. It’ll have to wait till we get back.”

Feeling terrible about lying, she continued preparing breakfast. Mr. Rayller said nothing but suspected that wasn’t it at all.

Soon, all the family was up and about. With washed faces and hands, they gathered at her kitchen table. As pleased as she was to have them, she wished they were together for a different reason.

CHAPTER 20

Phyllis sat on the side of the bed she shared with her occasional husband. He had decided not to come home again last night. This didn't upset her. In fact, she preferred he didn't.

I didn't have to put up with that fool last night, just the stinking kid. And today they bury the other fool, she thought.

She'd managed to get the deed on the thirty acres of farmland located between her house and Bill Breeker's. The only thing separating the two homes was a patch of thick forest. Her badgering and threats had also gained the deed to the house she lived in as well. He had even paid her monthly child support as long as she stayed out of court. This money went to her bank account in the next county.

That worthless heavy-handed husband of hers couldn't stay sober, or out of someone else's bed, or out of jail long enough to tend the land. As a result, she had leased it to a farmer across the county who paid at the end of each year, which gave her Christmas money.

Soon, she thought, she would have enough stashed away to disappear next time Mr. Perfect got himself locked up. But with Breeker dead, that might take a little longer. As for Timmy, he was only good till he was eighteen, then the money would stop. But she would still have the land, and Mr. Perfect didn't even know she owned it. If he did, he'd kill her then sell it. He thought they owned only the house and one acre.

When Roger walked into the bedroom, she was half-smiling.

This seemed to irritate him. In a half-drunken voice, he spoke.

"Get that smirk off your face.

You get your playboy out the door before I got here? Oh, that's right, he's dead."

He then laughed in his nastiest way, showing the few dirty teeth he had left. Phyllis was neither upset nor offended. He was right, Breeker had been her plaything, and he would pay for it until Timmy was eighteen, dead or alive.

After regaining his composure, he again looked at Phyllis.

"I don't know what you're smiling about. You and that baby reject in there are going to the funeral."

The flash of anger and dread mixed with defiance played across Phyllis's face. She could not help but imagine the evil and dirty stares she would receive from the other women in the county. Their husbands, sons, and boyfriends had been her entertainment for many years. She in no way wanted to be confronted with a church full of the "high and mighty" of this county, and she would tell Roger just that.

"The devil you say. There is no way I'm going anywhere near them high and mights in town."

Now on her feet, she stood with her hands on her shapely hips, defiant and facing Roger. He was in an evil mood, and before she could blink, he held his knife to her throat. In a voice equal to the hiss of a snake, he hissed his demand.

"You will go say goodbye to your old lover boy, or no other man will ever look at you with lust again. That is, if I stop cutting."

The feel of the sharp edge and cold steel caused her to quickly rethink her position. She knew the look in his eyes well. This was no joke. As much as she liked pain, she was in no hurry to die.

Without another word spoken, she stepped back and went to the closet to find something to wear, but Roger wasn't quite finished. With devilish delight, he spoke again.

"And remember, take the little reject with you."

Her head snapped around to look at him. The eyes had not changed. She knew from experience that to say what she wanted would result in more pain than she could bear. She said nothing.

CHAPTER 21

Funerals in small towns are usually a full-house affair. The funeral of Charles "Bill" Breeker Sr. was no exception. Being an old-timer and the former owner of the local newspaper, nearly everyone knew or knew of him. Word of his death spread across the county lines in only hours, and almost everyone knew which church to send flowers. Anticipating this action, Reverend Andrew Burns was waiting when the first arrangement arrived.

He knew there were many more to come. Reverend Burns called on the church secretary and elders to assist in the upcoming funeral. He also called the sheriff for traffic control. Many responsibilities were taken on by the good reverend and the sheriff. Charles "Bill" Breeker Sr. was the last of his family. There was no one left to handle the arrangements or carry on.

On the day of Mr. Breeker's funeral, the pews were full. No section had been roped off for family because there was none. Almost all the shops and businesses were closed at noon. Everyone, it seemed, would be attending the funeral.

Agnes Cornwell made it a habit of attending the funeral services of those near her age. Her and Gloria Knoll, both elderly women, saw this activity as their way of saying goodbye to those they knew and liked. If it were someone they did not care for, they would attend, just to be polite. Behind their backs, they were commonly referred to as salt and pepper. This was because Agnes was white and Gloria black. Neither of the ladies looked their age, and few people in town knew what that was. They did make note of the number of people attending the funeral and commented on it.

"It's a shame all these people aren't here every Sunday." said Mrs. Knoll.

"No one ever thinks they're going to die until they do, then it's too late." replied Mrs. Cornwell.

The casket was positioned at the front of the church, directly in front of the pulpit. Because of the flowers and the position of the casket, it was good the pulpit and choir were on a raised platform.

Michael and his family sat on the second row halfway along the pews. To his left sat Michelle and beside her sat Kathryn.

Mr. and Mrs. Rayller sat to the left of the center aisle. Their son and his family sat alongside them. When the church filled, Mr. Rayller felt Mrs. Rayller looking to his right and over her shoulder. This was very unusual for her because she seldom turned around in church to see anyone. Mr. Rayller, seeing her head turned, decided to turn and see what captured her attention. Her attention had been attracted by the two occupants in the third row— Phyllis and Timmy Scott.

Phyllis had cleaned up nicely, and Timmy looked about like every other little boy, but with a bruise on his chin. Phyllis knew the church was full, and she felt people looking at her, but she didn't care. Then she felt eyes burrowing into her, demanding she look. Look she did, right into the eyes of Mr. and Mrs. Rayller.

Mr. Rayller had a look of pain and sorrow on his face and in his eyes. Mrs. Rayller had the same, but her eyes told Phyllis how low she was considered, and respect for her would never be received from Mrs. Rayller.

Looking into the eyes of Mrs. Rayller, Phyllis could feel them boring into her. After a few seconds of eye contact, Phyllis had to look away. Through the remainder of the church service, Phyllis never looked into the eyes of the Rayllers again. She'd seen what she feared and dared not risk seeing—the scorn and hatred in the eyes of the other women.

Timmy sat to the left of his mother one row back from the Stones. He had been looking at the casket, and thinking about the shine and the flowers and wondering if there was some way to make Mr. Breeker not dead. He missed him. He looked back down at his shoes, old and unpolished. They hurt his feet.

Feeling someone staring at him, he looked up and around, right into Michelle's eyes. The eyes he saw were not afraid. They stared at him a few more seconds and then turned away.

Kathryn felt Michelle tighten her grip and begin to tremble ever so slightly. She too had seen the woman and boy. They seemed somewhat out of place, but this was a small town. Many different people would be here from all over. She made a mental note to ask Michelle about this later, and then the service began.

CHAPTER 22

Why are there so many flowers? Who would send all the flowers? Where did they come from? Timmy had never seen so many flowers in one place in his entire life.

The clear blue sky seemed brighter than he could ever remember. Standing at the gravesite, Timmy found himself sandwiched between two women he didn't know. Phyllis had pushed him forward so she could stand behind him. Confused by her action, he wondered what he was supposed to do now.

Watching the mourners, his eyes spotted a familiar face. There he was again. The face was that of the man who had been with the sheriff at Mr. Breeker's house. He looked at the man and then, looking between the flowers, he saw the girl. The same girl had watched him in church.

That's got to be her. What's she looking at me for? He thought.

Timmy didn't like being looked at. He always knew he was going to get hit if he was being watched.

He looked around at the other people. One by one, he saw faces, some he knew, and most he did not. He thought they all looked at him like he was dirty. He could see it in their sad and twisted faces. They looked at him like his mom and dad did, like he was worthless.

Timmy's heart began to pound, and his fear grew. He could still smell the flowers, their sweet smell, but more and more the odor of freshly upturned dirt came through. The smell of upturned earth gradually overpowered the sweet-smelling flowers. The earth that he stood on was now taking away his friend. The only one he knew that really cared.

He truly believed Mr. Breeker had been his only friend. He had no friends his age, not even in school. He had only one friend, and the ground was now taking him away.

He turned his head and looked past the other end of the casket and flowers. His eyes came across the eyes of Mr. Rayller. He was watching him. He was sure of it. His aged face was sad, but his eyes were angry. Timmy believed the anger was solely directed at him.

He wants to hurt me too, Timmy thought.

The fear grew stronger as Timmy looked away, right into the eyes of Mrs. Rayller.

She hates me too. I know she does, and she wants to hurt me like Mommy does. Timmy knew it. He felt it in every muscle and fiber. His eyes moved from Mrs. Rayller to her granddaughter, Shelia.

That girl beside the old woman is looking at me too, but why? I don't know her. She's going to laugh at me like everyone at school.

Timmy felt closed in, locked away in a small place. In Timmy's eyes, everyone began to look as if they were watching him, waiting for their chance to inflict their idea of pain and punishment or sick fun.

Timmy's chest tightened, his hands trembled, and his eyes flashed from casket to flowers to faces, over and over again. His young mind could no longer see the pain and suffering in the faces, only the mocking they directed toward him. Faster and faster his eyes moved, searching for a way out, someplace to run. In every face, he saw laughter behind their tears. Their faces and eyes made him feel like they were laughing at him.

Everyone was crying and acting like this was a big stupid joke. They were burying his only friend, and they thought it was funny. Then and there, Timmy decided one day they would all stop laughing.

I will make them stop laughing at me. I will make all of them stop laughing.

The thought circled around and around in his mind. It now became a part of him. The pressure and confusion became unbearable. Minutes later, Timmy became aware he had wet his pants, but he didn't care; he would make them all stop laughing.

Phyllis never noticed his discomfort, pain, or fear. Standing right behind her son, she ignored him slipping away. She was too busy enjoying the feeling she was getting from two men standing behind her. She never noticed her son's shoulders trembling for no apparent reason and then suddenly stop. Nor did she notice the puddle at his feet or the change in his stance.

She brought a battered little boy to the funeral of his daddy without telling him the truth about the man being buried. The child that would leave the gravesite would be different. This child wore wet pants, but the look in his eyes now portrayed a committed purpose. He had just become very, very dangerous.

CHAPTER 23

Kathryn and Michael stood with Michelle between them. Kathryn wanted to protect Michelle from the pain of any funeral, but finally decided it would be a learning experience necessary for Michelle's growth. She would need to learn and understand even this part of life and death. As part of life, Kathryn believed one day their daughter would have to say goodbye to them. Kathryn silently prayed it would not be the other way around.

At the gravesite, they had stayed back, allowing those familiar and acquainted with Mr. Breeker to get near to say their goodbyes.

Sobs and tears all around soon had Kathryn, Michael, and Michelle drying their eyes. They did not like seeing and feeling the sense of grief and loss the other people felt. The tears shed by his friends showed he would be missed.

Michelle had been holding her mother's hand tightly and wiping her eyes with the other hand when suddenly, she tightened her grip and stiffened.

Kathryn, drying her own eyes with a handkerchief, felt the pressure from the small hand. Looking down, she noticed Michelle looking through the flowers, over the casket. As the casket was lowered, she noticed the boy across the grave. Only a few years older than Michelle, his eyes were flashing from person to person. He looked terrified. She could see him trembling. Then suddenly, his trembles stopped. Michael had noticed as well. Ever so quietly, under blue skies, something had just happened to the little boy. Even if no one else noticed, the Stone family did.

CHAPTER 24

Mr. and Mrs. Rayller stared at the casket as the minister completed the funeral services. It was obvious to most present, their self-control was enduring its greatest test. The pain and sense of loss was not limited to just the Rayller family. Charles Breeker Sr. and family had been a part of the community. As the owner of *The Republic* newspaper, his observations and news stories were read countywide and beyond. The strong opinions and quick wit had entertained and informed readers for many years. Most of the mourners knew of at least one story that could have been written but was not due to The Breeker Standard: Report the news, ignore the gossip. The loss felt by the Raylllers was shared by most.

Mr. Rayller, with handkerchief in hand, steadily wiped his nose and eyes. To Mr. Rayller, all seemed to have happened too quickly. One day his oldest and dearest friend was here, and the next, he was gone. Even though he stood looking at the casket, hearing the words, feeling the pain, his mind refused to accept it as real.

Mrs. Rayller, also showing her emotions, stood dabbing her eyes, holding her husband's hand. She saw the years of friendship and association, the losses and the gains, the laughter and the tears of two families ended. Looking up and across the casket, she fixed her eyes on Phyllis and Timmy.

Within her pain and suffering she thought, *It is almost over. That harlot, strumpet, and worthless piece of trash over there used him and made him pay for a son he will never see become a man. She's the lowest of the trash, and everyone knows it. But she doesn't care.*

That little boy has no idea who he is or why he's treated so badly. To her, it's just a game. Any man will do, just as long as she can get him into her bed.

Phyllis looked around, avoiding eye contact with Mrs. Rayller. Try as she may, their eyes locked. The two women traded death stares with the accuracy of lasers. Phyllis knew if she was ever in danger, Mrs. Rayller would be the last to come to her aide, but she didn't care. She'd decided long ago to play men for her amusement and personal gain. The defiance in her eyes relayed her attitude to Mrs. Rayller.

The old bat is jealous. She wishes she had my body. She wishes she could get any man she wanted, dump them when she wanted, and have them begging for more. No, you old bat, you never did have it and never will. But I could take your man, use him, send him home, and you would never know the difference.

With tear-filled eyes, Mrs. Rayller continued to stare.

CHAPTER 25

With Mr. Breeker laid to rest, the town returned to normal. The damage from the tornado was cleared by Mr. Rayller with the help of friends known to the Breeker family.

The groundskeeper took care that the grass was always well manicured throughout the cemetery. The lawyer supplied the headstone for Mr. Breeker, paid for by Breeker's estate. In only a few weeks, the fresh flowers stopped appearing on all three Breeker gravesites.

Mrs. Breeker's was the first to lose fresh flowers, then Bill Jr., and finally the freshest grave, Mr. Breeker. A few people noticed the absence of flowers at first, and then gradually the town slipped back into a normal routine. Eventually, no one noticed the absence of flowers, but the Breeker memory did not erode as quickly.

The years passed, and the town grew as did the cemetery. The small town of Lake City gained a strip mall, four more stoplights, two more churches, and more people moved into town and the surrounding county. Many children grew up and left home, often to return with their offspring. Sometimes, they returned with their spouses in tow, but more often than not, without.

The winters gave way to springs. The springs surrendered to summers. The summers granted access to autumns. The autumns suffered to the heat shifts of Indian summer only to have to give way to the onslaught of winters. The springs arrived again to break the isolating grip of winters.

On one hot Indian summer night, Mrs. Rayller sat at her vanity table brushing her hair. Being of a curious nature, she was wondering why things had been so quiet around town, but still grateful it was. This was soon to change.

Mr. Rayller sat in his old recliner, reading *The Republic*. This gave him some comfort, not because he thought the articles and content were the greatest, but because he felt it was a part of his dear friend Bill he could hang on to.

With his feet up and the chair reclined, the old blue recliner was nearly too comfortable, and he was getting sleepy. After a few short catnaps, bedtime finally arrived. Besides, the wife hadn't been feeling well all day, at least that's what she'd said. He figured she hadn't felt well for quite some time.

Mrs. Rayller was in fact not feeling well and had not been all week. While attempting to brush her hair, her arm began a combination of aching pain and numbness. She ignored it and continued. Next, her stomach became more nauseated than before, forcing her to consider calling Mr. Rayller for help.

She hadn't eaten much dinner. The food seemed to have no taste even though she had seasoned it. The fact her stomach was now nauseated again made her afraid.

Mr. Rayller had righted the recliner and then forced himself up out of the chair.

"These old bones are getting tired," he said, speaking to his bones. He had only made a few steps toward the bedroom when he heard the cry of pain from Mrs. Rayller and a thud of her falling to the floor. He ran to her as only a loving husband could, no matter the age.

In the bedroom, he found his wife of many years on the floor near her vanity. Running to her, calling her name, she said nothing he could hear. Crouching on the floor beside her, he lifted her from the floor and placed her on the bed.

To him, she seemed to be a lot heavier than she looked. Her eyes were open, and she tried to move her arms with little success. Mr. Rayller asked her repeatedly what was wrong. She could only whisper, "I hurt so bad."

Mr. Rayller grabbed the bedside telephone and dialed the three-digit emergency number. He was in a state of near desperation. Mrs. Rayller said in a soft and light whisper, "Bill, remember the train ride?"

He said, "Yes," ignoring the operator. He remembered they had only taken one train ride together, and that was when they were very young.

She continued, "Thank you for taking me."

"I was glad you went," he said softly.

Mrs. Rayller whispered, "I love you, Bill. See you at the station."

He looked into her eyes. The voice of the dispatcher was getting agitated because there was no response. Finally, he said into the phone, "My wife is going to the train station. We need an ambulance."

The operator, not understanding the situation, said, "This number is for emergencies."

Mr. Rayller said, "She's dying! Please send me an ambulance. We are at 9131 Breeker Road."

The dispatcher continued to talk, but Mr. Rayller laid down the phone. He wanted to hold his wife before she left for the station.

CHAPTER 26

The emergency units arrived at the house. Being local, they knew Mr. Rayller seldom locked his back door. With speed and urgency, they entered the house, locating Mr. Rayller in the bedroom lying on the bed beside Mrs. Rayller.

Holding her in his arms, he retold about the sights and sounds of their only trip by train. With tears rolling down his face and a breaking voice, he ignored the emergency workers and continued talking to his wife.

He and Mrs. Rayller knew the nearest hospital would be fifteen miles away, and she did not think she would make it.

Before the emergency team or the sheriff arrived, Mrs. Rayller left for the station. Mr. Rayller talked to her all the way. Not wanting his wife to be alone and afraid, he could not see himself allowing her to make this journey without him. Try as he did, the only thing he could use was his voice. He was aware if he held her lifeless body and prayed, his voice may be permitted to travel with her soul. Joined in marriage by love, heart, and soul, he knew she would be waiting at the station when he arrived.

The EMTs struggled to save his wife, even though they had little hope, if any, of doing so. While the EMTs worked, Mr. Rayller called their son.

Bill Jr. and his family were just walking in from a family night out when the telephone rang. Bill answered, "Hello."

In a broken, tear-filled voice, Mr. Rayller could say very little.

"Son."

The only word Mr.Rayller could utter as he struggled to force the words to come together in his mind.

"Dad? Dad, what's wrong?" Bill Rayller Jr. barely recognized his father's voice; however, in that recognition he also heard pain and fear, in one word.

"Ma's gone, gone to the train station," said Mr. Rayller painfully.

Mr. Rayller could hold his composure no longer. For a minute or so he sobbed, and his son listened. Bill Jr. knew the meaning of 'gone to the train station.'

As a child, when discussions of the dead or dying arose, it was always referred to as taking a train ride. He knew but could not get his mind around the thought of his mother going to the station.

When his wife entered the room, he held the phone halfway down his chest, lost in thought and shock. She took the phone and said hello. What she heard was her father-in-law crying and in a broken voice talking about a train station. She said, "Papa Rayller, what's happened?"

"Ma's gone. You need to come home." Then his voice broke again.

"We'll be there right away." She said.

"Thank you." These two words relayed only a fraction of the confusion and agony raging within Mr. Rayller. Without saying another word, he hung up.

Bill Jr., his wife, and daughter were back in the car in fifteen minutes. Thoughts of his mother mixed with references of the train station filled his mind as he drove.

CHAPTER 27

Many adolescent girls have mixed dreams. They are in that time of life between childhood and teenage years. Everything begins to change. The dreams of climbing mountains and trees began to change to fashion shows and perfumes.

However, on this Indian summer night, Michelle's dream was one of the aforementioned. Having completed her homework after dinner, she said her goodnights and went to bed.

Shortly before eleven p.m., her first dream came. At the age of twelve, Michelle had become quite accustomed to her often odd dreams. On this night, they would forever capture more of her attention.

A lady stood on the platform of a train station waiting for someone. A man came from beside the station and started toward the woman on the platform. First, he walked, then he ran, but she only got farther away. The man was Mr. Rayller.

After midnight, she had her second dream. Sound asleep, she heard a train whistle, or was it the sound of skidding tires of an automobile that became the sound of a train whistle? She could not be sure.

Emerging from a dream fog, Michelle saw Mr. Rayller at the same station. He was very sad. He'd stopped running and stood at the train, looking at those on the platform. Mrs. Rayller, her son and daughter-in-law, were all on the platform.

Michelle recognized all that were present now, and she knew why. Struggling to awaken, she sat on the edge of her bed wiping her eyes. Her mind emerging from the dream world, she asked the empty room, "Do I tell Mom and Dad now or later?"

She heard a voice, "Let them sleep till morning."

This surprised her. She had not expected an answer. The voice was female, soft and gentle but firm. In moments, she recognized Mrs. Rayller's voice and understood that she was dead. The voice also asked her to help Shelia and Mr. Rayller as much as she could. They didn't have much time and would need lots of help.

Michelle replied, "Yes, ma'am."

Then she was told to lie down and go back to sleep. All that could be done was being done. Michelle did as instructed and soon was back asleep.

CHAPTER 28

Mr. Rayller stood heartbroken in the emergency room with Mrs. Rayller's body. His grief was clear, but his thoughts were repetitious and sometimes, he would simply say, "How do I tell our son?" A question no one could answer, not even him. He knew Bill Jr. would come to the hospital.

After a considerable amount of coaxing and pleading from the nurses and finally the doctor, Mr. Rayller permitted himself to be led to the hospital chapel. His reluctance to leave his wife was handled in the most delicate of manners. To ignore his loss would have only served to increase the injury he already felt.

Seated in the chapel alone, his mind jumped in spurts and dragged over things of the past. Alone with his thoughts and prayers, the death of his wife was being rejected by his heart and mind. In his pain and confusion, no one could have convinced him the lady sitting next to him was not his wife. The spirit of Mrs. Rayller, seated beside him, had not come alone. Standing in the aisle next to his pew were his son and daughter-in-law.

The gentle words of comfort coming from them soon helped him understand how much they loved him and that he would never be alone. He had God, the memory of them, and his granddaughter. The fact they were with him only in spirit, refused to take root in his mind.

At two forty-five a.m., Deputy Long stepped into the chapel. With hat in hand, he approached Mr. Rayller with dread and regret. Delaying his steps, he summoned the courage to follow through with his duties. Seeing no way to cushion his task, he approached and spoke to Mr. Rayller.

"Mr. Rayller."

Mr. Rayller looked up from where he sat in the pews. He did not look at Deputy Long; rather, he looked through him, but said nothing. Deputy Long, feeling sick, did not want to say what he had come to say, but it was his job. He had known the Rayller family for most of his life and did not want anyone but himself to bring Mr. Rayller the bad news. The family was special to him and because they were, he would carry as much of the burden as he could. Standing in the aisle, to the front and right of Mr. Rayller, Deputy Long continued what he came to do.

"Mr. Rayller. Sir, I have to tell you something that I really hate to say. Can you understand me, sir?"

Deputy Long looked back down the aisle to the doorway of the chapel. At Deputy Long's request, the E.R. doctor and nurse stood just inside the chapel door. They read his face and came forward. If necessary, they would be close by.

He tried speaking to Mr. Rayller again.

"Mr. Rayller, did you call your son earlier to come to the hospital?"

Mr. Rayller struggled to comprehend what was being said. After a minute, he finally spoke.

"Yes, I did."

Deputy Long swallowed hard and struggled to maintain control of his emotions. Knowing there was no way to break such news gently, Deputy Long continued.

"Mr. Rayller, sir, Bill Jr. has had an accident, and—"

Mr. Rayller came to his unsteady feet, saying, "I have to go to my wife. She needs me."

The doctor, nurse, and Deputy Long knew Mr. Rayller had lost his wife of many years only hours earlier. Now they must inform him that his losses had not stopped there.

Deputy Long emotionally braced himself and continued. "Mr. Rayller, please sit down."

Mr. Rayller, giving him a look of defiance, attempted to push past him. Deputy Long did not move but instead spoke in a firm but polite tone.

"Mr. Rayller, Mrs. Rayller would want you to sit down."

No one knew if it was the stronger tone, the mentioning of Mrs. Rayller, or the combination of the two but Mr. Rayller stopped pushing. Standing statue-still, he faced Deputy Long. He seemed to comprehend where he was and why. Deputy Long took the opportunity to continue and get it over with. It was going to be a disaster for this man that he respected and admired, no matter how he said it.

Speaking clearly and straight, he spoke directly to Mr. Rayller.

"Mr. Rayller, while your son and his family were en route

to the hospital, a driver in an oncoming car appears to have crossed the double solid line. The other vehicle struck your son's car head on."

"Mr. Rayller stared at him for a long moment. He appeared to understand, and then said, "Why are you telling me this? My son didn't have an accident. They were just here a few minutes ago. He and my daughter-in-law were with Mom."

As he finished saying the last few words, his voice trailed off. It became apparent he realized what had happened. Taking his seat slowly, his elbows settled on his legs, his face fell into his hands, and then he began to sob. He understood he had lost his wife, their son, and daughter in-law. Deputy Long, the doctor, and nurse left him in silence.

Deputy Long stood in the hallway outside the chapel fighting to control his emotions. At times like these, he hated his job. To serve and protect the citizens of this county was part of his oath. He thought, *I should have been out on patrol. Maybe they would still be alive.*

He knew he was blaming himself unnecessarily, but he felt powerless to stop the wash of guilt. With his heart heavy, saddened, and twisted in more grief, he left the hospital. The doctor would call if, or when, he was needed.

In his cruiser, on a deserted stretch of highway, Deputy Long parked in the driveway of an abandoned house. With engine, radio, and lights off, he laid his head on the steering wheel and cried for the loss of his friends.

He and Bill Jr. had been fishing buddies, hunting buddies, and drinking buddies. He had been told not to come to the scene; however, against orders, he had gone. Once there, he saw the car and knew at a glance who it was. After refusing to leave the scene, he was assigned to directing traffic until the accident investigation was complete. At first, he had hoped he could help Bill Jr., but in the end, he realized there was no hope.

CHAPTER 29

In the Stone household, the weekend was a time anticipated for five days previous. However, on this Saturday morning, Michelle was up early. When Kathryn entered the kitchen at eight a.m., she was startled to find Michelle already sitting at the kitchen table. A half full glass of orange juice sat on the table in front of her. Michelle's hands and forearms rested on the table.

Walking to the cupboards for the making of morning coffee, she looked at her daughter. What she saw was not something she was prepared for. Michelle's face was expressionless, as if she were sleeping, except for the tears. Her eyes were open, but not blinking. Surprised by Michelle's appearance, she questioned her daughter.

"Honey, are you alright?"

Michelle continued to stare, still in deep concentration. Nothing moved, not a hair, not an eyebrow, not a finger. She had all of her concentration on her dream of the previous night. She neither heard nor saw her mother enter the kitchen.

To Michelle, nothing existed at that moment beyond her latest dreams. The train station, the voices, the faces—all of this came flooding back to her. The memory of her dreams did not come alone. She also knew she would have to tell her parents they had lost a close and dear friend.

After a minute or so, Michelle blinked, returning her focuses on the present. Feeling her mother stroking her face with an open palm, she smiled. Looking up into her mother's face, she became concerned.

"Mom, are you all right," asked Michelle.

The question surprised Kathryn.

"Honey, I thought something was wrong with you. You were just sitting there staring off into space, like you weren't even here."

Michelle looked down at the table. She knew now would be the best time to talk to her mother. Summoning her courage, she spoke.

"Mom, I had another dream last night. You know, like the one I had about Mr. Breeker. Do you remember that?"

Kathryn felt the cold chill run down her spine. She remembered it. She remembered her daughter telling her about Mr. Breeker getting on a train with his dead wife and son, and then waving goodbye to her like they knew she was there and could see them. She rubbed her arms to hide the goose bumps.

"Yes, I remember that." She really wanted to know where this was going.

"Well, I had another dream, Mom." Michelle said, in a soft and timid voice. She knew the meaning of this dream, and she'd had more dreams than she mentioned.

The dreams came to her usually at night. She'd promised herself to say nothing to her parents unless it was someone close to them. The dream about Mr. Rayller's family was about as close as it could get around there.

The meeting of Michael and Mr. Rayller on the day of Mr. Breekers death developed into a friendship between the two families. Church committees and an occasional dinner together had produced an understanding of their differences and similarities. Michelle had tried to befriend the Rayller's granddaughter. Shelia only three years older, thought herself to be more mature than she was, and too often rude. Michelle tolerated her when it was necessary, but that was all. With her latest dreams, she knew they would be together much more often.

Michelle had not told her parents everything about the Breeker dream. Mr. Breeker had told her he was very tired and was glad to be free of his earthly body. The time he had spent away from his family was the worst of all. He had told her not to feel sorry for him, but to be happy. His life had been full and worthwhile. Now, he felt no pain and no loneliness. He advised her to be cautious who she told what she dreamed and could see. He also reassured her it was good she could see the dead because she was protected. Then, he said goodbye and went away.

Mr. Breeker was not the only visitor, but he was the first. She had received visits from firemen, farmers, a county commissioner, and many others. Not all were friendly and nice. Some were angry they had died; still others were confused and afraid. Michelle discovered she was quite comfortable communicating with the dead, and often directed them to the station. She quickly discovered they were far less complicated than the living. She decided to tell her mother only enough to encourage them to check on Mr. Rayller as had been done with Mr. Breeker, but no more. With her decisions made, she proceeded carefully. To tell too much may scare them, and too little, they may ignore her, so she spoke slowly.

"Mom, in my dream, Mr. Rayller is at the train station, and he's crying."

Kathryn interrupted her daughter, saying, "Ah, honey, I think your father needs to hear this also. Let me get him."

Kathryn remembered very well being told about the train station in Michelle's dream. If she had a train station in this dream, then Michael needed to know about it. She was about to rise from the chair when his voice came from the doorway.

"I'm here. Go ahead, Michelle, I'm listening."

Kathryn, surprised by Michael's presence, glanced at her husband. The eye contact told her he was as concerned as she. Michelle continued.

"Mom, Dad, it wasn't one dream, it was two." Kathryn and Michael again looked at one another.

Michael said, "Wait a minute, you had two dreams last night, not just one?"

"Yes, and they were both about the Rayllers," Michelle answered, looking at her father.

Michael said, "Let me sit down, I have a feeling this is not going to be good."

Pulling out the chair beside Kathryn, he took a seat. Michelle looked at her parents, noting the uneasy looks on their faces. She knew she would have to tell them nearly everything.

She said, "Last night after I fell asleep, the first dream came. In the dream, I was at the train station again. Mr.

Rayller and Mrs. Rayller were there. Mrs. Rayller was standing on the train platform alone. Mr. Rayller was approaching from the side of the station. She was more beautiful than I had ever seen her. She was dressed like she does when she comes to church, only nicer. Her face had a bright glow to it, and she moved like she was floating.

She continued standing on the platform as Mr. Rayller tried to get closer. When I saw his face, he didn't have the same kind of glow. He started walking toward her, and she didn't move, but she kept getting farther away. Then he started running, calling her name, but she just got farther away. Finally, he stopped running. That was when she thanked him for a wonderful life and told him she would be waiting on the platform for him when it was his time to go. Her exact words were, 'We love you, and we will wait.' Then, I woke up.

"I'm sorry I didn't wake you and tell you, but Mrs. Rayller said to let you rest, and that all was being done that could be done. I believed her and went back to sleep."

Michael and Kathryn sat quietly and listened to every word Michelle said. They were too stunned to do anything else. The confirmation of their daughter's abilities had come from their very own daughter. They did not doubt Michelle's ability to see and communicate with the dead. How much she knew and about what, they could only imagine, and they were both afraid to do so.

Michael looked at his daughter and saw not a little girl, but a very young clairvoyant that appeared to be as comfortable talking to the dead as she was talking to the living. He was not at all comfortable with this realization. When Michelle had told him of Mr. Breeker, he felt it was a blessing at the time. Now, some years later, he was not so sure. He said to her, "Honey, aren't you afraid of what could happen to you?"

Michelle remembered the words of Mr. Breeker as the train passed, "You are protected by the white light." She still didn't know what that meant. She said to her father, "No, Daddy, I'm not afraid."

Michael got to his feet, staring out the window for a few seconds. His mind pondered the possibilities and dangers, both real and imagined. He turned to Kathryn and said, "I need a cup of coffee. Would you like one?"

Kathryn, deep in her own thoughts and concerns, only mumbled, "Yes."

Michael stepped over to the kitchen counter, took down two cups and filled it, then returned with the full cups of coffee to the table. He set a cup before Kathryn while taking a seat.

Kathryn lifted her cup, with the intent of taking a sip, but stopped before it touched her lips. With a tone of confusion in her voice, she relayed her question to Michael.

"Michael, did you make the coffee?"

Now it was Michael's turn to be confused. He knew he had not made coffee and said so. They both looked at Michelle. Michelle stared back. This was not something she had planned or even hoped for. How was she supposed to explain this when she didn't even know what had happened?

Kathryn, seeing her confusion, asked,

"If I didn't, and your father didn't, and I know it wasn't made when I came in—did you make it?"

Michelle just shook her head, indicating no. She did not dare risk speaking just yet. She suspected one of the spirits had made it in an effort to help. But why? Was there more going on than she had seen or been told? Maybe her dad was right. Maybe she should be concerned.

Keeping her thoughts to herself, she replied, "Maybe one of you made it without thinking."

Michael, not very convincingly, said, "Yes, maybe. Now you said you had two dreams. What was the other one?"

Michelle, feeling relieved he didn't push the issue of the coffee, continued into the next dream before her mother could voice an objection and demand an answer.

She said, "Later in the night, I found myself back at the station again, except Mrs. Rayller was there alone, still standing on the platform. She looked the same as she had before. Then the door of the station opened, and two people came out, a man and a woman. When they stepped out the door, they appeared dull and seemed to have to struggle to move. With every step they made, it seemed they got lighter. It was like they were dropping stuff as they moved until they were floating. By the time they reached Mrs. Rayller, they were bright and floating like her. When the three were together, they turned and looked at me. That was when Mrs. Rayller said to me what she said about letting you sleep."

She paused for a few moments, looking down at the table. With a certain finality in her voice, she said, "Mom, Dad, I think they're all dead. Mrs. Rayller, her son, and her daughter-in-law. I think they're all dead."

Saying nothing more or moving, Michelle continued looking down at the table. Ever so quietly, she began to cry. The feeling of helplessness weighed on her in ways she could not explain, even to her parents. The tears she shed were for Mr. Rayller. He would certainly be lost without his wife, and Shelia, without her parents.

Michael and Kathryn sat and listened to what Michelle had to say, the mysterious coffee temporarily forgotten. Their daughter had relayed a lot for them to digest, and it was quite clear that Michelle was affected by the dreams.

Kathryn spoke first.

"Michelle, how long have you been having these dreams?"

Michelle would never outright lie to her parents, but avoid the whole truth, that she would do. She knew this was a trapping question. If she said exactly how long, then they would want to know how often, but not answering the question could get her racked over the coals. She didn't kid herself. She knew from experience her parents were as sharp as a Japanese sword, so she decided to give only precise answers and hope for the best.

She answered, "Since Mr. Breeker died." "Have there been others?" Michael asked.

Michelle knew she was about to be trapped, but she promised herself she would try to protect the spirits. She answered with a simple yes.

Michael and Kathryn shared a concerned quick glance between them. A message between them could be relayed in just a glance.

They both knew if they pushed too forcefully, Michelle would clam up and say almost nothing, and if they stopped now, she may think she had taken control of the situation.

Michael could not allow this to be the outcome of this discussion. This was his home, his family, and his only child. He would allow nothing to threaten or endanger his family, no matter if the threat was dead or alive, real or imagined. Now, standing by the kitchen counters, he turned on his heels.

Kathryn and Michelle had been looking away, not watching anything in particular, and only thinking their private thoughts.

Michael spoke in a sharper tone and low volume that always indicated he was very upset. He was losing control of his emotions and his temper. Still on his feet, he began to pace and talk.

To Michelle, he said, "You are our daughter, and we love you, but if you think I'm going to buy the storyline that you have only had three dreams, you are sadly mistaken. Now, I suggest you tell us about all the dreams and when they occurred."

Michelle, looking into her father's eyes, knew that telling half-truths and vague answers would not work. She saw he wanted answers, and he wanted them now.

Her father was normally a quiet man, but when he was like this, his being quiet could be the prelude to a serious butt-chewing.

Michelle had been biting her lower lip in an attempt to control herself. She looked to her mother. The expression on her worried face said there would be no help coming from her. She knew she would have to start talking.

Feeling herself under enormous pressure, she reasoned that lying would be the best way to protect the spirits.

She opened her mouth to speak, when the telephone rang. On the fourth ring, Michael lifted the handset from its cradle on the kitchen wall. The ringing of the phone had interrupted his getting to the bottom of Michelle's dreams.

Kathryn knew Michael was very upset, and he had a right to be. Something was invading their child's mind, and she was being protective. However, he was not nearly as upset as she was. She had kept quiet, waiting and watching, biding her time. She was thinking, *If Michelle will not reveal the truth, as our little girl always has, when I get her alone, then we will talk like she is quite a bit older. That could make her feel more comfortable. I'm her mother, but if it becomes necessary, I'll apply the pressure. We have to know the whole story.*

Kathryn, watching Michael over Michelle's head, toyed with the crystal salt shaker, which was part of the decorations on the kitchen table. She watched as Michelle's shoulders sagged as if under a great weight. The sagging only lasted for a second before she again straightened her back, squared her shoulders, raised her head, looked directly at her mother, and then smiled.

Michelle had indeed been feeling the crushing weight of her promise of silence to the spirits when she heard the soft, gentle, grandmotherly voice of Mrs. Rayller say to her it was all right to tell them everything.

The voice said, "They now see you as a young woman, not as a child. They are ready to listen. Yes, you can tell them all you know."

Then the voice fell silent. When she raised her head, she saw what she had never been allowed to see before. Behind her mother were two beings she could only describe as angels, one on her right and one on her left. They spoke in unison and said, "Michelle, you can speak, they are ready to listen."

This made her smile. She knew her house was protected.

Kathryn saw that Michael's once tense back and shoulders now sagged, as if he had just received a great weight from the telephone call. She wondered what was happening.

Did the weight move from her daughter's shoulders to his, or did it just look that way?

Michael said goodbye to whomever he was talking to on the phone and then hung up. Turning around, he faced Kathryn. She could see most of the fight had gone out of him with the call. Something he just heard hit him like a ton of bricks.

Kathryn said, "Honey, what was that all about?"

Michael, with a sincere look of sadness said, "I was hoping she was wrong. I was even ready to demand she admit she was wrong, but she was not. Janice just informed me that last night Mr. Rayller lost his wife, son, and daughter-in-law, and almost his granddaughter. He's at the hospital now. I think we need to get dressed and go there. He's going to need a lot of help."

In the car on the way to County Memorial Hospital, Michelle told each and every dream she'd had. Kathryn and Michael listened intently, as if listening to a master storyteller. Michelle relayed every detail she could recall: names, dates, and family members. When someone came to her, it was like she already knew their names.

As she talked, she felt lighter and more at ease with herself. To her parents, she sounded like she had aged ten years in an hour. They could hardly believe she was their daughter. She spoke so smoothly and with a never-before-seen confidence. It only took Michael to glance in the rearview mirror to be reminded. *Yes, she's our daughter*, he thought. The eyes his daughter inherited from her mother stared back at him.

CHAPTER 30

In everyone's life, misfortune will fall. Unfortunately for Mr. Rayller, he found himself both in the rain and the flood. While he sat in the hospital chapel awaiting the arrival of his son, he was handed a double blow to the heart when he learned his son and daughter-in-law died in an auto accident while en route to the hospital.

To lose a spouse is awful enough in that gone is a significant part of one's self, but to also lose your only child carries a considerably higher level of suffering and emptiness. Mr. Rayller sank quickly into the sea of despair. He was at his lowest point when the E.R. doctor came to him and said, "Mr. Rayller, your granddaughter is asking for you. Please come with me."

Mr. Rayller had not questioned what he had been told by Deputy Long. He simply assumed he had lost his entire family in one night. He examined himself, admitted his flaws, and prayed for the souls of his departed loved ones.

The news that he had not lost his granddaughter was a most welcome surprise.

With tear-filled eyes and unsteady legs, he got to his feet and followed the doctor. Around the corner and down a short hallway, he was back in E.R. Being led by the doctor, they passed station after station of the sick and injured. Finally, they came to the last bed, a nurse holding back the curtain to grant him access, motioned Mr. Rayller to enter.

Before him on the hospital bed laid his petite teenage granddaughter. Her right foot protruded from under the sheet. He could see that she had received injury there. Twisted to one side in an unnatural pose, one glance and he knew it was broken. The rest of her little body was covered with a sheet up to her neck. Around her neck they had placed a brace to keep her head from moving.

Did she have a spine injury? He wondered as he approached.

Her face was beginning to swell and turn black-and-blue. She resembled more a small prizefighter than a petite teenager. He could only see one eye, and it was closed. Standing beside her, Mr. Rayller took her hand and began to rub it. He would have loved to have reached down and cradled her in his arms, taken her place on that hospital bed or even given his life, so she would not have to suffer this way. He knew he could no more do that for her or her mother, or father, or grandmother than walk on the moon. At that moment in his life, he felt very old and worn.

The nurse told Mr. Rayller his granddaughter had been asking for him. Because of the medication, she drifted in and out of consciousness. The nurse also said she was glad he was still there because Shelia would need to see a familiar face after surgery. She then left the station to attend to other patients.

Shortly after the nurse had gone, Shelia opened her eye. She looked at her grandfather and seemed not to be able to see him clearly. Mr. Rayller began talking to her, totally ignoring her injuries. He did this to help them both keep from talking about what had happened. He could not risk explaining to her what had happened before surgery. She may not want to wake up ever again.

It seemed to take forever, but soon the doctor returned. He told Mr. Rayller Shelia would be leaving in a minute to be prepared for surgery. The doctor briefly explained the surgery. Shelia would have her ankle and clavicle reset with pins. They would have to wait to see if there were any injuries to her brain. At this time, he did not think so. Mr. Rayller waited rather impatiently, and then finally said, "Will my granddaughter fully recover?"

He had emotionally prepared himself for the worst possible news. The doctor was aware of this and was quick to say he would do all he possibly could, but he did not see any reason why she shouldn't, but she would still need more surgeries to repair her foot.

Mr. Rayller's stress and tensions lessened slightly. He would remain at the hospital for the rest of the night pacing, crying, and worrying.

At four a.m. the doctor entered the waiting room. Looking confident, he informed Mr. Rayller the surgery had gone very well, and he should expect her to be as good as new. He had not forgotten she had just lost her parents and grandmother. To try to offer some type of additional assistance, he informed Mr. Rayller he would be arranging for a nurse to come and assist once she was home.

Being unable to avoid the subject, he asked Mr. Rayller an important recovery question.

"Will Shelia be living with you or another relative?"

The reality of Mr. Rayller's losses again became clear. He looked down and away from the doctor in an effort to hide the tears. His mind remained embraced on one thought, *Grandma isn't going to be there to take care of her or me. She won't be there ever again.*

To the doctor he said, "We have no choice but to manage together. If you will send the nurse, I would appreciate it."

The doctor said, "I will see to it that it is done. Shelia is in recovery now. When she wakes and stabilizes, she will be taken to her room. Would you like to wait for her there?"

"Yes, I will wait in her the room. I want to be there when she wakes up."

With all the losses he'd endured on this night, he wanted to be no place else. The doctor bid his farewell and left. Within minutes a young and energetic nurse walked in to escort Mr. Rayller to the room.

As Mr. Rayller waited in Shelia's room, his heart ached for his lost family. He knew there was nothing he could have done to change things, but knowing this did not make it any easier. He could not imagine his life without his beloved wife or the love and respect of his son. He could not get his mind around the fact he would never hear their voices or feel their touch, and neither would Shelia. He understood his loss, even though he couldn't yet accept it, but for Shelia the loss was greater. She was so young, and to lose so much, so fast was bound to make her even more fragile. Would she be able to carry on? Would she want to? He didn't know.

CHAPTER 31

At the hospital, the Stone family was directed to Shelia's room. Mr. Rayller was there sound asleep, sitting in the only available chair. Mr. Rayller was not asleep because the chair was comfortable, but because he was exhausted. The pain and suffering drained him until sleep was all that was left. He had no more energy or tears for now. Sleep came as a welcomed escape and as a thief in the night. He had fallen asleep without expecting to. His last clear thoughts were the memory of his wife making Christmas dinner when their son was nine.

A much younger Mrs. Rayller, up to her elbows in flour and stuffing, joyfully labored away, preparing Christmas dinner. Their son served duty as her willing assistant trying desperately to help and doing an excellent job of supervising and testing pie fillings. That was tough work for Junior. He knew he could be caught and banished from the kitchen at any time.

This particular dream came without warning or expectation. Mr. Rayller, smiling, unexpectedly slipped into dreams of much happier times.

Michelle had informed Michael and Kathryn about all the dreams on their way to the hospital. They felt relieved to know all the details and asked Michelle to tell them if she saw spirits or whatever at any time or any place in the future. She had agreed. She hated keeping secrets, especially from her parents. Knowing she could speak freely about these things increased her awareness of becoming an adult.

Michael and Kathryn, on the other hand, were also relieved to have the openness again but felt apprehension about what they may be told in the future. They had learned so much in the last few hours, and now they were in the hospital.

They suspected Michelle was surely being bombarded from the other side.

Neither Michael nor Kathryn had any idea how to protect Michelle from the unseen, but they knew they would have to trust God, and their daughter's judgment concerning these matters.

The three of them stood just inside the door of Shelia's room. Kathryn looked over at Michelle. Having already decided to test the waters, she asked, "What do you see?" Michelle was prepared for the question.

"This is a very busy place. They're in the parking lot, the hallways, everywhere," Michelle replied.

Michael had his own question, "And in here?"

"Guardian angels, two of them, and they are glad we are here," Michelle answered.

Kathryn and Michelle stepped to the side of Shelia's bed. Shelia was still asleep or sedated. With tubes running out of her nose and IVs in her arm, she was a sight. That was bad enough, but they had her foot in traction.

Kathryn's motherly instinct took over. She reached over, brushing hair back off Shelia's forehead, and tucked her covers around her neck. Shelia never seemed to notice. She continued to sleep. With her face now swollen and discolored, sleep was the best thing for her.

Mr. Rayller was no longer asleep. He sat quietly, motionless, and quietly watching. He watched how a family he had only known a few years was the first there to offer aid. When he did move, it was accompanied with a groan. His old bones were informing him they did not care for sleeping in a chair. The three turned toward him. Michelle walked over to his chair, bent down, and kissed him on his cheek.

"We came here to help you and Shelia," she said with a smile.

Mr. Rayller felt a friendship from the Stone family that he had not really felt before. Their coming to help him counted for more than words could say.

Michael, standing at the foot of the bed, spoke to Mr. Rayller.

"We got word this morning of what happened and came right over. You may not have thought about what needs to be done, but there are things you are going to have to do. I hope you will allow us to help wherever we can."

Mr. Rayller was in no condition to think about the things he would have to arrange and handle. He had friends and neighbors that could help, but, as yet, the only offer of assistance was coming from a man he had first met at another disaster—the death of Bill Breeker.

How is it he always knows when I lose someone close to me? Mr. Rayller asked himself.

Standing stiffly to his feet, Mr. Rayller walked over to Shelia's bed. Leaning down, he kissed her on her forehead. Straightening his back, he looked around at the three of them and said, "If you will excuse me, I'll be right back." He then went to use the hospital room lavatory in Shelia's room.

When he came out, he walked back over to the bed, kissed Shelia on the forehead again, and then asked Michael to join him in the hallway. He then asked Kathryn to come and get them if she started to wake.

The two men stood only a few steps from the doorway to the hospital room.

Michael spoke first.

"Mr. Rayller, I hope you don't feel like we just barged in, because that was not our intent."

Mr. Rayller had been looking down at the floor. Looking up at Michael, he cleared his throat before speaking.

"I'm glad you and your family are here."

For a few moments, Mr. Rayller was silent. It appeared that he was gathering his thoughts and his composure before speaking again.

"Michael, Bill Breeker was my best friend. We had known each other all our lives. Until last night, I really did not understand the pain that he felt when he lost his son and then his wife. How could I have been so blind to the pain he was feeling?"

He paused. Michael did not know if he should speak or not. Mr. Rayller now stared off into space, deep in his thoughts. This lasted only a minute before he spoke again.

"Carol is my best friend, too. She is my wife, my lover, the mother of our son. She is everything to me. She really gets upset when promises are broken. What is she going to say when I tell her I couldn't protect our son?"

Michael did his best to hide his confusion. The only Carol he knew of was Mr. Rayller's wife, and she was dead. He could hardly blame the man if he was not ready to let her go and admit she was dead. He knew he certainly would have a tremendous problem letting Kathryn go.

Michelle stepped out of Shelia's room. She walked up to Mr. Rayller and touched his hand. The touch of her hand brought him back to reality.

Looking into his eyes, Michelle said, "Mr. Rayller, you need to come back to Shelia."

Gently taking his hand, she led him back through the door to Shelia's bed. Michael followed close behind, wondering how he could help Mr. Rayller and surprised by his daughter's gentle handling of the man. She had certainly changed, and he didn't know if he liked it.

CHAPTER 32

Someone should have warned the Scotts about possible outcomes. But if they had, would they have listened? Then again, someone may have, but they felt they knew better.

Timmy received the minimum of all that was supposed to be due him as a child. However, he received in abundance a twisted discipline, far beyond what was acceptable.

He endured many long years of pain and suffering at the hands of not only his parents but also classmates. On one particular day while riding home on the school bus, his life became even darker.

While sitting in the back of the bus, he remembered he had not cleaned the storm cellar as his father had ordered to be done. Knowing his father seldom came home before midnight, he felt he had time. Still, he knew if his father had mentioned it to his mother, she would check to see if he had in fact completed the chore. She would take great pleasure in promoting another beating for him.

His beatings had not lessened in severity or frequency over the years. This had only served to increase his hatred for his parents. Often in dreams, his imaginary friend, Nats, would comfort him.

In the early years, Nats would encourage him to be strong, and he would be alright. Often, he would say, "They are just stupid grown-ups." As the years passed, Timmy became more dependent on his imaginary friend for companionship. He withdrew more and more from those his own age.

On the bus, Timmy quietly hoped his father would not come home early. If he did, it would be a first in six months. As the bus neared his stop, he saw his father's pickup truck round the curve, approaching the rear of the bus.

Fear struck him like a wrecking ball. The knot in his stomach formed instantly and began to grow. He attempted to relax by reminding himself he was now seventeen. He didn't need to be afraid of the old man because he was also a man now.

Brave thoughts, but his stomach rolled and tightened with fear, nonetheless. His intestines seemed to become liquid steel rippling in his abdomen.

The more he watched the pickup truck, the worse it got, until he could contain his bowels no more. The mess he made was slight, but the smell was enhanced by his fear. The odor drifting through the bus only served to trumpet his event to all its occupants.

The timing was at its worst. His father's pickup approached then passed the school bus. He could clearly see the driver was his father. He did not look up as Timmy looked down from the rear seat of the school bus.

Looking ahead again, Timmy saw they were nearing his stop. He dreaded having to get up and walk past the students not getting off at his stop.

Standing quickly, he walked briskly toward the front of the bus. As he passed each seat, each student rewarded him with more pain and insults than he was prepared to take. Each step he took was a movement in a torturous dance. Having no place to hide, he was forced to walk the aisle in shame.

All eyes were on him, and the comments cut like razors to his heart. To have such an embarrassing thing happen only served to increase his feeling of worthlessness and anger. Before he reached the front of the bus, the laughter began. They had even given him a most unwanted nickname. From that day on, he would be referred to as Turd Boy. By the time he reached the front and exited the bus, most of the kids were laughing at him.

Once off the bus, Timmy ran with all his might across the field to get away from the laughing bus full of kids and the driver.

As he ran, his father watched from the roadway in front of the house. He suspected Timmy was running, hoping to get home and clean the storm cellar before he got there, but he was too late. With an evil smile, he turned into the driveway. Parking his pickup, Roger Scott got out and walked directly to the storm cellar. He wanted to see for himself if Timmy had done what he said. If he'd done as ordered, he did not care. He'd just find some other reason to beat Bill Breeker's bastard kid.

Roger opened the door and looked into the cellar. He was right. Timmy had done nothing.

Casting his words into the storm cellar, he said, "Well, well, well, Timmy boy, looks like you think you are finally big enough to ignore me? Then, let's see if you can take an attitude adjustment."

He slammed the door and turned looking for Timmy, but he was nowhere to be seen. He had not run home.

Timmy had run across the field from the bus stop, but stopped and squatted behind an old tree stump in the middle of the field. The tree had broken off years earlier, leaving a stump four feet in height. No one had bothered to remove the stump. Squatting behind it, in a field of half-grown corn, he rested and watched his father.

The fear of what would happen when he finally got home, mixed with the anger of being laughed off the bus, whirled within his mind. He knew who had called him Turd Boy first, and the little rich boy would pay. Timmy talking to the stump, said, "I will beat him until he wishes he was a turd. Every single one of them that laughed at me will pay."

It never occurred to Timmy the boy he had in mind was not the one that made the name up.

Believing he was right about who called him Turd Boy first, only gave him another reason to hate the kid even more. He decided to give a beating equal to the one he was sure to receive, and do it with pleasure.

Seeing his father go around the corner of his house, Timmy got up and sprinted toward home. He nearly reached the backdoor when his father stepped from around the corner.

"Hey," he shouted.

Timmy skidded to a stop short of the backdoor. In a few quick steps Roger was near enough to deliver the first blow

to Timmy's head, taking him off his feet. When Timmy crashed to the ground, he rolled over onto his stomach. With his hands under him, he attempted to push himself up from the dirt. Roger stood towering over him with clutched fists, shouting down.

"So, you think you're big enough to do what you want, huh? Well butthole, when I finish kicking the dog crap out of you, then you will know different."

With that, Roger delivered a sharp, hard kick to his ribs. Tim, suspecting the kick was coming, had attempted to roll away; however, he was caught in the ribs by the force of

Roger's boot. The impact of the powerful kick rolled him over until he came to rest face down in the dirt.

His mother, Phyllis, came out the back door in no hurry. Standing on the steps, she laughed at the lopsided fight going on in her backyard. Through the pain in his ribs and stomach, Timmy clearly heard her words.

"It's 'bout time you let him know he's not grown. He's been getting too big for his britches."

Roger turned to face her and delivered an acidy treat. "Shut up, before I finish with you."

Oddly enough, the treat of a beating excited Phyllis. She put the palms of her hands on the sides of her thighs and slid them up until her hands were resting on the tops of her hips. Turning sideways, she stepped down one step, saying to Roger, "Bring it on when you're finished."

Phyllis loved playing rough, and Roger loved giving it to her. Sex, for them, was violent and painful—before, during, and after. Unfortunately for Timmy, the beatings he took and hated, were warm ups for the beatings she took and loved.

Once again, he was the warm-up. How much he hurt was of little concern to them, but they did not want him to die. They enjoyed using him too much to let that happen.

Seeing Phyllis's legs spread open spread in short sundress excited Roger even more than beating Timmy. He turned his back on Phyllis and went back to what he called fun.

From what he had just heard, Timmy knew this beating was going to hurt worse than the rest. Feeling another kick to his side, he curled into the fetal position, covering his head.

Soon Roger had worked up a good appetite for Phyllis, at the expense of Timmy. Roger's desires rose to their highest level, and he abandoned beating Timmy. His interest now lay inside the house.

What sounded like an argument erupted immediately, followed by sounds of slaps and punches. This was not an argument, but the ending to Rogers warm-up. A door slammed inside the house, and then there was silence. The sounds of birds singing, insects buzzing, and traffic passing along the highway replaced the ruckus coming from inside the house.

Lying in the dirt, filled with anger, pain, and hate, Timmy again wept.

CHAPTER 33

Mr. Rayller stood in the kitchen he once shared with his wife Carol for over forty years. They had moved into this house on their tenth wedding anniversary. As a shared dream, they worked odd jobs along with their regular one to get the down payment. After that, they bought the house and continued their odd jobs and extra work until the mortgage was paid in full. Even Bill Jr. added where possible. They had bought and paid for their home in less than fifteen years.

Mr. Rayller looked around and listened. In every aspect of the house, Carol was present. Everything had her touch, from the linoleum on the floor to the eggshell white ceiling. This house had her essence from door to door. Even the yard was undeniably hers. The shrubbery, flowers, and even the lawn furniture bore her style and taste. This had been their home— the three of them— and now he was there alone.

Mr. Rayller had come home from the hospital the previous night. Too exhausted to focus on his surroundings, he had simply walked in the backdoor and aimlessly wandered about the house before settling into his chair.

He had not driven himself home, but at the insistence of his older sister Gladys and her husband Frank, he allowed himself to be chauffeured, leaving his car in the hospital parking lot. Too distraught to decline the offer, he accepted, and regretted it five minutes into the ride.

Gladys, his only surviving sibling of a family of seven, should have made him feel closer and warmer toward her, but this was not the case. In his view, she was overbearing, bossy, mouthy, sneaky, and underhanded. The same way she was when they were kids.

When they were children, she would do something wrong, and then get someone else blamed for it. From what he had seen over the years, little change had come her way. As a young woman, she was not all that attractive but appeared to have good qualities, as long as she was on her best behavior. This best behavior had been her mask the entire time Frank dated her. But when the proposal was made and the marriage complete and with baby on the way, Frank discovered her other side.

The baby was supposedly a month premature, but to Mr. Rayller's young eyes, he looked awfully healthy to him. Mr. Rayller was a teenager at the time and talking to his mom about where babies came from was not advised, but the wedding did seem rather quick.

What Gladys got for her trapping was a short, opinionated, self-serving, womanizing, know-it-all bigot, who thought himself a legend in his own mind. They were a perfect match of misery.

On most occasions when Mr. Rayller found himself trapped in their presence, with no hope of a quick escape, he equated the experience to an old storm door without a latch, flapping in a strong storm of hot air.

Now, with most of his family gone, they were there to supposedly comfort and assist him in his time of greatest need. What Mr. Rayller decided he needed was his granddaughter at home with him, and his sister, along with her husband, back in Chicago. Even though he resented the presence of his sister and brother-in-law, he decided that for the sake of Carol he would be nice. To accomplish this would require him holding his tongue and hoping they left early. Besides, they were only going to stay till the day after the funerals.

Thinking of the reasons behind the three funerals, he looked at the coffee maker given to them by their son two Christmases ago. Standing at the counter, he realized he held two empty coffee cups in his hand.

The rule of the morning was, the first up made the coffee and took out two cups—one for you and one for the slowpoke. That had been the rule since their first week of marriage, and it was clear to Mr. Rayller that it still held.

He stood in the kitchen holding the two cups, feeling the weight of an aching lonely heart. He caught himself listening for her to come along the hall. But he soon forced away the hope and longing desire. She would not be coming into her kitchen ever again.

Frank and Gladys had taken up their temporary residence in the guest room. He was grateful that they had kept to themselves.

By his sister and brother-in-law staying in the guest bedroom, this left Bill Jr's room unoccupied. He was relieved Junior's childhood room remained empty of guest. Knowing why only added to his pain.

This being his first time home in a few days, he'd walked down the hall toward the bedrooms shortly after getting home. Frank and Gladys had followed with a discomforting silence. After seeing to it they had what was necessary, Mr. Rayller stopped in front of the door to Bill Jr.'s room. He wanted to open it and see his son as a small boy or even a teenager doing his homework, but Bill could not bring his trembling hand to turn the knob. The door had remained closed. In fact, he had not even opened the door to the bedroom he had shared with Carol for so many years. As his sister and brother-in-law fell silent in their room, he fell asleep in his recliner.

His sleep was the kind that came from exhaustion. The kind you have when you are too tired to dream or move. He had awakened in the same exact position in which he had fallen asleep.

The sun's rays came in sharp and clear. No cloud, as he could see, had dared intrude. As he stood, still holding the two cups by their handles, as he'd always done, he spotted a blue jay landing in a grassy part of the yard and beginning to intently peck at something. Without a second thought, he began to speak to his wife Carol.

"Hey, Ma, your blue jay is back, and she's digging in that same spot. You need to come see this."

His words abruptly stopped, remembering Carol couldn't come and see. Feeling the rip in his heart, he continued speaking to the empty kitchen.

"No, you can't come see. You are waiting on me. Well,

honey, you wait right there. I'll be on shortly, but for right now, I need to take care of Shelia."

He fell silent for a few minutes, pondering his situation. When he finally came to a decision, he spoke to his wife.

"You know, I been married to you almost fifty years, and in those years, we have talked almost every morning over coffee. Even those mornings that one of us was still mad with the other. Well, honey …"

He paused, gathering himself.

"Well, I just be darned if I'm gonna let your dying stop me from talking to you." Mr. Rayller then filled two coffee cups and walked to the table. First, he set his cup in front of the chair he usually sat in, and then he reached over and sat Carol's on the table in the spot she occupied for most of their married life.

Yes, he could see her in his heart, mind, and soul. She was still there. He was going to have coffee and talk with his wife, just like he had always done. No matter who saw it, heard it, or cared. He knew she would be there just as long as he was.

Gladys had risen and was coming down the hall when she heard a voice. Slowing her pace and not wanting to be seen in her nightgown, she peeked around the corner to see who else was in the house at this hour of the morning. She was stunned to see Bill sitting at the kitchen table, talking to himself. As she listened and peeked, she noticed there where two full coffee cups on the table, one he was sipping from, and the other at the chair she had seen Carol sitting in on the mornings of her visits. With a pinprick of pain in her heart, she understood. Bill was having coffee with his wife as he always did in the mornings.

The pinprick became a rip when she heard the crack in his voice, but he continued. For the first time since their arrival, she allowed herself to feel the absence of her sister-in-law. She hadn't liked her, but she certainly admired her for being the woman she was. She had to include envying her, also. Unable to evade her own mind, a thought occurred to her.

If I died tomorrow, would Frank want to talk to me?

As she thought about this, tears ran down her face. She had accidentally witnessed more than she was prepared to handle. Her hard outer shell not only cracked, it shattered. Her younger brother had lost the woman he had loved all his life and couldn't bear to part with her, so he continued talking to her, even in death. Her tears were for herself. She knew she had not been the kind of wife or woman that deserved a man that could love her that much. That is why she had Frank. He was the outer ugly of her inner pain.

She no longer wanted to listen. She silently returned down the hallway and entered the bathroom to cry alone.

CHAPTER 34

Shelia lay in her hospital bed quietly crying. With lights down low and the sun long gone, no one would see. She had been through three surgeries and two months of therapy, traction, IVs,visitors she hardly knew or didn't know at all, and hospital food.

With her arm finally out of the sling because of a broken collarbone, she enjoyed more freedom of movement. The ability to reach up and touch her lips with her own fingertips of her left hand made her happier for a short while. Being able to touch and brush her own hair offered a surge of joy she hadn't expected.

The joys and satisfactions she felt were fleeting. In only seconds after each accomplishment, she felt the absence of her mother's loving hand. The pain of not feeling her touch became more and more unbearable with each successful step toward a complete recovery. The physical pain came first, making its presence known as soon as the anesthetic wore off.

Shelia had been asking for her mom and dad in recovery again after her first surgery. Mr. Rayller could not be with her until she was in her own room, so that was where he waited. When she was fully awake and could understand him, he pulled his chair next to her bed, took her good hand, and began to talk.

"Shelia, I need to tell you some things, and I want you to listen to me and try to understand."

Having had some time to think and grieve, he had prepared himself to tell his granddaughter the worst news of her young life.

"When your daddy was a boy, he and your grandmother would talk for hours about trains. They would look at books and read all kinds of stories about trains and train stations. They really had a big time with it. They even got me involved and talking about them."

Shelia always listened closely to her grandfather because he told great stories.

Finally, she said, "Grandpa, can you make the pain stop?

Can you or somebody go get Mom and Dad?" Mr. Rayller held her free hand and continued.

"Their interest in trains got to the point that one day Junior said to your grandma, 'When I die and go to heaven, will God take us up on a train?'"

Mr. Rayller had been able to keep the tears from falling up to this point. Shelia said, "Grandpa, why are you telling me about a train and Daddy when I need him here?"

Mr. Rayller, with tears running down his face, said, "Baby girl, Grandma, your daddy, and your mom are all at the train station."

Being unable to continue to speak, he hung his head while the tears rolled down his face.

Shelia first shed tears because her grandfather did. It hurt her worse than her injuries to see him cry. She had never seen him like this. She wondered in her medicated mind, *What do trains and train stations have to do with my family? Why is Grandpa so upset?*

Gradually, the words he said came together in her mind. When the reality made its way through the haze, she understood. Her father, mother, and grandmother were all gone. They were waiting at the train station of the dead.

The pain that hit her heart was worse than her physical pain. Now, she cried for and with her grandfather. They had both lost everyone that mattered except themselves.

In the darkness, she was hidden from the exposure of light. In the late night, pain did not have to be concealed from others. No one was there to ask her if she needed something. Quietly she thought, spun in darkness, pain, and regret, *What stupid questions people ask. My mom, dad, and grandma are all gone. I couldn't even attend the funerals, and Grandpa is facing this all alone. Just like me, he is locked away inside himself. Unable or unwilling to tell others how bad he hurts.*

This was not completely true. Michelle Stone had become a regular visitor. Shelia was not entirely comfortable with Michelle. They had become casual friends but not the die-hard lifelong inseparable type. With Michelle being two years younger, they had similar interests, but with the similarities, Shelia held back. Michelle had something Shelia did not and never would have again—she had parents.

With the passing of each day, the value of her parents became even clearer. She now saw the errors of her rebellion and objections not as a statement of her individuality, but as the expressions of a spoiled brat and selfishness. A brat that would not be given a chance to say, "I'm sorry, I was wrong. Will you please forgive me?" She had lost her opportunity and resented it. Feeling she had been robbed, she unfairly struck out at Michelle. Having done so, she felt bad and wanted to say she was sorry, but Michelle had not been back for two days.

Shelia lay in the dark crying. She was alone and wishing she could hear her mother's voice just once more. Again, tonight she fell asleep with her eyes wet with tears, and she dreamed.

In her dream, Shelia found herself walking on the edge of a jagged cliff. The footpath was narrow, only six or eight inches wide.

"Why am I here? Where am I trying to go?" she asked.

She looked down and saw only blackness. She looked up and saw heavy dark clouds. The winds ripped at her, trying to tear her away from her path and down into the blackness. She clung to the cliff face and inched along, one fear-filled step at a time. The fear grew stronger and stronger until she could not move a muscle.

Clinging to the cold rock face, she squeezed her eyes shut, too afraid to move or take a second look. She heard the wind scream and howl in her exposed ear, but the ear pressed to the rock heard something as well. She listened more closely. Yes, the rock had a voice.

She opened her eyes, and she was no longer on a cliff's edge. She was hugging her mother, and her mother was hugging her back. In her dream, her mother looked down at her and said, "You are my daughter, flesh of my flesh, and blood of my blood. Don't ever think I'm out of reach."

Her mother took a handkerchief and began wiping her daughter's face, drying her tears. Speaking again, she said, "Your father and I gave you our love, and now we give you our strength. Hold fast to the knowledge that you are not alone. Jesus is with you and so are we."

As she dried Shelia's eyes and wiped away her tears, Shelia closed her eyes again. The dream softly and quietly ended with her mother wiping away her tears and stroking her hair. The feeling she so dearly loved.

The next morning, before the nurse made her rounds, Shelia awakened. Lying on her side, she awoke clutching her pillow. She lay still for a moment, thinking of the dream, and then decided it was just a dream. When she removed her right arm from under the pillow, she found she was holding a fine linen handkerchief. Its dampness and the smell of her mother's perfume came as a double shock to Shelia.

She lay absolutely still and began questioning her sanity, *Where did this come from? Who would come into my room to play a joke like this on me?*

Still afraid to move, she again thought of her dream, *Is this her way of telling me I am not alone?*

Finally bringing the handkerchief to her nose, she inhaled the smell of the perfume her mother had worn. The fragrance had an unexpected effect. With each inhalation, she gained confidence and comfort.

She has been here with me. I am not alone, she thought.

Shelia held the handkerchief like the most precious jewel in her world, because it was. When the nurse made her rounds a half-hour later, the room she walked into held a patient much different than the one she had left a day before. She found a girl with a new light in her eyes and a never-before-seen softness in her voice, holding a handkerchief that she had not seen before.

It had an odd quality about it. It was something special and made with unusual care. She had seen unexplainable things in the hospital before and chose to keep silent about them. If this little girl had gotten outside help, then God bless her.

The Saturday morning had started with an unexpected gift from her mother. Shelia could not understand how, only that it had come during the night.

The sun had announced its presence with the arrival of a new day. Shelia lay in bed, looking out the window. Her view of her circumstances and the world had changed only slightly. Positioned on the fourth floor, she had a view of the sky with highflying birds and slow-drifting clouds. Day after day, she watched the repeating scene.

A cloud drifted by, a bird flew by, and then came the setting of the sun and the rising of the stars. No matter who came by, this scenario changed only slightly. Her bitterness steadily grew as her physical pain decreased, but now she was confused.

How could her mother come back and give her this gift and yet leave her here alone again?

She was stewing over this question, when Michelle and her mother, Kathryn, walked in. Kathryn in a sundress and sandals and Michelle in jeans, tennis shoes, and an oversized T-shirt, looked to be comfortable.

Walking into the hospital room, they greeted Shelia with big smiles and a genuine cheerfulness. As cheerful as Michelle and Kathryn were, Michelle could see Shelia was not totally alone.

Michelle focused her attention on the window. They watched as she walked in, and she watched them.

Shelia greeted them with a lukewarm reception. Her confused and irritated mind showed through her plastic smile. Both Kathryn and Michelle saw it, yet they inquired about her condition and how soon her release may be.

After a few minutes, Kathryn excused herself, saying she wanted to discuss something with the nurse. Michelle had earlier stated to her mother if Shelia was in a foul mood to give her some time with her alone to clear the air. Michelle silently indicated to her mother it was time for her to go. This didn't upset Kathryn. She also noticed Shelia's chilly mood getting worse.

As Kathryn left, she closed the door behind her. Kathryn was well aware of the sharpness of her own tongue and had no doubt that her daughter's was equally so. What was about to happen was not going to be pretty or nice. There was no need for it to be heard outside the room. Kathryn walked down to the nurses' station.

The girls' watched Kathryn leave, Michelle ensuring the door was closed, and Shelia wondering why Kathryn left so quickly.

Now, they were alone, or so Shelia thought, but Michelle knew better. Michelle had seen the spirits in the room when they entered, one good and full of hope, love, and joy, the other dark and full of anger. The angry one was usually closest to her bed. When that occurred, Shelia was usually in a foul mood.

Today was different. In addition to the single good spirit already there, two more had entered with Michelle when she entered the room. Shelia's mother and grandmother had taken up positions to protect Shelia. The dark spirit was being forced outside, away from Shiela. Michelle had watched this take place while talking with Shelia and her mother. With the angry one gone, Michelle knew it was time for an attitude adjustment. Stepping to the foot of the bed, she stood exactly in the middle. Unseen by Shelia, her mother stood by her right side, and her grandmother on her left side of the bed.

Michelle, having positioned herself as instructed, began her delivery of correction.

"I am very sorry you lost your mother, father, and grandmother, but I will not allow you to mistreat or disrespect me or my mother ever again. You are a selfish, self-centered, arrogant little twerp that thinks the world should spin just for you the way you want and when you want. Have you not learned anything?

Your life, our lives are too short to be all tangled up in self. Your grandmother had a long life. Your mother and father had a shorter one. But do you know how long yours is going to be? No. You have no idea, but you are acting like it's going to last forever. You should be advised, Miss Nasty, that your ticket could have been punched in that car wreck also."

Shelia, angry at being attacked so boldly, was ready for a fight. Sitting up in the bed, she fired back with a viciousness that would not have been expected by an outsider but was expected by Michelle.

"Who the hell do you think you are? You come prancing in here with your mother like I want to see you or anyone else and think you are going to set me straight. You, in your hand-me-downs, you look about as cool as a bag lady. And on top of that, you have the nerve to bring your mother in here, knowing full well that mine is dead. How do you think that makes me feel?"

With tears from anger streaming down her face, she continued.

"You've still got your father and your mother and a school with friends and someone to make you a birthday cake and open Christmas gifts with. I don't have any of that anymore. So don't come marching in here and think you are going to tell me what's good for me when you don't even know me."

Michelle stood still and listened, she watched both sides of Shelia's bed. Then she spoke, softly, evenly, and without anger.

"Miss Nasty, I was asked to be your friend and help with this rough time you are in. I was asked to be here for you. I was asked to offer support. I was asked to help, but what I'm going to say now, I was not asked to say.

And that is this: you had better grow up a little and start taking responsibility for your actions and attitude because if you don't, you are going to see this place again or some place much worse.

As for, who do I think I am? Well, I'm just like you, a girl trying to learn to be a woman, but the difference is, I did not have to lose the most precious women in my life before I could see that I didn't have all the answers. You think you do, but you are dead wrong. Before you fire another angry word, I suggest you think about where and how you got that handkerchief in your hand."

Shelia was readying herself to return her own barrage of words, until she heard the last sentence. Instantly all her waiting words vaporized. The only thought remaining in her mind was, *How does she know?*

Michelle fixed her with a knowing stare and said, "Don't ask how I know, but when you're ready for a friend, your grandfather—you know, the one you just disrespected—he knows how to find me, and you better get a lot closer to him. He's all the family you got left."

Seconds later, Kathryn returned to the room. A quick glance at both girls said it all. Noticing the hard unrelenting stare Michelle had on Shelia, she asked, "Is everything all right here?"

Michelle answered without hesitation or taking her eyes off Shelia, "Yes, Mother, everything is all right here. Isn't it, Shelia?"

Shelia, still reeling from the verbal right hook she never saw coming, could only murmur softly.

"Yes."

Michelle, now looking at her mother, said, "Mom, Shelia doesn't seem to feel like having visitors. It's time for us to leave."

W*ow,* Kathryn thought, *This is a big power play coming from my sweet little girl.*

Kathryn said, "In a minute."

Walking over to Shelia's bed, she again inquired as to how she felt today and if they could bring her anything from the mall. This time Shelia's response was much more pleasant and easy to stomach.

"Thank you for the offer, but I'll wait till later." She said.

Kathryn, taking note of her answer said, "Very well, then. We'll be going. We'll be seeing you soon. Heal quickly."

She then turned, giving Michelle a hard, quick you-better-have-a-good-explanation-for-this-sweetie look and then walked to the door.

Michelle, still rooted at the foot of the bed, said, "When you feel like talking, let me know. See you 'round." She then turned on her toes and followed her mother out of the room.

In the hallway, the two of them walked to the elevators. Once inside the elevator, they were alone. Kathryn, looking up at the numbers, said, "When we get inside the car, start talking, and it had better be really good."

To an outside observer, they would have appeared to be just another mother-daughter team but to Michelle, she knew she had overstepped the line by a Nebraska mile, and the only way to quell the explosion that was coming was to start talking, in detail, when her mother said to talk. She could only hope the explosion did not come before they reached the car. She knew that by the time she finished talking, this would be one trip to the mall her mother would not soon forget. She kept silent all the way to the car.

As soon as Shelia's visitors left the room, a chill moved into the room. Shelia could not determine where it came from, but her concern was short-lived.

She soon began to cry, this time in frustration, anger, and confusion. Minutes later when her tears stopped, she was finally able to think, and think she did.

CHAPTER 35

With doors closed and seatbelts unfastened, Kathryn waited not a second longer than necessary before giving the order to start talking. Anger boiling within her did not come from the confrontation between Michelle and Shelia; rather, because of the take-charge attitude exerted by Michelle toward her. This would have to be dealt with immediately.

Kathryn started the car and turned on the A/C for the cool air, which did nothing for her boiling temper. She decided on the way to the car that she would set their roles straight before she demanded answers or the car moved. She was the mother and would not allow her child, gifted or not, to tell her what or when she was going to do anything.

"Okay young lady, let's get something understood. I know and accept you are gifted, and it makes your life more difficult, but don't you ever make the mistake of thinking you can give me orders. I am the one who brought you into this world and nearly died doing it. For you to use that tone of voice and behavior on me is one thing I will not tolerate, for any reason. I know your discussion with Shelia was not pleasant, but don't you ever make the mistake of bringing it in my direction ever again. Do I make myself crystal clear?"

Michelle cleared her throat and closed her eyes while leaning her head against the headrest. She decided the time had arrived to explain the rest to her mother, straight, clear, and without pretense.

"Yes, mother I understand, and I really am sorry for what I did. I was wrong." Michelle replied.

"For you to do something like that, really burns me up and what did you two have going on in there for you to use that tone on me? That I would really like to know, so start talking young lady, and it better be good."

Kathryn's anger cooled only slightly, but she was still determined to get to the bottom of whatever it was that got Michelle in the state of mind to commit such an offense.

Michelle remained silent the entire time she received her reprimand. While she listened, she also came to a decision.

She reasoned the best way to get completely through this discussion would be to plunge right in.

"Mom, are you sure you want me to tell you what's going on?"

"Yes, I do," Kathryn said shifting in her seat.

"Okay. Remember, you asked," Michelle said with a twinge of regret.

"Last night I had a visit from Mrs. Rayller. She came to me before I fell asleep. The room was dark, and I was just about to doze off when a soft breeze moved through my room. I opened my eyes, and Mrs. Rayller was standing at the foot of my bed. She was wearing the dress she was buried in, but she looked so alive and vibrant. My bedroom took on a strange kind of glow. The light had life to it. It pulsed and vibrated and seemed to be alive and full of life itself. She told me when we came to see Shelia today, she would be with us, and so would Shelia's mother. I asked why, and she said Shelia's room had a dark spirit that came and went, but now was taking control. That is why she was so nasty the last time we were there. I told her I had seen it and asked her what she wanted me to do. She said, 'Allow us to help her through you. We would not ask, but she is in a dangerous time.'

"I said, 'So you want to speak through me?' She said, 'No. Let us speak with you.' I said I didn't understand. She said, 'You will know what to say when the time comes, and we will support you.' Then things changed. She said, 'There are other things you need to understand and tell your parents.' You see, Mom, they knew you would be upset.

"Then my room changed, and I was looking at the train station. I saw the name on the front of the building. It is called Destination Junction. There were souls of all kinds and types, and they were coming from all directions, one at a time. No one soul seemed to be aware of another as they approached the station. They all were going to their own personal station, even though it appeared to be the same place. Then, I saw the inside.

"They would come in alone and step up to the ticket window. The clerk would always be waiting for them and address them by name in their language. I can't say if it was a he or a she, only the clerk. Some of the people would ask how they were to pay for a ticket. The clerk would say, 'It's been already paid.' Then they would say, 'How?' The clerk would say, 'Your ticket was paid by the life you lead. Now your train is waiting through that door.'

"There was always only one door. Once you entered through the train station's front door, it no longer existed from the inside. It became a solid wall, and you would have to use the door marked 'Platform' to leave the ticket counter. There was no other choice. You had to use that door. A person—I call them people even though they are dead—would go out the door and some would find themselves on a dark and scary platform. On the platform waiting for them would be their worst deeds. They could not run or hide or seek help. The evil life they led would be there and serve as escort, dragging them to a dark dreadful-looking train.

"The windows were black with eyes looking out—evil unfriendly, hate-filled eyes. The person, the soul, would beg and plead and cry all the way to the door of the rail car. Then the door opened, and in the same instant they would be both shoved and yanked inside. Then, the windows would show shadows, awful evil shadows of things happening on the train.

"Always after the door closed, the whistle blew. It sounded like a scream of a thousand souls in terror and agony. Then the train would start to move down the track."

Kathryn sat in the same position as before. She had forgotten the car was running. She had forgotten everything. Her mouth hung open. She was too baffled to speak. Michelle continued speaking with her eyes closed.

"Another person who'd lived a good life would enter the station and stand before the clerk. After receiving their ticket, they would leave through the platform door, the same as the others before them. Outside their door, they would find as beautiful a station as they could have imagined. Waiting for them on the platform would be one or more loved ones or even loved pets that had passed on. They would all be happy and pleased to be together. The loved ones would escort the newcomer to the train, where they would join other loved ones and journey together. All the cars were well lit, comfortable, and filled with rejoicing souls.

"It was made clear to me that the train of darkness and the train of light both went to the same place. They both went to meet our maker, the God of gods, at the end of the line.

"Mom, Destination Junction is at the intersection of Alpha Street and Omega Avenue. All life travels Alpha Street with its curves, stop signs, and forks in the road. All life passes near Destination Junction Station many times. All roads eventually led to Omega Avenue. Mom, Omega Avenue ends at Destination Junction. Sooner or later we all must take Omega Avenue and enter Destination Junction."

Kathryn was speechless. She could only sit and stare at her daughter and wonder who she really was.

CHAPTER 36

The weekend is the most treasured and sought-after time of the week. Almost everything planned is for the weekend, the time for self, family, and relaxation.

For Mr. Rayller, this weekend, like all his weeks and weekends for the past two months, would gain no support or any rest and relaxation. Today he was picking up his only grandchild from the hospital.

Driving to the hospital, he made use of the time to think. His desire to be there when Shelia was discharged was tempered by the knowledge that he would be responsible for the rearing of a teenage girl, even if it was his own granddaughter. He recalled all too well the challenges he'd had with her father. Feeling certain he knew Shelia, he did not kid himself about the whims of a teenage girl. This concerned him greatly.

It had fallen upon his shoulders to arrange the funerals of his family after the death of his wife Carol at home in his arms, and the deaths of his son and daughter-in-law, by auto accident, on the same night. The events of that night left him guilt-ridden and depressed. He thought about the events that had put him in this position as he drove.

Mr. Rayller had always seen himself as a strong and independent-minded man who provided for his family and prospered. The home he and his wife shared was free of any mortgage. The vehicles they had driven were fairly new and paid for. However, three months ago, he had thought Carol was in good health. That had all changed in one long and torturous night.

The day of the funeral was an ugly, rainy day. The church he'd attended all his life was overflowing with mourners. The floral arrangements were too numerous for display. In the middle of the beautiful floral arrangements sat three coffins.

Mr. Rayller was positioned between his two nephews, Bruce and George, to ensure if grief was too great to bear or his legs gave way, they could support him. Those were the instructions given them by their mother, Gladys. Mr. Rayller didn't have to hear her say it to know she had arranged the seating.

As Mr. Rayller pondered these thoughts for the hundredth time, another thought occurred to him. His sister Gladys had been quite subdued and seemed to be genuinely mournful of the losses to the family. Not with screams and uncontrollable tears, but quiet suffering, isolated from all others, locked with her pain inside herself.

In fact, he was sure of it. After the second day there, she had been someone different, not her usual bossy self. He asked himself, *Did I notice that, or am I imagining it?*

Steering into the hospital parking lot, he found the closest parking space available to the front door. This would ensure a lesser walking distance for him.

In Shelia's room, he was greeted by an eager teenager ready for discharge. Shelia had seen as much hospital as she wanted to see. In her mind, any place was better than being there.

Mr. Rayller observed, in his casual way, that his granddaughter was up and dressed. Impatiently, she waited to be released by the doctor. That was really not a surprise, considering she had endured three surgeries and one staph infection, with a name that sounded like a sexually transmitted disease. The whole time, she was never allowed to leave the hospital.

Paperwork done and bag in hand, Shelia was wheeled downstairs to the curb by an orderly. This was one wheelchair ride she had long waited for. She observed Mr. Rayller bringing the car up to the main entrance. When he stopped, she felt an urge to sprint from the wheelchair, dive onto the hood, and scream, "Drive anywhere, just away from here!" This she may have tried, if she'd had the benefit of two good feet to support her. Instead of reenacting the role of some unknown Hollywood stuntwoman, she sat patiently and waited for her grandfather to park and open the rear door of the sedan for her.

Being helped up by the orderly, Shelia positioned herself in the open car door and lowered herself down onto the seat.

It appeared he had tried to think of everything to make her trip comfortable. Against the door, on the rear driver's side were two pillows. Once in, she slid across the seat to the other side against the pillows. She noticed a small cooler sat on the floor and inside, she found a soft drink and a bottle of water. Across the rear dash laid a blanket.

Mr. Rayller, first making sure her feet were in, closed the door. There was no fanfare, only a few goodbyes and best wishes from observers, and they were gone.

The trip home was fairly quiet, neither one wishing to discuss where they were going or why. Mr. Rayller drove, and Shelia slept, or appeared to. What she was actually doing was quietly crying, trying not to let her grandpa hear.

Arriving home, Mr. Rayller helped Shelia onto her crutches and, with bags in hand, helped her into the house. Once inside, neither could bring themselves to speak a word. Mr. Rayller led her to her father's old room. This pleased her.

Inside the room, Shelia felt a little closer to her dad. His old desk, bed, and books were all there. Mr. Rayller cleared his throat to get her attention.

"I hope this is all right."

It was more than all right. It was what she had been hoping for.

"It's just what I wanted. Can I keep his room?" Shelia asked in choked tears.

Mr. Rayller, anticipating her request, said, "Yes, you can. I was hoping you would want to. We'll get the rest of your stuff when you feel up to it."

He then put her bags on the bed and walked back out of the room. Shelia sat down on the bed. Wrapping her arms around herself, she could not restrain the tears and loneliness of the missing arms of her mother, father, and grandmother.

With a fertile imagination and longing heart, Shelia remembered the sounds of her grandmother going about her business in the house. The sounds of her in the kitchen with pots and pans rattling, the vacuum's whir, even the rhythmic sounds of the washing machine—all this was missed and replaced by the silence of the departed. As much as she tried to ignore it, her grandmother's absence was accented by the silence.

Mr. Rayller stood on the back porch with an aching heart. He was only a few feet from his favorite fishing rod and gear. He recalled all the mornings he'd gone fishing before first light and had dinner caught before breakfast. Knowing Carol was not there, he had little desire to try his hand at catching dinner.

CHAPTER 37

Nats became quite a close friend to Timmy. They spent many long hours together. With Nats, Timmy never feared being struck, kicked, or called painful names and worse. Nats always treated him the way he liked to be treated, but he would argue with Timmy quite often, until the day Timmy was beaten and kicked, then left in his own waste in the backyard of his home by his father. That was the day Timmy stopped trying to hide his hate for his parents.

After the beating and crying stopped, Timmy struggled to his feet and entered the house. No one offered help. They were still having fun. In the bathroom, Timmy relaxed slightly while pondering a thought, *If what they are doing is making love, I would rather be whipped with barbed wire.*

Even while in considerable pain, he showered and went to his room to dress. Being both soiled and bloody only multiplied his hate and magnified his desire to be free. The dream of being away from his parents carried him when his injured and battered body could not. In his mind, he often imagined their destruction but after this beating, he no longer needed to be asleep to see them dead in vivid color and detail.

Finding his room in the same destroyed manner as always, he quietly dug through the mess until he found clothing that appeared cleaner than the rest. Dressing again, he left the house, and again, no one noticed.

With considerable difficulty, he made his way toward his castle. Even though the fall sun disappeared earlier in the evening, he had no trouble seeing the trail to his castle.

Did he see himself as a knight returning from battle with a powerful and unrelenting foe? No. Rather, he saw himself as one of the toys or tools his parents used for their enjoyment. It was clear to him it mattered not one bit to them how he felt. Their only concern was his being there for the warm-up for them to have fun. Their fun was all that mattered to them.

As this clear fact replayed itself in his mind, his eyes filled with tears. However, as his eyes filled with tears, his heart filled with more anger than ever before, and for the first time, he accepted whole-heartedly the desire to strike back. Not just in an, I'll-teach-you manner, but in a manner that said killing-you-will-make-me-very-happy. The idea of giving back to them all the pain they had given him had taken root. But he knew he would have to give this a lot of thought. This was a challenge he was going to like.

The challenge at hand was found in making the journey. From head to toe, the pain screamed its presence. In the shower, he'd felt and seen the bruises start to show all over his body. Every place his father's boot made contact with his body, his body announced the injury.

Timmy knew very well his father could have killed him if he had intended to. This would have been Timmy's preferred condition at the time, but then dear old Dad would have lost his warm-up "whipping post."

The idea of a whipping post stuck in his mind and united with his anger, formulating into a rather vicious thought.

How would dear old G.I., tough-as-nails, I-could-whip anybody-in-my-platoon Dad like to be tied to the tree in the backyard and whipped?

With these thoughts, Timmy's mind perked up a bit. In the midst of the pain, more severe than he has had to endure before, his mind began to imagine. With each step, the images grew clearer and more defined. This continued until he had his own personal movie playing in his head.

The movie Timmy was seeing was not only visual, it was interactive. Roger was tied to a high limb of their tree in the backyard. With his arms above his head and spread apart, he appeared to be attempting to pull himself up onto the branch. This would have been amusing, until you noticed the blood running down his arms. The blood was because, in Timmy's dream, Roger was being repaid with a whipping or flogging with a cat-o'-nine tails whip made of barbwire and leather. His hands were bound to the tree limb with barbwire around each finger and thumb, around the wrists and palms.

This would be quite punishing alone, but to add to it, he could only reach the limb while standing on his tiptoes. Any attempt to relieve the strain to his legs would be met with immediate and terrible pain to his hands and wrists.

In Timmy's dream, his mother received the same degree of mercy she had offered him—none. She was the partially suspended occupant of an opposing limb. Only slightly lower, Timmy thought she would be able to stretch higher, considering her love for four-inch heels. For added amusement, he placed her in her favorite short sundress. He liked the idea of beating it off her with a cat-o'-nine tails.

Timmy knew all too well the pain that could be caused by using a piece of wire for punishment and particularly enjoyed the idea of barbwire for his parents. In his dream, he easily saw himself as the disciplinarian.

As most people know, good movies are best enjoyed in the company of a close friend. This movie was not only enjoyed by Timmy, but also by his best friend, Nats. His role in all this was as the cheering squad.

He sat on the first limb supporting Roger, and because the limbs were set at forty-five-degree angles, their captives could see each other by turning their heads. They were even suspended far enough from the trunk of the tree that Timmy could walk completely around them with no fear of encountering the tree trunk.

In reality, the tree in his backyard was large, but not nearly large enough for his dream, so he expanded it.

Timmy imagined himself walking around his parents as they hung from the limbs with barbwired hands. He listened with joy, even glee, as they screamed obscenities at him. His father tried to kick him and was rewarded with excruciating pain for his movement, and more blood ran. He used threats, but Timmy only looked at him and smiled. He finally tried begging, and Timmy mocked him with laughter.

On the other hand, Phyllis started with her womanly charms. She tried to sweet-talk him into letting her go. When that failed, she also chose profanity and threats.

When he ventured close enough, she wrapped her legs around his waist as quickly as a serpent capturing its next meal. Her intention had been to capture and swing to her husband for more kicking; however, the second she locked her heels, she could not unlock them. For only one second, she thought she had him, and then discovered he had her.

Timmy imagined himself becoming red hot, not blazing as if on fire, but the red hot of a cook stove. This was unfortunate for Phyllis because she could not unlock her legs. He enjoyed her screams, not of or for her pleasure, but from the pain. He kept her locked to him until her legs were burned to the bones.

When he finally released her, she hung limp, no longer able to support her weight. Timmy said, "Now your legs are really hot."

Nats said, "Cool. I didn't think you had it in ya. She's smoking."

They laughed. This was the first Nats had ever spoken in these dreams involving his parents, but this was the first time Timmy had been awake. Timmy didn't care why he hadn't spoken before, but he was glad he did. This gave him a conversational audience and partner.

Speaking to his parents, Timmy said, "Mom, Dad, I hope you enjoy this game. I will."

Timmy reached down and picked up the cat-o'-nine tails, and without warning struck his father across the face. To Timmy's delight, his father screamed from the pain. The barbed wire had cut into his eye, nose, and forehead. The appearance of blood and bone delighted Timmy, so much so, he struck Roger in the face until he was unrecognizable. Not feeling satisfied, he continued striking Roger, working his way down his body. This continued until he had beaten all the clothing off Roger, and every inch of his body was a mass of bleeding flesh. Roger no longer begged for mercy, he only stared out of his one eye and whimpered. Timmy showed no mercy of any kind. He continued his attack until Roger died. He then turned his attention and attacks on his mother. Her end came the same way.

Now exhausted from his efforts and pleased with the results, his dream ended. Thinking himself exhausted from his dream, Timmy soon realized he had reached his castle.

Timmy's injuries would gradually heal, at least the ones on the outside. The bruised ribs were still tender, and the other injuries had not required medical attention but quick movement was not likely.

Timmy missed two days of school after the beating, but he didn't care. The other kids didn't care if he showed up or not. They considered him to be a bully and a loser anyway. Feeling humiliated about the incident on the bus and not wanting to be seen with his injuries, he rested in his hiding place, his castle.

Some kids build tree houses and christen the structure their castle or clubhouse, "No grown-ups allowed."

In Timmy's case, his clubhouse was not in a tree, where he could overlook the vast expanse of his kingdom, but instead, it was in a place that felt to him more like his standing in his family and life.

His clubhouse and place of privacy was in the remains of Mr. Breeker's fireplace. The remains of what was once the only place he felt safe and welcomed. Now it was an abandoned plot of land being consumed by the wild growth of nature.

The top of the chimney could not be seen beyond the young pine trees. Many years earlier a tornado had taken his only living friend as it completely destroyed the house. The only thing remaining of the house was its large fireplace and its chimney broken off four feet above the point where it narrowed. Timmy salvaged a piece of old plywood and a couple of mason blocks for use on the chimney. With care and determination, he closed off the opening at the chimney's top. The plywood on the top of the chimney kept out the rain.

After cleaning out the ash and debris, Timmy lined the interior with panels of cardboard. He used the fireplace grates positioned outside the entrance on the sitting ledge to serve as sentinels. Their job was to guard the castle.

After stealing a different piece of plywood from Mr. Rayller's barn, he created his gate by laying it lengthwise on the edge across the front. Of course, no castle or clubhouse was complete without a skull and candle. The skull he found in a trashcan behind the drugstore in town after Halloween with a number of damaged candles.

Within his castle, as he thought of it, he had made it quite comfortable by his standards. To him it was more comfortable and safer than being at home. At his castle, no one could find him or hurt him. This was his place; he was king and supreme ruler. Trespassing in his domain was punishable by death, no appeals.

Within Timmy's domain, no small rodent, lizard, or animal escaped his punishment. His executions were performed with haste and delight.

The location was hidden, isolated, and ignored. In hunting season, only a hunter or two ever noticed it, and then it was forgotten. For Timmy, it was safe and dry. In winter, it could be fairly warm with a small fire. Winter or summer, he could spend hours there, just himself and Nats.

With some effort, Timmy slid back the plywood that served as his door and entered. With equal effort, he again closed the entrance.

Knowing the layout and contents of his castle, Timmy soon had a candle lit and settled into a corner. Too sore to go farther, he tried to rest.

Looming close by, Nats was completely satisfied his young friend had made the journey. He fell silent and let him rest. Nats knew there would soon be other opportunities to teach, and he was in no rush.

Timmy fell asleep carrying the events of the day into the night, the trip home on the bus after school, then the beating from his father, and finally the walking daydream. With all he'd endured that day replaying in his head, his sleep was not restful.

Awakened with the sunrise, he lay still and tried not to think of the soreness in his stomach and ribs. As much as he would have preferred to remain still, a nature call was making its demands known.

With considerable pain and stiffness, Timmy pushed himself upward until he was on his knees. Fighting against the pain and stiffness, he was able to eventually stand on his feet with his head in the mouth of the chimney. Sliding open his doorway, he was greeted by the morning air. The sounds of morning would have been welcomed by other people in other places, but for Timmy, he wished they would all just shut up.

With aching muscles and ribs, he made his way around to the rear of the chimney. There, in seclusion, he relieved himself. Feeling better, he now noticed the extent of his soreness with every move he made. The pain was not to the point of demobilizing him; however, speed would not be available to him. To be able to see his dream come true, he knew he would have to first heal before enacting any plan.

Back in his castle, he returned to his makeshift bed. This he preferred, and Nats's company was welcomed more than anyone else's. Cradling his ribs, Timmy thought, *No school today*, and fell asleep.

Phyllis walked down the hallway of her house, dodging items and trash she thought beneath her to pick up. She looked at the door to Timmy's room and laughed. Mumbling under her breath, she said, "At least you are good for getting the old man warmed up."

She had no fear or care of being overheard. Roger had already left; she didn't know where he had gone and didn't care. As for Timmy, she didn't care where he was, as long as she didn't have to put up with him.

For two nights and days, Timmy remained in his castle. The pain on the second day was worse than the first; however, he knew sooner or later he would have to eat.

CHAPTER

38

On Saturday, Shelia sat on the bed in the room that had once been her father's. The tears came as if poured from a bucket. The tears came until her head ached, her ribs hurt, and her eyes were puffy. Finally, she simply ran out of crying power and fell asleep.

Sleep had always been Shelia's preferred avenue of escape from stress and reality. She had reasoned as a child, when asleep, the dreams you had were yours and whatever happened in the waking world didn't affect your dreams.

On the night of the car accident, she had been asleep, happily in dreamland and ignoring everyone inside the car. She first heard screeching of the tires and felt the braking of the car in her dream. Opening her eyes, as she quickly sat up, she saw the headlights directly in front of them. She heard her father shout, "Oh my God!"

Not comprehending what was happening, she saw her mother turning and grabbing her by the sweatshirt, yanking her down toward the floor. With strength she never knew her mother had, she found herself being forcibly driven toward the floorboard of the car, then the explosive impact. She heard her mother scream in harmony of terror with her father, as the two cars became one mass of twisted metal. She saw in her dream, as if in third person, a slow-motion reenactment of the collision.

The car crossed the centerline, not being corrected, and plowed into their car so quickly her father jammed the brakes only seconds before impact. Headlight to headlight, bumper to bumper, and grill to grill, they collided.

On impact, the hoods buckled and crushed back into the windshields, causing them to implode. The dashboard vibrated, jerked, and twisted a fraction of a second before it was forcibly shoved into her parents in the front seat, killing them both instantly. For good measure, the engine and transaxles followed the dash, being forced into the front seat of Shelia's car by the impact of the heavier car as it plowed into them head-on.

Shelia saw her shoulder and head slam into the back of the front seat as the seat's bolts ripped from the floor. The momentary driving force of her body assisted in ripping out the seat bolts, only for a second before the driving force of the impact and her parents shoved back, sitting her up straight again in the rear seat. When her back came to rest against the rear seat, the front seat, her parents, and the engine compartment all rested on her right leg and foot.

In the accident scene, she was unconscious, but in third person she could look at herself in her dream and wonder why she was still alive. No one in the cars moved or spoke.

She was unconscious, her parents were dead, and the man in the other car did not survive.

She awakened trying to pull her parents free of the wreckage, only to find herself pulling at her sheets.

This dream had become a regular occurrence. Sometimes it came nightly, other times not as often. Shelia had not had five consecutive nights of sound sleep since the night of the accident. This night had been no different. Restful sleep had lasted only a few hours.

Lying in bed, feeling she had failed her parents, she gave into the grief, loneliness, and pain of loss. Lying on her side, she cried, but when she raised her hand to wipe her eyes, she found the same handkerchief from the hospital in her hand. She wiped her eyes, looked at the handkerchief, and knew she was not alone. After a few minutes of remembering the good times she had with grandma and her parents, she fell asleep. This time she was blessed with no dreams.

Shelia awakened Sunday morning to nature's concert. A blue jay was busying itself with the tree outside her window, and a butterfly rested on the wire screen. The butterfly sat for a minute or two, and then flew off as Shelia watched.

"Thanks for dropping by to say good morning," Shelia said.

The sun was up, bright, and screaming to all daytime creatures large and small, reminding them the day had started.

Her Sundays once consisted of hanging out with friends at the mall or playing with her hair and clothes and gossiping on the phone. The accident had changed all that. She thought her popularity at school and being in the right clique would get her lots of visitors, but she was wrong. As the weeks in the hospital dragged on, her friends disappeared. Few came to the hospital for visits, and eventually, none even called. Her school counselor arranged with the hospital a daily delivery of her homework assignments.

After learning she had lost her parents and her friends dropping away one by one, her anger and resentment hit with full force.

Who needs them? She thought, with tears of pain and loneliness.

The only girl that even acted like she cared was Michelle Stone.

Shelia had regretted the way she acted on their last visit, but when Michelle and her mom came to visit her in the hospital, Shelia learned just how much a mistake it was to make Michelle an enemy.

Shelia sat on the side of the bed thinking of her last conversation with Michelle, if you could call it that.

Speaking to herself, she said, "How could she have known about the handkerchief?"

This question puzzled Shelia since the last hospital visit. Now she wondered if knowing Michelle was an advantage or a disadvantage. Michelle was a little younger, but she was also different.

Shelia's thoughts were interrupted by the sound of her grandfather walking along the hall. Listening to his footsteps, she could tell he was wearing his usual boots. The muffled thud resounded in her ears many times, but this morning it was different. They sounded heavy, and the timing between the steps was slower.

Sitting on the side of the bed, she wondered if it would be wise to go out and greet him now, or should she wait a while? She decided to wait.

Mr. Rayller was indeed moving slower that morning. His sleep had not been restful; his mind spun with questions well into the early hours of the morning. The questions came to his mind in rapid fire as he lay in bed.

How do I raise and care for a teenage girl? Does she know how to take care of a house or even cook? Who can help me with a girl her age? How do I get her into school?

He had far more questions than he had answers. After one a.m., he finally fell asleep, but even in his sleep the questions persisted.

Shortly after sunrise, he had awakened with many of the same questions he fell asleep with and only one sure answer. He knew he would not allow his granddaughter to be raised by someone else; he was the last of her immediate family. He knew he would have to seek the help of his friends to see this through.

Standing in the doorway of his kitchen, he saw everything the same as Carol left it. The dry food canisters with flying birds sat on the counter where they had always been. The dishtowels hung on the wall rack by the kitchen window; she liked the rack there. It dried the damp dishtowels in the sun and was easy to reach. The range-top oven needed a good cleaning, he noted; he would have to clean the stove today. All the pictures and reminders where stuck to the refrigerator by bird magnets, still hung there reminding. Coffee maker, toaster oven, and microwave all still as they were when she left. The kitchen had always been the gathering place for the family and visitors. Mr. Rayller decided it would remain so.

After putting on coffee to percolate, he set about cleaning the kitchen, wiping down appliances, cleaning up in general. He did not hear Shelia when she entered the kitchen on her crutches.

Positioning herself in the doorway, she watched her grandfather doing the housework. Sure, she had seen him put away his newspapers or hang his work coat back outside but never engage in detail cleaning as he did now.

Not wanting to startle him, she tapped the bottom of her crutch on the door jam, as if she was just entering.

Mr. Rayller looked up to see her and smiled.

"Good morning, Grandpa." Shelia said.

Her face in the doorway was one of the best sights he had seen in a long time. He returned the greeting, and then remembered he had put on coffee.

"You want coffee?" he asked.

Without thinking, she answered, "No, Mom doesn't allow me to drink it."

Realizing what she had just said, she hung her head, then said, "I'm sorry, Grandpa, for saying that. It just came out."

Mr. Rayller straightened and looked at her. "That's all right. We both have to get used to them not being here. I'll get you a glass of milk. We still don't want to make them upset with us."

He walked over to the cabinets and removed a clean glass for Shelia. While he filled the glass, Shelia took a seat at the table, the same seat her grandmother once sat in. Mr. Rayller turned from the refrigerator with the full glass of milk and nearly dropped it.

Shelia, sitting in Carol's chair, looked so much like her grandmother when she was a young woman, it startled Mr. Rayller. For a second, he thought Shelia was Carol. With a tremble in his hand, he set the glass on the table, and then turned away. Speaking under his breath, he said, "This is going to be tough."

Shelia, hearing what he had said, chose to remain quiet. She did not know what had caused the comment, but figured she would find out soon enough. Retrieving her glass of milk from across the table, she sat quietly sipping. Mr. Rayller turned around and took a good long look at his granddaughter. Not wanting to add worry to his granddaughter, he measured his words carefully.

"It's been a while since anyone sat in your grandmother's chair, and it took me by surprise how much you look like her when she was a young woman. She's always been a young woman to me. She never slowed down, always baking or out in the yard or going fishing with you. I don't remember her sitting very much for very long. No, she didn't slow down much. Always some project she wanted to see finished and then on to the next one."

The two remained silent for a moment, Mr. Rayller standing by the sink, Shelia sitting. She noticed he appeared to be thinking about something. She hoped he would not bring up her parents. She was not ready to start talking about them yet. For her own sake, she changed the conversation.

"Grandpa, you ready for breakfast yet?" she asked.

Mr. Rayller, pulled from his thoughts, responded quickly, "Do you know how to cook?"

Shelia, taking note of his expression, said, "Grandpa, my cooking is not restaurant quality, but we will survive." Then, she smiled.

Mr. Rayller worked in the kitchen, helping Shelia make breakfast. For their joint efforts, they were able to enjoy a feast of bacon, eggs, and pancakes. This made Mr. Rayller feel better. *She could at least cook breakfast*, was his thought.

With breakfast complete, Mr. Rayller instructed Shelia to get off her foot, and he would do the dishes. Shelia, having been on her injured foot longer than ever before, gladly accepted the offer. With Shelia sitting at the table, their conversation continued.

CHAPTER 39

Kathryn could not believe her ears. Had her daughter just told her there was a place that we all went when we died? She didn't call it Purgatory, but that's what it sounded like. She even explained it in detail.

Unable to find her voice, she sat and watched Michelle. Minutes passed and neither spoke or moved. Finally, Michelle turned toward her mother and said, "I'm sorry, but remember, you asked."

At last, Kathryn found words.

"Who are you, and what have you done with my daughter?"

There was no humor or sarcasm in her voice. She was dead serious. The car continued to idle, and the air conditioning blew cold air, but that was not the reason why goose pimples covered Kathryn's entire body.

She had just been told what she had always believed to be. It was more than she expected and certainly more than she was ready to comprehend. All this came from left field, and she didn't know which way to go with it. Sure, she had accepted the fact that her daughter could see and talk to the dead, but for them to give her detailed information such as this was too much. Now she feared the dead had taken over her daughter. She was possessed—or was she? She didn't know.

Michelle sat quietly, allowing her mother to try and digest what she had been told. For her, the idea of an afterlife was not difficult to grasp, considering she had been seeing the dead for as long as she could remember. She also understood at an early age, there were good dead and bad dead. She even learned the difference between spirits and souls, even though it was hard to explain to a layperson like her mother. But she was told to be patient, and they would learn and understand.

Now, she wondered when that would be.

Michelle, knowing all the signs and signals of her parents, said, "Mom, I'm still your daughter. The same one you and Dad made, the same one you gave birth to over fifteen years ago. And, before you start thinking I'm possessed or something, my soul belongs to the one and only true God."

Kathryn sighed with relief but still remained confused. *How could she have such a religious base when we seldom go to church?*

Michelle, still leaning her head against the headrest, continued watching her mother and began to speak again.

"Mom, remember when I was little, about three, and you or Dad would come and tell me a bedtime story?"

Kathryn, remembering those short years, smiled and said softly, "Yes, I do."

Michelle continued, "Well, one night you and Dad were tucking me in, and Dad asked me if I was afraid of the bogeyman, and I said, 'No.'

"Then you asked me why. And I said, 'Because I have an angel.' You and Dad laughed, kissed me goodnight, and I went to sleep."

Kathryn, remembering so many of those nights, was trying to remember that particular one.

Michelle, sensing her confusion, said, "That particular night is not important, but what is, is this: I do have a guardian angel. You have a guardian angel, Dad has a guardian angel, everyone has a guardian angel. Believe me, Mom, they are real. Some of us have additional angels to help us do things or give us extra protection. Our family has extra angels to protect and help us."

Kathryn slowly began to relax. This was a line of discussion she could feel better about. Michelle, seeing the tension relaxing a bit in her mother's face, continued, "Mom, remember you and Dad said you were really sick when I was born?"

Kathryn began to slowly nod her head. Speaking out loud, she said, "I was in my last trimester. Nearing your delivery date, I developed an acute appendicitis. It ruptured and filled the both of us with poison. Your dad nearly lost us both."

Michelle tried to remain calm, but her excitement was building, and she spoke as calmly as she could.

"You told me that after the surgery and my delivery and stuff, you went to intensive care, and so did I, right?" Again, Kathryn nodded. Michelle continued.

"Did you ever ask Dad what he was doing, while all this was going on with us?"

All the events had been clearly recalled in Kathryn's mind.

She said, "I know exactly what he was doing. He was praying for our survival, the same as me. What does this have to do with anything?"

Michelle cleared her throat, "Dad's prayers were answered by our survival. I was told he had even offered himself to die, instead of us. Mom, the angels around us came because Dad was willing to give up everything to save us."

Kathryn knew Michael loved them, but hearing how deeply his love ran was bringing her to tears. If it had been coming from a stranger, she would have been able to hide the effect all this had on her, but coming from their daughter, the value and love of her husband was being driven home with ten-inch nails. She could hide her emotions no more. Her heart swelled to the point that her eyes could not restrain the tears. They rolled down her face.

Michelle, still barely in control of her emotions, said, "Mom, there's something else."

Kathryn, now looking down at the tissue she used to wipe her eyes, said, "After all you have said, what else could there be?"

Michelle now had a tear rolling slowly down her cheek. Speaking slowly, she said, "My grandparents have come to see me also. They said I look like you did when you were fifteen. They said you may have doubts, so I'm supposed to tell you, 'Words spoken even underwater still travel the universe forever.'"

Kathryn felt like she had just been kicked in the gut. She knew exactly what that was meant to say.

When Kathryn was six years old, she had climbed the fence that enclosed the family swimming pool. After being told repeatedly she could not play in the pool unless her parents were present and receiving two spankings, she decided she in fact was going to play in the pool. With the aid of a large clay flowerpot, she was able to climb over the fence and safely enter the pool area. The only evidence of her entry was a fresh footprint in the potting soil. Her mother had not yet planted a flower in that pot. In the pool area, she selected the five-foot depth section and dived in.

She was an excellent swimmer for a six-year-old, but she soon grew tired and developed leg cramps. Unfortunately, she developed the cramps in the deep water. As she began to lose her ability, she panicked and started fighting the water. Losing that fight also, she found herself underwater and drowning. The last words she could gasp out were, "Daddy, save me." Then her small lungs filled with water.

Her father, working in the backyard, noticed her absence. Knowing his daughter's stubbornness, he headed for the pool area. At the fence, he spotted the flowerpot and the fresh footprint. Running around the fence and through the gate, he immediately saw Kathryn floating just below the surface at the deep end. Screaming for his wife to call the ambulance, he dashed for the deep end of the pool and dove in.

With an ambulance on the way, he struggled to force air back into Kathryn's lungs till they arrived. She was rushed to the hospital and spent a week learning to hate hospitals.

Two days after the incident, her father drained the pool and hired a contractor to return the area to a lawn. When Kathryn returned home from the hospital, there was no longer a pool in her backyard, just grass.

Kathryn felt Michelle had truly spoken with her parents; there was no one underwater to hear her speak. With her parents having passed on, there was no one living to inform her of the events, and she had never told her of the event. There was never any need.

Kathryn, drying her eyes, said to her daughter, "I believe you, Baby."

She then reached over and with both arms embraced her daughter.

After another round of tears of understanding and joy, they jointly decided the mall could wait. They were going home to enjoy the company of the man they loved.

CHAPTER 40

Timmy knew he could not remain in his castle forever. On the morning of the third day, he left the safety of his castle as he had done the morning previous and returned home. Not wanting to see either of his parents, he chose the predawn hour to reenter. He needed not have worried, neither Phyllis nor Roger was home.

Discovering the house empty, he showered and peacefully dined on cold cuts and leftovers. He didn't know where his parents were and didn't care. His intentions were to eat, shower, and go to school. The idea behind going to school was not to get an education; it was to find and keep track of Andrew, better known as Andy.

Timmy was certain it was Andy who gave him the unwanted nickname, Turd Boy. He was sure, and so was Nats. Keeping track of Andy was important while he came up with a suitable plan for revenge.

Andy, being from one of the affluent families in town, was known for getting out of school early for family trips. His parents could always afford what they wanted. This made Timmy extremely jealous and filled him with hate for them.

Looking through the pile of mixed laundry, Timmy found enough clean clothes to dress. Ignoring the soreness, he managed to make himself appear like the other students that would be at school. That was in appearance only; he knew he was different. He knew there was no one else in the world that had to put up with the things he did.

Having come home the previous morning before his parents awoke and made sounds of getting ready for school, he felt certain they did not care if he went to school or not. Then he left the house in the direction of the bus stop, only to bypass it and return to his castle.

On the morning previous, he had not seen them, but had heard their snoring. On this morning they were not there, and he was happier about their absence.

After dressing and pacifying his hunger, he headed for the bus stop. This time he would get on the bus and go to school. He did not need to rush to catch the bus. He was early and knew very well when the bus would arrive. At the bus stop, he was soon joined by three other students.

Timmy and Andy were the same age, but not the same size. Andy was fair-skinned with blond hair and blue eyes; Timmy had a darker complexion with brown hair and brown eyes. Not his hair, eyes, or physical build matched either Phyllis or Roger in any great detail. They both had sandy hair and blue eyes. The slight differences were enough to make it easy for them to make sure he saw and knew the differences in private and public.

Phyllis, being his mother, ignored him when the three of them were together. Timmy looked like a tag-a-long, and his parents made sure he felt that way also.

This difference did not escape the attention of the town's gossip clubs. They passed the rumors back and forth on a hot and heavy basis. One of their favorites was guessing the real identity of Timmy's father. Most could not figure out who Timmy resembled, and those that did were fortunately not part of the gossip club. They had narrowed it down to three men and were right about one.

Timmy, being tall and solid build for his age, was three inches taller and twenty pounds heavier than Andy. The feelings of inferiority, in spite of his size, always put him on the offensive around those close to his age. He would fight, as boys do, but not often and never with witnesses. He was withdrawn, but would use the sly approach when he wanted to get even.

Andy, on the other hand, was shorter, and because of his family's influence and wealth, thought he was superior to others his age. He did not take kindly to being teased about having to ride the bus. He thought he should have been driven to school or in his own car rather than ride the bus. His arrogance was not easily stomached by most kids. Timmy hated him.

As the other three kids horsed around, Timmy waited in more silence than usual and farther away. When the bus arrived, the last one to board was Timmy.

With one foot on the first step and left hand gripping the rail, he looked up at the driver. What he saw made his stomach curl with anger. The driver had a sarcastic grin on his face. The kind displayed when someone is about to say something offensive.

Timmy looked directly into the eyes of the driver. As their eyes remained locked, the driver's grin faded. It was replaced by a cold chill that ran down his spine. This was not the same kid that got off his bus with dirty underpants. This kid was ready and willing to fight.

The eyes said it all.

Timmy boarded the bus. When he turned from the driver and started down the aisle, only a few snickered. One of them was Andy.

Following Nats's instructions, he only gave Andy a glance when he passed by. He had been told that doing anything more would give away his intentions.

Other kids that laughed or made comments were given a stern look and ignored.

When he reached the back of the bus, Timmy took his usual seat. Looking to the front, he noticed the driver continued to stare at him. He felt he had made a major success; he had shut down a grown-up. If he could stop the driver from laughing, then he could stop the rest.

For the next week and a half, he repeated his routine until there were no longer any laughers. Those who had chosen to ignore his evil stare were later caught in the bathroom or other isolated places and persuaded into silence with a quick punch to the ribs. Timmy knew all the places that could hurt. His father, being combat-trained in the military, had taught him many of the painful blows while kicking the crap out of him for warm-ups. Timmy had learned to force the appearance of respect born of fear from others through pain.

On a bright and sunny Monday morning in late fall, a new stop was added to the bus route. It traveled the same route on the same roads; however, on this morning it stopped in front of the Rayller's house.

Standing in the driveway were Mr. Rayller and Shelia. With little difficulty, Shelia boarded the bus. Making her way to the rear, she took a seat, in Timmy's seat. A few of the students knew who she was spoke as she passed, but none really wanted her to sit with them. Shelia didn't care; they were too far behind the times for her liking. They lacked the cool she required to be their friend.

Mr. Rayller watched as she moved to the rear of the bus carrying her crutches and walking on her cast and heel. He wondered why she had chosen the rear of the bus. He decided to ask about this when she got home.

One kindhearted freckle-faced girl turned and said to Shelia, “That’s Timmy’s seat. He’s not going to like you sitting there.”

Shelia, giving her a nasty look that only girls can give each other, said, “Ask me if I care.”

The younger girl, noting the indignation, said, “Okay, it’s your funeral.”

Shelia, wanting to end the conversation, immediately shot back, “Don’t send flowers.” Then she rolled her eyes, snapped her head, and looked out the window. She didn’t like the school or its students. They had no idea about how to be cool.

The bus pulled in its stop sign and proceeded to its next stop along the route. That next stop happened to be Timmy’s.

The first three students that boarded the bus seemed happy and normal, ready to go to school. The fourth student was tall, lean, and mean looking. This was the new Timmy.

He boarded the bus and immediately spotted the intruder. Timmy was obviously surprised by the newcomer.

How dare anyone intrude into his private sitting area! He was convinced he had established his authority on this bus. Who did she think she was? All this ran through Timmy’s mind in a matter of seconds.

With long strides, Timmy was quickly at the back of the bus. Towering over Shelia, Timmy stared down at her. Shelia, in an act of defiance, turned and threw both legs up onto the seat cushion, then slid her back against the wall. With her left hand on a crutch, she stared up and back at him and at first said nothing.

Timmy slowly began to lean toward Shelia. "This is my seat."

Feeling as if she had lost all that was worth living for and ready for a fight, Shelia said, "I don't know who you are, you knuckle-dragging neanderthal, but your name ain't on this seat. Mine is, so get lost."

Timmy's temper now at its boiling point, he said, "I don't know who you are, but if you don't get out of my set, I'm gonna break your crippled little neck."

She stared at him. By now he was ready to drag Shelia, crutches and all, out of his seat.

"Timmy, Timmy, relax. Let the little Phyllis-looking dog sit there. We'll get to her later," Nats whispered in his ear.

The driver yelled back while looking in the mirror, "Sit down, Timmy, or the bus doesn't move."

With reluctance, Timmy sat down in the seat across from Shelia.

Thinking she had won, Shelia said, "Wise choice, caveman." Timmy gave her a smile that could kill and then looked out the window as the bus pulled away from his stop.

The rest of the way to school, he neither looked at her nor spoke. Shelia kept her leg, with the cast partly covered in blue jeans, on the seat and continued with her own evil stare.

The first school stop was for high school students. Timmy noticed she did not move to get up nor got off at this stop. Now he knew she was in junior high.

The school day for Timmy went as usual—show up to class but have little participation. Just after lunch, Timmy was in the smoking area when he overheard Andy, who was not a smoker, say to another student, "I heard Turd Boy had to back down this morning on the bus. He's so tough that a junior high girl can put him in his place."

His back was turned to Timmy, so he didn't realize Timmy had arrived. When he turned around, he was greeted with a death stare.

Timmy stared eye to eye with Andy. Tendrils of smoke flowed out his nostrils and up through his line of sight. He appeared as if he was exhaling smoke from an internal fire. This only represented a fraction of how angry he really was.

Timmy thought, *Keep talking, Andy. What I have planned for you will make you wish you were dead. Then we'll see whose laughing.*

After giving him a death stare, he snubbed out his cigarette and left the smoking area. A half dozen other students saw the look he had given Andy. They knew he was not joking. Andy was too arrogant to see the need for caution in a crowd or alone.

Shelia had been in the new school for only a week. She felt she was too cool for even the coolest of the cliques in this small hick school. When she saw a classmate wearing an identical top to hers, she gave the unconcerned girl a nasty look. This was her only reason to dislike someone she didn't even know. A few girls in her classes tried to talk to her but were soon displeased with her attitude. They then ignored her.

Day after day, she went through classes basically ignored and shunned. This treatment she had brought upon herself, but she didn't think so.

On the bus ride home, the first to board were high school students. After picking up the students, the buses went to the junior high school and completed the boarding.

The afternoon of Timmy's return to school, the buses loaded as usual. Timmy boarded the bus and went directly to his ruling seat. Making himself comfortable, he knew he would enjoy the look on her face when she saw he had reclaimed his seat.

When the bus stopped at the junior high school, the students loaded. Shelia discovered Timmy in her chosen seat, and she exploded.

"Who told you to put your worthless backside in my seat, caveman? Can't you see that I'm on crutches, and I need to sit where I want?" All this she said near the top of her lungs. Some of the students on the bus laughed at her. None laughed at Timmy.

Timmy, keeping a blank look on his face, watched her as she neared the rear of the bus. When she was three rows away, he lifted his legs and spun around, putting both his long legs across the seat and partway into the aisle. This made it very clear he not only was giving up the seat, but she would need to make adjustments to get past his feet.

Near the last row, Shelia stopped to give him another blast of her sharp tongue.

"You are a nasty little—no, big—piece of white trash, and I demand you get out of my seat."

Timmy, enjoying her anger, just sat and watched.

"Timmy, she looks like your mother, she sounds like your mother, and she acts like your mother. You know, I even hate her like your mother. Wonder how she would like being tied to the tree and beaten?" Nats whispered in his mind.

With this thought, Timmy smiled.

The smile made Shelia even angrier. Seeing Timmy was not giving up the seat she demanded, Shelia pushed past his feet and seated herself across the aisle. Putting her feet up on the seat, she sat and stared at him. Wanting to give him one more piece of her mind, Shelia said, "Your mother should have aborted you."

The bus had now moved away from the school and was headed out of town. Timmy continued to listen to her comments and imagine beating her to death with his cat-o'-nine tails. Nats spoke again. "Does she ever shut up?"

Finally running out of steam, Shelia went silent. Even in her silence, she gave off an air of anger. Timmy continued to smile. He was enjoying his imagination and her anger.

When the bus came to a stop at Mr. Rayller and Shelia's house, she again got to her feet and pushed past Timmy's feet. Before going up the aisle, she fired her most dangerous verbal shot at Timmy.

"I heard your old man beats you. Maybe next time he'll beat you to death." She then hobbled up the aisle.

Timmy watched her leave the bus, then settled his eyes on Andy. Nats said, "Little Rich Boy is the one I want right now."

At his stop, Timmy was the last of the four off the bus. He walked only a few yards before stopping behind a tree.

When all the students were out of sight, Timmy came out of the woods, crossed the road, and reentered the woods on a footpath in the direction of town. Using the path, it would take only fifteen minutes to trot back into town unseen.

Timmy knew Andy cleaned and stocked shelves every evening at his father's hardware store, but on Mondays he would be at his father's hardware store till six thirty, and then walk six blocks to his mother's flower shop. Nats thought it was good Andy walked. He usually biked into town to his father's hardware store, and then walked to his mom's shop.

At six thirty-five, Andy left his father's hardware store en route to his mother's flower shop. Coming out the front door, he turned right, went to the corner, and turned right again. Andy would need to help put away the fresh stock and help with the wedding arrangements for the next day at his mother's shop. Andy only wanted out; he knew his father had hired a fresh new girl for the summer season as a cashier. The only thing he wanted to see that was pretty and smelled good was her.

Timmy had covered the one-and-a-half-mile trail quickly through the woods. He knew Andy's route and shortcuts.

After turning right, Andy walked two blocks then cut down the alley, between the pool hall and the furniture store. This route would save him a block and a half of walking. The alley was little more than three feet wide, with a small gap between the rears of the buildings.

Timmy arrived in the alley five minutes before Andy.

Looking around, he spotted a broken barstool next to the trashcans. Working quietly, he freed one of the legs from the broken stool. With the stool leg in hand, he knew he only needed to wait.

Timmy heard footsteps coming down the alley. Peeking around the corner of the shaded alley, he recognized Andy's silhouette. Listing to Nats's instructions, Timmy waited. With the stool leg in the swing position like a baseball bat, he waited. The steps came closer and still closer. "Wait, wait, wait… *now*!" Timmy did not step out before he swung, he just swung.

The stool-leg-turned-bat caught Andy squarely across the bridge of the nose. The impact instantly crushed the bridge of his nose and rendered vision impossible in both eyes. After the initial shock of the impact, Andy would have screamed from the pain had it not been cut short by the second blow landing across his diaphragm. A hand yanked him in between the buildings. His shoulder slammed painfully against a brick wall. He was still holding his shattered nose. He felt another blow to his head before losing consciousness.

Timmy beat and kicked Andy until he felt certain Andy would remember this for some time to come.

With no witnesses, Timmy was satisfied. He exited the alley as he had entered—unseen. In another alley at the edge of town, he picked up a discarded sweatshirt and wiped off the blood, then placed the bloody rag in a different garbage can.

Taking a different route, he passed the back of the building that housed the newspaper offices. Michael Stone had just closed the door to his jeep when Timmy appeared, walking down the alley across the vacant lot. Michael could see he had something in his hand. At that distance it could have been a stick or a cane or something else. Michael could not tell for sure.

To him, Timmy was walking like he didn't have a care in the world. Michael started his engine and headed home.

Timmy continued his casual stroll all the way out of town. At the woods' edge, he took another footpath, not the one he had entered town on, but the one that would take him to the lake.

At the water's edge, he used the cover of the woods to toss the stool leg into the lake. Along the way, he had taken time to pick up a plastic bag, scoop in three handfuls of dirt, and then tie it to the stool leg. When the stool leg hit the water, it immediately sank out of sight.

When Andy didn't show up at his mother's shop by seven o'clock, his mother became concerned. By eight o'clock they had called the county sheriff. At midnight, when the pool hall was cleaned and the trash taken out, Andy was found in the alley. At one fourty-five a.m., Andy was admitted to the hospital, and his surgeries began.

Timmy was right; Andy would never forget the beating. He would have to learn to walk all over again with one eye.

At ten thirty p.m. Timmy went to bed. He was happy with himself and Nats. Nats was delighted.

CHAPTER
41

Shelia, on her crutches, slung the backpack of books over her shoulder. Exiting the bus, she made her way up the driveway to her house. She had no idea if Mr. Rayller would be at home, but no matter, she had a key.

Long before she got out of the hospital, Mr. Rayller had started transporting things he felt she would need from her parents' home to his. The home she had always known now stood empty of life and locked up. Mr. Rayller had said they would have to go over soon and get the remainder of what she needed, and the rest would be put into storage and saved for her.

As she approached the house, she noticed the pickup truck was gone. Making her way across the loose gravel on crutches was a little tricky, but she thought she had managed it quite well.

At the back door she turned the knob and found the door unlocked. To no one present she said, "When is he going to learn to lock the doors when he's gone? Anyone could get in here."

For Mr. Rayller, locking the back door or any door was not a problem. His wife Carol was usually there, and as far as he was concerned, she still was.

Shelia entered the kitchen, calling for her grandpa. Getting no answer, she understood she was alone. Dropping her book bag on the floor, she focused on the refrigerator.

As she opened the fridge, she complained, "Lunch was a joke. How could these people eat that garbage?"

Quickly scanning the contents of the refrigerator, her eyes rested on leftover cold chicken. She grabbed a thigh, knowing that would satisfy her taste buds. Standing in the kitchen, eating cold chicken, she began to think, *How on earth could anyone stay in that stinking school? They have no idea of fashion or style. They think cool is a soft drink. All the girls dress like old maids, and I can't find a joint. Not a single person has even offered.*

Thinking of the joint gave her pause. She remembered the question her mother had asked her when some of the kids found themselves busted at school for smoking grass. Yes, she had been involved but had only moments earlier walked away from her friends after getting a good hit. Turning the corner, she was out of sight when the principal rounded the opposite corner and caught four of her friends sharing a joint. Their punishment started with a stern lecture, a call to their parents, and finally, suspension from school.

Word spread through school like a bad odor in a packed room. The principal did not call the cops, so no one got arrested, but instead, they were all suspended for three days. Shelia missed being snared by only seconds.

Word spread equally fast among the parents. When Shelia was asked about her involvement by her mother, she lied to protect her own skin.

"Shelia, do you know these kids?"

"Yes, Mom, I know a couple of them."

"I thought they were all friends of yours."

"No, Mom, they're not all my friends, just two of them."

"Well, I don't want you hanging around with them anymore."

"Yeah, yeah, whatever you want Mom!"

She had not only continued hanging around with them, she continued to smoke at their homes every chance she got. She had lied through the entire affair and walked away untouched.

Feeling the weight of guilt, she lost her taste for food. The act of swallowing was akin to trying to ingest sand. This, combined with the fact that she saw no way to correct her lie, served to choke her. From the kitchen sink's faucet, she drank water like a dying man in the desert— with no glass but with both hands.

In the back of her mind, a clear voice said, *They should have left when you did. It was their fault for getting caught. You were the smart one. You left.*

This voice spoke to her often, and when it did, she usually felt better about anything she had done. Drying her mouth, she looked around to see if her grandfather or anyone else had seen what she had done. Reassuring herself she was still alone, she gave a sigh of relief, and then went to her room to change. Guilt departed her mind as quickly as it had arrived.

Mr. Rayller had looked forward to his retirement, but now with the loss of his wife, son, and daughter-in-law and the gain of his granddaughter; he felt emotionally shipwrecked.

It had been nearly three months since the deaths of his wife and most of his family, but with the new responsibility of having to raise and provide for Shelia, he did not think twice before stepping up to the plate. She was the last of his line, and seeing her to adulthood was now his only goal.

Having made a trip into town to seek advice on the rearing of girls, he headed home with much on his mind.

How was he supposed to understand the whims of a teenage girl? Mrs. Proctor, a widow, seemed quite concerned about Shelia being able to fit in, being new to town and all. This was completely opposite the opinion shared with him from Kathryn and Michelle. They delicately informed Mr. Rayller of their opinion concerning Shelia, and the likelihood she would have problems.

It was easy with boys, thought Mr. Rayller, *they meet the new kid, fight to see who is the toughest, and become lifelong friends or teenage enemies.* That was simple to him, but girls and females in general were more like cats. They could rub their fur up against you one minute and be ready to claw your eyes out the next. He began to see just how much he really needed Carol. Accepting the reality of what he'd been dealt, he drove on toward home.

Shelia changed into more comfortable clothing, and in truly careless style, she neither picked up nor hung up any article of clothing. As she had done all her life, she left her clothing and anything else she had her hands on in the middle of the floor. She was not interested in cleanliness. The bedroom her grandmother had insisted on keeping clean and later her father refused to get out of order was a disaster area. Mr. Rayller had not seen her room in weeks. This was done to give her the privacy he thought she deserved.

For weeks, Mr. Rayller made breakfast and dinner for them. On the way home, he wondered if Shelia would even consider making dinner. In fact, he would like it if she would even start dinner. Her lack of concern over house chores was starting to bother him also. Her injuries were serious, but she was healing well and quickly, so in his thinking, she could do more around the house than she was doing.

As he neared home, he realized there were a number of things going on he didn't care for. This he would deal with at home, tonight.

Shelia felt at home enough now to stretch out across her bed with the door open. No good afternoon for a teenager is complete without music. For Shelia, the music had to be listened to at deafening levels. The bass was loud enough to be heard down the road with the doors and windows closed. That would explain why she did not hear her grandfather when he pulled in and parked. That would also explain why she didn't hear him when he walked into the house, nor when he walked into her bedroom and yanked her one-thousand-dollar stereo off its stand and smashed it on the floor. The sudden death of her loud music was the first thing she noticed. The second was the look on her grandfather's face. He was angry.

The look on his face told her this was not the same sweet gentle grandfather she had been manipulating for the past month. This man she saw now was old and tough looking.

Mr. Rayller spoke in a tone void of gentleness and cordiality. He said, "This is my home, and until you are old enough to live on your own, it is yours. For many years, your grandmother and I lived here in peace and quiet, but you come here, and I can hear this crap you call music a half-mile down the road. The first thing I hear is boom, boom, boom from the bass, then a guitar that sounds like nails down a chalkboard, and you call that music."

A clearly stunned Shelia said, "You busted my stereo. My dad gave me that, and you busted it."

Mr. Rayller, still with plenty of steam to go, said, "I'm sorry about your stereo, but you showed no consideration for me, my house, the neighbors, or anyone else, and you want to complain that your stereo is busted. Maybe you should have considered the effect your actions would have on other people, and speaking of that, you may be hurt, but that does not keep you from cleaning up this pigpen room or cooking dinner. No one good wants to be around a lazy person, and you are lazy. You are my and Carol's granddaughter, and I will not allow you to bring shame to your parents, my wife, me, or yourself without doing something about it. That does include what you do in school. I know you lied to your mother about your friends getting caught smoking dope, but that lie is for you to live with. From today on, you will act like a young lady. Also, no more sitting in the back of the bus. That Timmy Scott sits back there, and he's nothing but trouble, so don't sit back there. Now I'll be back when I cool off, but until then get off your butt and get dinner started. Do it now!"

Shelia, feeling like she was just dunked in cold water, said, "Yes, sir," and began quickly getting to her feet.

Mr. Rayller spun on his heels and left the room and the house without saying another word. Passing through the porch, he grabbed his fishing rod and basket on the way by. He felt he needed to be alone, so he went fishing. Three hours later when he returned with a mess of fish, Shelia had indeed cooked dinner and cleaned the kitchen, all while on crutches.

When Mr. Rayller entered the kitchen, he looked around and raised an eyebrow. The kitchen looked much cleaner, and the meal—hamburger steaks and mashed potatoes with gravy— actually looked tasty.

After washing his hands and sitting at the table, he looked at Shelia and said, "Thank you for dinner." After saying grace, he began to eat.

Shelia felt he should have said more, but she kept quiet. She wasn't ready for round two. She knew that would come soon enough.

CHAPTER 42

Michelle Stone was shocked to hear the details of the Andy-Orbank beating from her father. Andy shared one of the classes she took and was not the best person in the world, but certainly not deserving of something like this. For someone to administer that severe of a beating was something that got the attention of everyone in school and town.

According to her father, Andy was beaten before eleven o'clock at night, but was found by the owner of the pool hall at about 1 a.m. This meant he had lain in the alley for at least two hours before he was found.

Michelle listened carefully and considered the dream she had the night before. After her father finished relaying the details, Michelle returned her attention to her bowl of cereal. This action did not escape the watchful eye of her mother Kathryn, who was standing beside the coffee pot. Michelle's reaction prompted her to speak.

"Honey, what's bothering you?"

After the conversation Michelle had with her mother in the parking lot, their communications were much more mature and friendly. Kathryn clearly understood her daughter was no longer a child and would enjoy much abbreviated years as a teenager. She was approaching maturity and adulthood with no intermission. Kathryn was aware her daughter was still a teenager on the outside, but she also had to admit, inside, she had more to deal with than even she could comprehend. Having settled all this with her husband and herself, she chose to deal with the waning teenager in Michelle while assisting the gifted side whenever she could. Gifted or not, Kathryn was determined to protect her daughter at any price.

Michelle positioned her eyes on the contents of her bowl and hoped the gut feeling or woman's intuition was wrong about her dream. Deciding she needed help with her confusion, she turned to her parents.

"I had a really troubling dream last night." Michelle's words changed the conversation completely.

Michael was about to sip his coffee, but now he set down his cup. Looking first at Kathryn then at Michelle, he said, "Is this connected to the beating of the Orbank kid?" Still looking at her bowl, Michelle replied,"No, Dad, this is not. The dream last night was different and very confusing."

"Tell us about it," Kathryn said, while taking a seat.

Michelle, now looking at her parents one at a time, began to relay her dream.

"This one was not like the others. In this dream, I'm floating above the ground, but not above the trees. The area looks like it's around here somewhere, but I'm not sure. There's a huge storm brewing all around, and it's converging on this one spot. It looks like a house, but everything is dark and dreary. The house can't be seen clearly, so I don't know where it is.

"Suddenly, it begins to rain. Not a clear rain, but a dirty, evil kind of rain. It's a rain that does not come to cleanse, but to claim. This rain brings more dirt and bad stuff with it.

"A tornado comes down to the ground. It's larger than any of the others that I've seen and more dangerous. People are running from it, but they get snatched up before they can reach safety.

"Inside the funnel cloud, I can see things moving. The people are being beaten and tortured by whatever is inside the tornado. I try to get closer, but the white light won't let me. Then I see the demons in the storm.

"The funnel cloud is full of them. Some appear shadowy and dark, eyes changing shapes and colors, never staying the same. These demons with their mouths agape seeking and searching for something to consume remained held within the tornado. Their clawed hands grasp and tear at one another, only to instantly heal and show no sign of injury. They seem to consume one another, only to spew them out again. The sounds were like screams of a thousand souls. They were the home of disease, illnesses of all kinds to the body and mind. And most of all, they were hungry. They were hungry for souls, especially corrupted souls of the good and kind. Evil is the source of this tornado. The people inside the tornado can't escape.

"I find myself feeling great pain for them, but I know they have made their choice and that cannot be changed by me. I am not afraid of them, but reject them and their evil master. My rejection angers them, and they reach out at me, but their way is blocked by Jesus Christ and the Holy Spirit. The demons within the funnel cloud are angry because I can see them, and they can't hurt me. Then I'm forced to leave, and I wake up.

"I don't know if they're after me, or if they're coming for someone else. It's so confusing."

Michael sat looking down at his coffee cup. He had heard something he didn't want to hear. The demons knew who she was. She had been identified. Now she was in danger, more so than ever before. His time in Third World countries as a reporter and reporting on crimes had taught him that demons and the residents of the dark side were very real. Attracting their attention was not something anyone should want. If it came to doing battle against the dark side, the warriors could be quite vicious. He hoped and prayed the white light and God's protective arms would always be with them.

Kathryn was staring out the window as she listened. She knew in her bones that, sooner or later, Michelle would see more than she could handle. This was an inevitable event. Now how did she protect her daughter from what she couldn't see or hear? She knew she would be wasting Michelle's time to pretend the demons weren't real in her dream. So far, there had been no reason to disbelieve her dreams, and starting now was out of the question. How were they supposed to handle this? She had no idea.

The three of them sat quietly. No one spoke or felt like speaking. The unspoken question hung in the air.

"Is the beating of Andy and Michelle's dream connected?" Michael broke the silence with a question.

"Who would have a reason to attack Andy Orbank like that?"

His question attracted Kathryn's attention.

"What did the sheriff say?" She asked.

"The sheriff said whoever gave him that kind of a beating is carrying a ton of anger. To shatter his nose, put out his eye, and give him head and upper-body injuries like those. It would take one or more people continuing to beat him after he was down. Plus, the fact that no one heard anything would indicate he was silenced almost immediately."

Michelle asked, "What did they use?"

"The sheriff said he did not find a weapon at the crime scene, but it was probably a ball bat or something similar. They are still investigating."

With the tone of a mother concerned about a child, Kathryn asked, "Who could do such a thing?"

Michelle, finishing her cereal while standing by the kitchen sink, said, "I can think of a few people with that much anger."

"Well, who do you think could have done that?" Michael asked.

Without hesitation, Michelle said, "Roger Stone and his friends, or Timmy Stone. He hates Andy and a few others."

"The sheriff told deputies to find Roger, but he didn't say Roger who," Michael replied slowly.

Kathryn turned and looked at Michelle.

"You seem awfully sure in your opinion?" Kathryn questioned.

"Mom, they have an awful lot of darkness about them, and they seem to hate everyone," Michelle said.

In a reflective tone, Michael said, "I did see the Stone kid yesterday evening, as I was about to come home from the paper, but he was on the other side of town. He seemed to not have a care in the world, just walking down the alley bouncing a stick off the ground. I even think he may have been whistling."

Thinking of Timmy Stone in a pleasant mood, Michelle said, "If he was in a good mood, it would likely have been because he had done something."

"Do you think he could have beaten Andy Orbank?" Kathryn asked.

This was a thought that got Michael's attention. He replied, "I'll call Deputy Long and mention it to him."

To Michelle, Timmy Stone beating Andy Orbank with a stick seemed very possible, even likely, but she would keep quiet and let the sheriff do his job. As she had noticed in school, Timmy Stone could be mean, nasty, and strike without warning. She didn't want him coming in her direction. Something bothered her more than the beating; she didn't know who to warn about the coming storm. Even if she could, this tornado was driven by evil. Who would know how to deal with that, and this included her.

The dream, this time, carried a sense of warning, but to whom was the warning intended? How soon would it occur? Where would it strike?

These questions ran through Michelle's mind. Over and over again, she replayed these questions but still came up with no answers.

Listening to her father speaking to the sheriff's department, she felt no sense of direction about her dream. After much thought, she decided this one she would have to wait out and hope for the best.

CHAPTER 43

The beating of Andy Orbank sparked a firestorm of calls and visits to the sheriff's office. This contact was not limited to the residents of town, but included half the county also.

It appeared that word of the severe beating of one of the area's prominent and wealthy citizen's child caused a sizeable degree of concern. Mainly, if someone was willing to attack the child of the wealthy, then who was safe? The assumption made as a whole was that the attack was without cause. Deputy Long was not so sure. If there were a cause for the attack, it was likely minor but taken to the extreme. This was based on the lack of any reports to the sheriff's office of serious criminal or no criminal incidents involving Andy Orbank.

A beating of this degree would most likely be the administering of a lesson being taught to Andy for others to see and fear. This was only the opinion of the sheriff. Based on his experience and longevity in the county, he suspected the best place to start would be with those having reputations for such acts.

Behind the closed doors of his office, the sheriff informed the deputies and reliable citizens that he wanted to talk to Roger Scott and his boys. The tone in the sheriff's voice made it clear he would like for them to come in peacefully, but he would prefer they resisted.

Deputy Long, having a good idea where to find Roger, returned to his patrols with a particular purpose. He didn't like the guy. He didn't like his lifestyle or his family. In Deputy Long's mind, the Scott family would be missed by very few if they moved to another county or state.

On a clay and gravel dirt road twelve miles from town, Deputy Long parked his cruiser in front of a shack of a house. The house was an illegal liquor-selling establishment, and sometimes gambling house. This particular illegal establishment had been raided at least once a year for as long as he had been in the department, but it was only out of business at most thirty days before they started again. So far, no one had been killed there; however, the number of knife fights and fistfights were beyond the count of anyone currently living.

After surveying the area around the house, he spotted what he was looking for. Roger Stone's pickup truck sat parked by a tree and positioned for a quick and easy exit.

Stepping out of his car, Deputy Long could clearly see the other dozen assorted vehicles parked around. Some he knew, some he didn't. In his usual casual pace, as if walking across his backyard, he moved toward the front door. You didn't have to be at the front door to hear the music coming from the house. With all its lights on and blaring music, the party seemed fully underway.

As Deputy Long approached the door, a thought crossed his mind, *Lively crowd, I hope they feel like playing nice tonight. I'm getting tired of cracking heads.*

Deputy Long, in his younger life, had been a weightlifter and a tough guy, but after two tours in Vietnam, he'd had his fill of dispatching the living to the realm of the dead. As a sheriff's deputy, he'd never had to draw his weapon but was still willing and able to use it, if there was no other choice. Otherwise, most people in the area knew him as a kind and gentle but no-nonsense cop.

Walking in through the front door, a half-dozen set of eyes settled on him, most of which he knew, and they knew him. The other half-dozen tried to hide their faces or slipped quietly into another room. They all hoped he had not come for them.

A beer belly with a man attached approached on short, squatty legs. His name was "Big Bobby" Watson. It only took one glance to see why the nickname.

Big Bobby was the unofficial and illegal operator of the liquor house. He appeared to be, and really was, one of those people who spent too much time in all the wrong kind of places, doing the wrong kinds of things.

A man in his early forties and a full growth of beard walked up to Deputy Long. Having taken only three steps inside the house, Deputy Long did not feel threatened. He knew where he was and what they did here. This was not his first time there. He expected the same icy welcome as his last visit.

It was said Big Bobby always had a can of beer in one hand and a cigarette in the other. Tonight was no different.

To Deputy Long, Big Bobby always appeared to be returning from a bear hunt. Not the kind of guy anyone should trust too far or for too long, and having his hands slightly occupied did not make him any less dangerous. Deputy Long did not like him and never had. He knew too much about Big Bobby's past.

Big Bobby positioned himself so Deputy Long would have to step around him to advance farther into the house.

The icy welcome began.

"You here to be a problem or lookin' for somebody?" Deputy Long looked slightly downward at the man. "Looks like you got a nice crowd here tonight." Big Bobby displayed no sign of being intimidated.

"That depends on how long you're here and what for. So, what's on your mind?"

Deputy Long detected a sense of irritation in his tone and mannerisms. For Bobby to act like this was not unusual; after all, the place was illegal. The tone implied to Deputy Long there was probably a cash card game going on in the back room, or maybe something else. Tonight, he was not interested in any of that. Tonight, he only wanted Roger Stone and his boys.

"You seen Stone?"

"Why you want him?"

Deputy Long, already in no mood to play games, replied with the one answer he knew would make Bobby angry enough to fight or answer the question and avoid a confrontation. "Unless you have him hung on your other nipple, that's none of your business."

When Deputy Long spoke of his nipple, Big Bobby got angry because Deputy Long was one of the few people in the county that knew he had only one nipple and why.

Big Bobby Watson, in his early twenties, had been caught in bed with a very wrong woman, his uncle's wife. She was twenty years younger than his uncle, putting her closer to Bobby's age.

After beating them both to a bloody mess, his crazy uncle cut off Big Bobby's right nipple, telling him it was a permanent reminder to keep his business to himself. Then, as if he had not done enough damage, his uncle started the rumor Bobby had been caught by a woman in another county with her husband.

Eventually, Big Bobby was able to silence the rumor, but he still only had one nipple and a not-so-nice little secret. His uncle strangely died in a house fire, leaving his wife free to move out of the state, which she did very soon after the funeral. Deputy Long knew why she moved quickly and who likely set the fire, but without proof, the investigation went nowhere.

"Why don't you wait right here? I'll see if he's around. I don't want you stinking up the place, cousin." Bobby growled out the words through gritted teeth.

The crazy uncle no one wanted to talk about was Deputy Long's father's brother—his uncle. For obvious reasons, the relation was known but seldom discussed or acknowledged. Having family standing on each side of the law, the illegal liquor house was a major sore spot. The liquor house had a long history, and, in addition to that, the real estate was owned by the uncle of a state official. Well-connected and buffered from shut down, this particular establishment really angered Deputy Long. Because of all the Roger Stones that came this way and made themselves at home, it had become a regular snake pit.

Big Bobby spun on his heels, as much as a pumpkin-shaped man could spin, and walked out of the room.

Deputy Long, being left with the three remaining occupants of the room, slowly looked directly at each person. As he watched the three—two men and one woman—he felt the familiar warning signals creeping up his arms. This warning had kept him alive in Vietnam and in law enforcement. He suspected he had been asked to wait because something was being set up, cleaned up, or hidden from his prying eyes.

Big Bobby Watson became angrier with each step. When he reached the room occupied by Roger and his friends, he did not hesitate with a knock. He shoved the door with force.

Entering the room, he did not distort his extreme dislike of having an interruption at this stage of his carefully planned and quietly run operation.

With scales and plastic sandwich bags on the old dining room table, Roger Stone and one of his friends were carefully cutting out nickel bags of marijuana for distribution. This had been Roger and Big Bobby's main source of income for over three years.

For Deputy Long or any other cop to show up now caused serious nervousness. Roger stood by the table with the shipment of product, ready to disappear out the back door, when Bobby entered. He had already learned a cop was out front.

Bobby's appearance in the room only confirmed Roger's idea to take the product and make a run for it.

Bobby closed the door behind him and looked at Roger.

"It's only one cop. Put that back down. Besides, if it was a raid, how far do you think you'd get?" He shut the door behind him.

Roger looked at Bobby, then at the back door, fifteen pounds of marijuana in a garbage bag under his arm. He looked unsure but determined.

"Put it back on the table. He's only interested in talking to you," Bobby said in a tone of disgust. "Have you done something else stupid? 'Cause Long don't make social calls."

Putting the garbage bag of product back on the table, Roger shifted a nasty look in Bobby's direction.

"What do you mean he wants to talk to me? I ain't done nothing."

“Then go talk to him, and do it outside.”

Roger glanced at Bobby, who was packing nickel bags into a backpack.

“Long is a prick. He’s been trying to find something to hang on me, anyway.”

Roger, looking at Skip, one of the few gofers they trusted to help with the cutting, realized he had quietly watched the whole scene. He needed to get him out of the room before anything else was said.

“Go to the corner of the house, just in case he’s not alone.”

After Skip quietly slipped out the back door, Roger threw on his jacket. Walking in his usual swagger, he made sure his body language said don’t mess with me. At the end of the hall, he entered the room and saw Deputy Long.

For a brief second, his hatred for law enforcement and the legal system in general surfaced. That second was all it took for Deputy Long to conclude he had been right. The expression and look in Rogers’s eyes said he was truly up to no good again, but the question was, up to what? The appearance and demeanor of the other three people in the room had given him a good idea, and he knew all three had been busted for possession over the last two years. Was this where they were getting their supply? While still looking at Roger, Deputy Long smiled. This was not a happy smile, but a knowing one. The smile unnerved Roger. He thought, *What is he smiling about?*

Deputy Long said nothing. He simply waited for Roger to speak.

“You looking for me?”

“Sheriff wants to talk to you.”

Roger, not being the sharpest knife in the drawer, stepped within inches of Deputy Long. Deputy Long, remembering the sheriff's orders, welcomed the intrusion.

"You tell Barney that if he wants to talk to me, he knows where I live. Right now, I'm busy."

Deputy Long had amassed a vast amount of knowledge about the activities in the county. He decided now was a good time to relay some of that knowledge.

"The sheriff would rather not come by your house, since he would have to stand in line for a chance to beat your wife."

At the mention of his wife, Roger's temper exploded like a house at ground zero. He made the welcome mistake of swinging at Deputy Long. In a fraction of a second, Deputy Long sidestepped and slapped to the side Roger's punch, spinning Roger off balance. This move left Roger's back to the deputy. Deputy long placed two more expert punches.

The first landed directly on Roger's lumbar plexus. The perfect placement of the punch disrupted the nerves and nerve endings so severely, Roger lost his breath from the excruciating pain. The second punch landed directly on the ileum, located in the pelvic area, dropping Roger to his knees.

With equal expert movement, Deputy Long extracted his cuffs and had Roger in brackets in seconds. Pulling Roger back to his feet, he half carried and half dragged Roger out the front door before anyone could react.

"I've been told you could whip any man in your platoon. Well, I wasn't in your platoon."

Roger's barely functioning legs were of little help getting Roger to the car. Deputy Long stuffed him into the backseat of his cruiser for the ride to the sheriff's office.

Being so completely and decisively defeated in a fight he started, Roger did not make the ride to the sheriff's office in silence but instead whimpered and whined about the pain. Deputy Long, feeling quite pleased Roger would attempt such a stupid and predictable move, allowed him no relief from the pain. In hand-to-hand combat training, his instructor had educated him personally on the pain of receiving such a blow in those two areas. He knew how much pain Roger was in and made sure to hit every pothole and rough spot he could find on the way to the sheriff's office.

In a small office also used as an interrogation room sat Roger. Absent was his tough-guy bravado, absent was his foul mouth, and absent was anything of the old Roger. This had all been replaced by a shallow breathing, pale-faced man slouched over onto the table in an attempt to relieve the pain surging through his body.

With only a small portion of the pain easing, Roger had stopped asking to go to the hospital; instead, he concentrated on how much he hated Deputy Long and how he could arrange things to get his revenge. The humiliation of having been beaten so quickly and easily now festered like an open wound and motivated him to find his strength.

The two other deputies had not been in the office when Roger came in, only the sheriff was present. In the private office, the sheriff asked Deputy Long what happened. Deputy Long gave a brief and detailed description of events, concluding with quick explanation the sheriff enjoyed hearing.

"He took a swing at me and missed. I didn't."

After the sheriff finished a good laugh, he said, "Let's go ask some questions."

The two men walked into the interrogation room and stared at Roger, his head and chest lay on the table. Like a schoolboy, he'd been crying.

The pain Roger felt was like none he had ever felt before. Hearing the sheriff and Deputy Long enter the room, he opened his eyes. With as much of an evil look as he could muster, he stared back at them. The staring contest lasted a full two minutes, and then the sheriff said, "Mr. Roger, you don't look so good."

The desire to spew tons of profanities at the sheriff gushed from his mind to his sealed lips but went no farther. He had no desire to see what else Deputy Long could do until his pain stopped; instead, he just stared.

The sheriff, glancing over at Deputy Long, said, "He's

got nothing mean and nasty to say. Well, maybe he'll be nice enough to answer some questions."

Roger thought, *The only answer I'm going to give you, pricks, will be written in your blood.*

Barely able to hold himself upright, Roger faced the two officers. For a second, he thought of the last time he had been whipped so completely, and the thought made him grimace.

When he was fifteen, he had stepped in between his mom and dad in the middle of a fight. That was when he decided he would never lose another fight. He could almost hear his dad laughing again. He grew angrier at the thought.

With Deputy Long standing by the door, the sheriff's questions started.

"Roger, thanks for coming in. Where were you at about nine o'clock last night?"

Roger just stared at him, trying to think. Remembering he was picking up a bale of weed in the next county, he decided to say nothing.

"Roger, do you know Andy Orbank?"

Rogers's eyes betrayed his answer. His confusion showed through his anger. He had no idea why they would be asking about him. The sheriff looked over at Deputy Long, and they both saw the confusion on his face.

"Roger, were you in town at nine o'clock last night?"

Roger was thinking the only Orbank he knew was the want-to-be-rich guy he sometimes sold weed to on the other side of town. He thought he had a kid, but he wasn't sure.

The sheriff, not liking his silence, decided to make known the need he had for coffee. This would leave Deputy Long alone in the room with Roger to continue the interrogation. "I could use a cup of coffee, so I'll let you give your answers to Deputy Long here."

The sheriff delayed leaving for a few seconds before turning toward the door. When his hand touched the doorknob, Roger cleared his throat. The sheriff released the knob and turned to face Roger. Roger now sat a little straighter and seemed ready to talk. It appeared he was not willing to give his answers to anyone but the sheriff, or rather, anyone other than Deputy Long.

"Did you say something?"

"Why are you asking about this Orbank guy?"

The sheriff walked back and took a seat at the table, and then he returned to his question.

An hour and a half later, Roger was back in Deputy Long's patrol car being driven home. He now understood why the questions about Orbank, and the sheriff knew Teddy Orbank had some illegal habits. Roger never specifically fingered Teddy Orbank but did give sufficient cause for suspicion. The most important thing Roger understood was that Andy Orbank was in the hospital in critical condition from a vicious beating, and he knew who had done it. He was not going to tell the sheriff that his son, Timmy, was the guilty party. He decided to let them figure it out, if they ever did.

All the way home, Deputy Long found potholes, the roughest spots on the railroad crossings, and every rut possible. Roger, determined to give no further satisfaction to the deputy, never said a word.

At the Scott's residence, Deputy Long turned into the driveway and drove to the back door of the house. After parking the car, a noticeable distance from the door, Deputy Long opened the rear door and waited as Roger gathered enough strength to remove himself from the back seat. With noticeable difficulty, Roger made it to the back door and onto his porch. Deputy Long closed the car door and got back under the wheel but did not wait to see Roger's painful assent to his rear porch.

When Deputy Long turned into the Scott's driveway, he noticed a pickup truck parked across the road opposite the house. Its dull and faded paint blended well with the tall grass and under growth. He did not think Roger had seen it. Coming out of the driveway, he turned and drove only a few yards before steering his car to the shoulder of the road. Parked with his lights off, he watched in his rearview mirror and waited.

The front entryway of the house had no porch light. It was, however quite easy to see the male figure exit by way of the front door, and the door immediately shut, leaving a half-dressed male on the porch in the dark. In seconds, a shadowy figure crossed the road behind Deputy Long's car. Another few seconds, and the engine started, brake lights came on, and the truck left its parking spot going in the opposite direction.

Deputy Long recited a verse of an old Motown hit as the truck rounded the curve moving away from him.

"Who's making love to your old lady, while."

He started his car and proceeded home. It was time to rest.

Entering the house, Roger called for Phyllis. Coming from the front of the house in a bathrobe, Phyllis made no effort to rush to his aid. She looked at him, then said,

"You're drunk again, you jackass. You get the sofa."

Faking anger, she spun on her heels and went into the bedroom, locking the door behind her. Roger was left on his own to get to the sofa.

In the bedroom, Phyllis looked around to make sure nothing had been left behind by her play-toy lover. She also thought she heard Timmy come in, so she would have to deal with him tomorrow. Feeling her secret was safe, she went back to bed.

CHAPTER 44

Timmy slept, uninterrupted and unencumbered. This was his most restful night's sleep in many weeks. On this night, Timmy was the only one to rest well in the Scott household.

While Phyllis and Timmy slept, Roger struggled. Using the walls, door jams, and furniture for support, he eventually made his way to the sofa. This would serve as his bed for the night.

The level of pain introduced to him with only two punches from Deputy Long had served well to remove his desire for any additional confrontations. In fact, Roger decided, in his current condition, he didn't want to physically fight with anyone for any reason. In the darkened and quiet house, Roger was left alone with his physical pains and childhood memories.

To most people in the county, the sun rising brightly in the fall morning sky was a beautiful and welcome sight, but to the Scott family, it was unwelcome.

Phyllis opened her eyes from her slumber and looked around. She had not enjoyed the same benefit of a restful night's sleep as Timmy. She was certain Timmy had heard the romping and snorting in her bedroom earlier in the night with a partner, not her husband.

Phyllis lay in bed looking around her bedroom. The room was a mess, she was a mess, and without having to move to verify, she knew the house was a mess. Knowing the cleaning had been done by no one, including herself, she dreaded getting out of bed and facing her house and her chosen standing in life.

Her house was always a mess. Her marriage to an animal of a man she had stopped caring about long ago offered nothing in the form of motivation. Their marriage was not worth the paper the license was written on, but she knew exactly how and when to use him for what she wanted, and a son she hated from conception for destroying her perfect figure. Phyllis thought of all this before she got out of bed.

Rising from her bed, she placed her feet on the floor and faced the mirror. She was disgusted with the image she saw in the mirror mounted on the dresser across the room. Between the perfume bottles and dirty clothes, she looked into the angry eyes of her reflection. Once, she thought herself to be the most beautiful woman in the county; now at the age of thirty-four, she could see Father Time was working his evil spell on her.

Ten years ago, she knew her looks could turn any man's head at any time and in any place. Time and fun living had begun to collect its payment for her lifestyle, even to her eyes. She refused to accept the blame. It was the fault of Roger, Timmy, and men in general. As she watched herself in the mirror blaming everyone else, she structured a plan in her mind.

First, I will ignore Roger on the sofa and walk straight into Timmy's room. Then I will use my baseball bat to give him a couple of good whacks across the arms. This will keep him from trying to raise his hands to protect himself or stop me from hitting him.

Then, when I have his undivided attention, I will put my lips really close to his ear, and whisper.

I'm going to enjoy the look on his face when I tell him, 'What I decide to do in my house, you have no say-so over whatsoever.' Then I'll hit him in his gut, just to make sure he understands. If Roger wakes up and ask questions, I'll tell him I was just practicing on kicking his butt when the time comes. If he asks Timmy later what the beating was for, Timmy will lie, because he's not going to want another dance with my bat.

I run this house. Besides, Roger's too busy trying to be a big dealer to figure out what's going on. If it weren't for me, he wouldn't even have a supplier. Man, he's a big idiot.

Satisfied with her plan, the comforts of her bed were traded for the necessities of the bathroom. Looking at her reflection, she wished, for the thousandth time, life had given her more than she deserved.

"Mirror, mirror, on the wall, who's the most beautiful of them all?"

Hearing what she expected, which was nothing, she turned away and prepared to take a shower.

Standing in the hot shower, Phyllis's thoughts returned to Timmy.

Timmy, you're as dumb as your daddy, the old fart. I used him to make you so he would have to pay me, and now I get to beat up on you whenever I like, and today I like.

Timmy lay in bed enjoying the best sleep to come his way in weeks. Even in his sleep, Nats did not leave him unguarded, nor did he let him totally rest in peace. In his dreams, Nats was usually there, coaching, directing, and as always, giving advice. Always ever-present in one form or another, in one place or another, he always kept himself near Timmy. Timmy preferred Nats's company to real people of any age or status. In fact, Nats had remained his best friend and his only friend. Even now, Nats again was inside his dreams.

Timmy slept, dreaming of battling a mighty spinning beast with many arms of steel. The beast moved faster than any force known to man and was determined to see him dead. Timmy, forced to fight for his life, saw himself casually dressed in jeans, T-shirt, and tennis shoes. For protection, a battered breastplate of steel covered his chest to below his waist. For his defense he had a mighty sword and shield.

Nats served as his partner, guide, and advisor.

Timmy fought the beast with strike-and-retreat maneuvers until it was lured into a deep crevasse in the rocks. In the large crack, Timmy made his stand.

Using the walls of rock for protection on three sides, the beast could only maneuver a few of its deadly blades at a time. Timmy had the advantage of smaller size and Nats's wit.

As the battle wore on, Timmy was able to sever the arms one by one. At this point, Timmy was beginning to feel the battle could be won, when Nats shouted, "Protect your head!"

When Timmy raised his arms with shield in hand to protect his head, he felt a jarring blow to his arm. Still in his dream, Timmy delivered a fatal blow to the beast. The scream of agony from the beast could only be heard in Timmy's mind.

That was when Phyllis struck his other arm with her bat.

Denied the joy of seeing his enemy die in battle, Timmy was snatched into reality by the second blow from Phyllis's bat. Sudden and sharp pain in both arms got his immediate and awakened attention. When he opened his eyes, he was greeted with the pretty face of evil that was his mother's. Unfortunately, she was in mid-swing, delivering her third blow. This one landed across his midsection, causing Timmy to curl in the fetal position for protection.

Three parts of his body were sending pain signals to his brain. These signals were coming in loud and clear. He was hurt, and he knew it. Curled in the fetal position with his back turned, he tried to protect himself. Again, Phyllis delivered a blow. And, as quickly as the attack started, it stopped.

Phyllis placed the end of her bat on Timmy's temple lobe and leaned into it. The pressure of Phyllis's weight against the top of the bat pressed Timmy's head deeper into the dirty sheets. She held him there, waiting for him to beg her to stop.

With her weight bearing down on the top of the bat, she delivered her message to Timmy in a soft whisper.

"What I do in my house is my business and none of yours. I will sleep with who I please, where I please, and you ain't got nothing to say about it. You say one word to Roger, and when he's finished with me, I will finish you. Do you understand me, son?"

In a pain-riddled voice, Timmy could only answer in a whispered, "Yes."

He understood. He understood he had just been beaten again for no apparent reason. To her, he said nothing else.

Looking sideways and back, he could barely see his mother, with her bat drilled into the side of his head. He knew how she was dressed. He knew how she always dressed. He did not dare tell her what he really thought of her now. He did not want to even be in the same world with her anymore, let alone the same room.

Nats whispered, "Just lie still. She'll be gone soon." Taking Nats's advice, Timmy didn't move a muscle.

Phyllis, feeling herself victorious, took her weight off the bat. As she turned from his bedside, she clipped his shin with the bat, just to make sure he understood. Timmy flinched, but otherwise did not move.

Walking out the room, as if she had done nothing more than remind Timmy to take out the garbage, she casually walked back to her bedroom and ignored Roger on the sofa. He appeared to have slept through the entire event.

Motionless, cradling both arms, he heard Phyllis's bedroom door close. Finally able to relax his muscles, he remained still. Listening to his own pounding heartbeat, Timmy fought to silence the pain in his arms and head. Slowly, very slowly, his racing heart calmed. He asked Nats a question.

"Why did she have to come in and beat me?"

"Why do you ask why? You know she likes to see you in pain. But my mighty warrior, best friend, do you hate her enough to kill her and that pile of garbage of a father you have? Because you can't kill her and let him live. You would have to kill them both. You are strong enough and powerful enough to take them both out and no one will ever think it was you who did it. You are a mighty warrior. Nothing can defeat you, not even that mother of yours."

"I don't care who she's sleeping with or where. Anyone that would crawl in bed with her is a fool anyway."

"Women like her think all men are fools. To her, you are a fool also, even though you are her son."

"Oh, God, how I hate her." Timmy whispered.

Nats had no problem promoting Timmy's hatred of his parent; however, he had a huge problem with God and anyone who believed.

With these words spinning in his head, Timmy struggled to his feet. The pain, running through his body like a bullet train running wild, caused him to lean against the wall.

Looking down, he realized that during the course of the beating, he'd wet his bed. This only served to increase his hatred. After finding clean underwear, jeans, and T-shirt, he made his way to the bathroom.

As he cleaned himself, dressed, and prepared to leave, he again noticed her underwear and pantyhose hung in any and every area conceivable. The only bath in the house was his mother's domain, as was the whole house. She always kept her clothes in order and clean; no one else got that treatment. However, the cleaning of this room, as well as any other part of the house, failed to rank as necessary to her.

Timmy dressed as quietly as possible. Leaving the bathroom, he heard his father still snoring in the other room. Pausing momentarily, he considered the value of his parents.

My father is a beer-drinking, drug-selling thug. My mother—she worships herself.

As Timmy thought this, he walked to the back door. The sun, high in the sky, offered little light and cheerfulness to the Scott house. Even the interior of the house was dark and depressing. Once outside, he looked back at his house and spoke to his parents, beyond their hearing.

"I wish you both were dead."

Holding his arms across his chest, he made the journey to his castle.

When safely inside his castle, Timmy lay on his side, facing the front of the hearth. With the pain in his arms and leg, he drifted off to sleep again.

In Timmy's dream world, he was master, he was king, he was in control, and all answered to him. He slept, and he dreamed.

Again, he dreamed his favorite. His parents hung by their hands from a tree limb, and he beat them to death, except this time he and Nats took turns delivering the lashes. Nats's enthusiasm increased with each strike, and Timmy's desire for vengeance showed no bounds. As a team, they delivered the punishment they thought was deserved. Blow after blow brought more joy to Timmy. In his sleep, his joy showed outwardly; he giggled out loud.

Fall is the time of year when creatures of all kinds seek out shelter for the coming winter. It is the time of year that warm and cold-blooded alike are about. The beauty of the forest sounds was interrupted only by the occasional giggle from Timmy. The giggles had attracted the attention of some inhabitants of the forest, especially one in particular.

CHAPTER 45

The snake slid in silently, as only snakes can do. With forked tongue constantly testing the air, it knew there was warm blood in the enclosure. It also knew it was large, too large to eat.

Entering Timmy's castle, it slowly traveled over his feet, along the back of his legs and back across his waist, all the time testing the air with its tongue. As it slithered nearer Timmy's head, it grew nervous and became more cautious. Slowing its movements, the snake began to coil.

Wrapped in the joy of his dream, Timmy was unaware of the snake only a foot away from his head. Nats knew it was there. Nats was the only thing standing between Timmy and a deadly snakebite. Nats could not and would not allow this to happen. Nats, being what it is, quietly and quickly convinced the serpent attack was not necessary and his assistance was not needed.

The snake uncoiled and turned away to the opening of the castle's entrance. When half its body passed through the opening, Timmy opened his eyes, with Nats's prompting. He saw the back half of the snake pass through the opening.

Nats, a master of his craft, selected now to stake his claim, "I fought for you and protected you. Now you owe me."

Timmy, seeing the color patterns on the snake, knew it was poisonous, and he felt Nats was right. He did owe him his life.

Timmy lay still for ten minutes, allowing what he thought was sufficient time for the snake to be well on its way. Finally, the rumble in his stomach motivated him into action. Much to his regret, the only place he had to eat was at home. With arms and leg swollen, he accepted the fact that he would have to return home.

As he approached his house, he saw two vehicles in the backyard; there had been none there when he left. One was his father's pickup truck, and the other belonged to one of his father's friends. He watched from the tree line as a man got into the passenger seat beside the driver of the car. In seconds, the car was on the road and gone.

With the car gone, he knew one or both his parents would be at home and awake. He didn't want to see either of them. Looking past the house to the garden, he decided a fresh vegetable would taste better than anything his mom had cooked.

With his sights set on the garden, Timmy passed the rear of the house, hoping he would not be seen. At the edge of the grassy rows, he fixed his eyes on the largest, reddest tomato there.

"Yes, that will do just fine. Within the tall grass is the lair of many dangers. Proceed with caution," whispered Nats.

In true stalker fashion, Timmy made his way through the grasses while watching the house for signs of movement. With every step the chance of another encounter increased.

Standing above the tomato plant, he studied the fruit. Larger than his fist, round and so full of the juices of his desire, it weighted itself to the ground. The red of the skin could nearly reflect the surroundings, capturing and holding his attention like the embrace of a starved heart.

Timmy reached down and with great care plucked the fruit of his current desire. Timmy, the king, had evaded his enemies and captured the elusive trophy. It now was his to consume. The fullness and beauty of the fruit begged for his consumption. Within its skin, Timmy knew the flesh would be tender, and with its juices, it would be delicious. Timmy studied and protected his captive as he worked his way back through the grasses of danger.

Safely returned to the backyard, Timmy decided the storm cellar would be a safe place to consume his capture and enjoy his reward in peace.

Phyllis stood in the kitchen before the sink. Her intention was to prepare breakfast for herself, but movement beyond the window drew her attention. She witnessed Timmy's exaggerated movements through the weeds and tall grass in the vegetable garden. She had figured he was doing something stupid that she could beat him for later. Watching him pick the tomato, she instantly flew into anger. That tomato he had taken was the exact one she wanted. If it had been a handful of dirt, it would have belonged to her first.

Still looking out the window, she watched him walk toward the storm cellar in a weird and exaggerated manner.

She watched until he was out of sight.

Standing at the entrance of the storm cellar, Timmy felt a brief cold chill before reaching for the door handle. He ignored the feeling of warning in his spine. Opening the door, he smelled the cool, damp, stale odor of the storm cellar. Built a couple of feet below ground level and into the rounded portion of a small hill, the storm cellar remained at a constant temperature. With its bunker-like design, it shed water easily and was accessible quickly from the house.

Timmy, leaving one door open, seated himself on the wooden bucket that had been there since he was a child. For no reason at all, this wooden bucket had never left the cellar, and he was now ready to enjoy his tomato.

Phyllis had an idea as to his destination with her tomato. After turning off the water, she left the kitchen and stepped to the back door. Seeing Timmy as he entered the storm cellar, she remained still.

That's where you're going. That's where you will stay.

Quickly leaving the back door, she walked across the yard to the storm cellar.

Timmy, having taken the first bite of the tomato, leaned his back against the dirt-and-plank wall. The tomato tasted delicious, fit for the enjoyment of a king. Enjoy it, Timmy intended to do.

With his head and shoulders resting against the wall, he closed his eyes and began chewing. Phyllis's silhouette in the doorway blocked the inflowing sunlight. Timmy stopped chewing. His mouth hung open, the juice of the tomato running down his hand and arm, his eyes wide and fully aware of her presence. Danger had arrived; he said nothing.

Phyllis, standing in the doorway, looked into the cellar down at Timmy. With an icy gaze, she said, "I wanted that tomato, and you took it. Well, big boy, why don't you stay in here and enjoy it?"

With her usual degree of no concern for her own son, she slammed the door shut and slid the handle of the shovel through the hopped handles of the doors, locking Timmy inside. At once, Timmy realized he was trapped. This reality was both confirmed and compounded by Nats.

"She may have locked you in, but you can take that stick and lock her out."

Timmy thought about this for a minute. Locking them out would be a surprising turn of the tables. Rising from his bucket, Timmy picked up the broken rack handle he was once beaten with and inserted it through the inside handles of the double storm cellar doors. He, in effect, locked them out. The storm cellar was now his; they couldn't get in, and he couldn't get out. Feeling a sense of accomplishment, he returned to his seat and continued to eat.

From his survival stash, Timmy knew he could weather a couple of days with ease, if it became necessary. In a mason jar, he stored a bag of dried beef jerky, a candy bar, and a soft drink. This was only one of his carefully placed containers within the storm cellar. In the semidarkness, he opened the soft drink, then the beef jerky, and completed his meal. Looking out through a small crack in the door, he noticed the sunlight fading faster than usual.

"Well, Nats, looks like it's going to be a long day. Mom locked me in, and I locked them out. I know she don't care if I drown in here, so I hope it don't rain much."

Nats smiled an evil grin, which Timmy could not see.

"Don't worry yourself, my friend. People like them always get what they deserve. Now take your nap and rest."

Timmy became sleepy. Taking up his old teddy bear from a low shelf, he curled up with it for a nap. In only a few minutes, he was asleep.

Phyllis spent most of the day trying to push Roger into a stimulating fight but was only able to elicit a slap across the face. This came as a result of insulting his most loved—his manhood. Seeing she would get no satisfaction from him, she returned to her bedroom.

Roger lay back on the sofa, groaning from the pain movement had rekindled in his body. He did not know how Deputy Long knew where to strike to cause this much pain, but he was determined to remember it for later use.

After lying on the sofa for much of the day, Roger's empty stomach forced him to the kitchen in search of food. Peering into the refrigerator, using the door for support, he saw and smelled the old food containers and rotten fruits. He knew the refrigerator should have been cleaned, but reasoned it was not his job.

With disgust, he took out a plastic container that held a single fried pork chop.

I'11eat this before it's ready to kill me. He thought.

The pork chop was one of three from the café he had put in the refrigerator two days earlier. He was surprised it had made it through two days with Timmy around.

Resting his elbows on the edge of the kitchen sink, he ate the fried pork chop with his hands. He did care enough to use a plate, but did not find one clean. Looking out the kitchen window, he observed the pounding rain. There was still enough light to see the trees twisting and bending in the strong wind. Speaking to no one, Roger said, "This is a storm from hell."

Across the open field, Roger saw the tail come down from the clouds. Even between the sheets of rain, he knew what it was. As not to obstruct his view, sheets of rain parted. He was granted a clear line of sight to watch the arrival of the funnel cloud. When the tail reached the ground, Roger's chewing stopped.

The tail struck the ground and appeared to spin as if it were a gigantic carving bit in a hell-sized router. Dirt, trees, and fence line alike were ripped from the ground. Then it turned toward Roger. Only a few hundred yards away, it grew larger and faster. For reasons Roger could not explain, he knew it was coming at him.

Roger swallowed his mouthful of food, and then said, "Tornado."

Hearing the word come from his mouth and enter his ears only served to verify what his eyes were seeing. With his mouth empty and dry as desert sand, he said in a loud voice, almost a shout, "Tornado." He then turned from the window and started for the door.

Phyllis, in the bedroom watching TV, thought she heard Roger say something, but all she could understand was, "Torn …" The word or words were drowned out by the sound of hailstones hitting the top of the house. Thunder and lightning were not a concern for Phyllis; however, the pounding on the roof and the fragmented word from Roger captured her attention. She thought it wise to first check the window. What she saw told her to run or die. She chose to run.

Grabbing her usual bathrobe and slippers, she was out the bedroom door and running for the back door. Roger was already out and crossing the back porch when Phyllis shoved past him, causing him to fall against boxes of forgotten items stacked on the back porch. Phyllis hit the ground running for the storm cellar. Roger regained his footing and was following only five yards behind her.

Timmy lay asleep on the floor of the storm cellar. He was dreaming of fighting an army of reptile-looking creatures attacking his castle. Nats was on the top of the castle wall, dispatching each and every creature to its death as quickly as they came over the wall. Timmy had been outside the gate and had fought his way inside. With superhuman strength, he managed to close and bar the gate. Climbing the stairway leading to the top of the wall, Timmy encountered another enemy. The fight was quick and bloody, resulting in the creature being delivered into the hands of death.

Now atop the wall, he too engaged the enemy. With the skill of a master swordsman, Timmy took on the enemy with a sword clutched in each fist. He and Nats severed, chopped, dismembered, and decapitated their enemies one by one as they defended the castle. To their surprise, the enemy withdrew, but that was short-lived. They returned with a battering ram and began pounding on the gate. Timmy was confident the barred gate would hold. From the top of the wall, he and Nats took up bows and arrows in an archery position. Letting the arrows fly from opposite ends of the wall, they picked off their enemies on the battering ram, one by one. As quickly as one fell, another took its place. The army was large, but Nats and Timmy's strength was mighty. They felt they could fight as long as there were enemies to fight.

Phyllis reached the storm cellar first. Yanking out the shovel handle, she thought the door would be free to open. To her surprise and bewilderment, the door refused to open when she pulled the handle. A moment later, Roger arrived. Wet from the rain and being battered by hailstones, they both pulled on the handles with no success. When pulling failed, Phyllis shouted Timmy's name and demanded he open the door. Roger cursed him and demanded the same. The roar of the tornado grew louder like an approaching train.

Timmy felt the vibration of the battering ram each time it hit his gate, but he and Nats continued to fire arrows. The screams of death were loud as a chorus echoing into the distant hills with the delivery from each bow. They screamed his name as they attacked, and they whispered it as they died.

Timmy was the name they hated and were bent on destroying at all costs. The attack continued.

Phyllis and Roger, stomping on the doors and screaming Timmy's name, continued begging to be let in. Timmy continued to dream. When the screams and demands brought no entry, they both cursed him intently. They begged and cursed a little too long. They could not hear their own voices over the noise. The tornado, with the noise of a thousand freight trains, was upon them.

Roger saw it first and knew it was too late. The tornado indeed had the noise of a thousand trains, but what Roger saw was far worse than the sound of freight trains.

Roger was frozen, unable to run or even move. His eyes focused on the sight of his father riding a black horse, with no legs and working a barbwire lasso. He saw the souls of his dead friends, all with eyes of hate for him. He saw the past and knew it was his. He saw the devil in himself and himself in the devil.

From out of the black of the tornado came a long strand of barbwire. It wrapped around Roger's arms and chest and took him into the storm. Before he was allowed to die, the tornado from hell took out his left eye, then ripped open his stomach and filled him with dirt and wrapped him in a barbwire spin. He was ripped, rolled, and wrapped repeatedly until he was presented to death like the present he deserved to be.

Phyllis had her back turned when she was received by the tornado. She pounded on the door until the tornado took her off her feet. Lifted into the air, she was spun round and round and disrobed by the hellish fingers of the tornado, not with the gentle caress of a lover, but rather like being clawed at by a thousand rapists. She received the romance she had earned and the respect from hell she deserved. Before her last breath, she felt herself swirl into death. She was taken as a deserving and welcomed addition into darkness.

The tornado took with it the back half of the house, leaving behind Timmy's room, Roger and Phyllis's bedroom, and the front porch. As the winds and debris spun around, Roger's body was slammed into the lowest limb of the tree in the backyard, which had been broken in half and stripped of its leaves. The broken limb entered his stomach and exited his back, leaving him bent backwards as if he was in mid backflip. His dog tags hung from his lifeless neck. He had a fixed stare on heaven, which he would never see. He did in death what he refused to do in life—look to the heavens.

Phyllis was carried by the storm to the old Breeker place. The winds used and tossed her body like a piece of garbage. At the Breeker chimney, Timmy's castle, she was shoved headfirst through the plywood into the chimney. This crushed her skull, which she never felt. She would not be a pretty face when buried. Her legs were broken and hung in an unflattering manner. The storm had finished with her and thrown her away. Her body was now of no value.

The battle raged on, Timmy and Nats delivering one death blow after another.

The enemy, sensing defeat, withdrew and left the land where Timmy was king. Feeling the sweetness of victory, Timmy slept peacefully another half-hour with his teddy bear.

CHAPTER 46

When Timmy awakened, the storm had passed, taking the clouds with it. The setting sun cast a fading light into Timmy's dungeon. One door stood open, offering a shadowy view of the sky beyond. Sensing something was not normal, Timmy placed his teddy bear on the upside down bucket and got to his feet.

From the open door, light of the setting sun came through. Timmy was confused. In all his life, when he was punished by being put in the dungeon, they never just left the door open and walked away. His eyes adjusted, and then he could see clearly the wreckage outside. He was now fully awake.

Coming out of the storm cellar, he noticed the debris scattered across the field before him. Memory of the day he found Mr. Breeker gave him a cold chill.

As he surveyed the field, he turned toward his house. First, taking in the missing front, and then as if looking through a camera's eye, his eyes and brain focused onto the rest of the house. He said, "What happened?"

His mind was still stunned when his eyes came to rest on what was left of the tree in his backyard. He saw that most of the tree had been destroyed the same as the house, but what had been added to the tree got his attention.

The whipping tree, as known in his dreams, had been broken off halfway up and all its limbs ripped away except the lowest one. No longer in existence were the thick leafy limbs supplying shade—a place for birds and the place he so often dreamed of hanging his parents before beating them to death. What was left was a stump half the height of the original tree. A body hung from the limb. The body was pierced through the stomach with what had been the limb of his dreams. The body of his father hung limp, leaking very little blood. Timmy stood for a long moment and stared at the body. He knew he should feel pain and loss, but instead, he was feeling a building sense of relief.

Standing almost underneath the body, Timmy looked at it dangling from the feet to the head, paying particular attention to all the cuts and rips in the flesh. Touching an ugly gash in the back of the left calf, Timmy said, "I wish I had done that."

Nats made his presence known by speaking in Timmy's head.

"You did. If you count his wounds, you will see there is one for every time you dreamed of killing him. You did beat him to death, and you did a very good job of it too."

Timmy stood still and absorbed what he'd heard. He liked it. In fact, he liked it so much he first began to smile, then he laughed out loud for anyone to hear.

When his laughter stopped, he noticed hanging from Roger's neck were his dog tags.

"Take them. They're yours now. You earned them because you are a mighty warrior, and you should have a trophy for your suffering at his hands. Take them. They're yours."

Timmy reached up, and with both hands, spread the chain wide and lifted it over the head of Roger's body. In one smooth and continuous motion, he placed them around his own neck and stuffed the tags inside his shirt.

Looking up at the body, Timmy said, "I would rather have your head stuck on the end of my sword, but this will have to do, Daddy. I do hope I find Mommy in the same condition."

With that said, he walked away. It was time for him to go find his mommy.

As Timmy turned, his eyes followed the path of the tornado. It had remained on the ground for over a half mile and cut a path straight through to the old Breeker place. Timmy could see the chimney some distance away, but something about it didn't look right.

As he stood trying to focus his eyes to clearly see over the distance, he heard a car slow to a stop and turn into his driveway. Looking in the direction of the sound, Timmy clearly saw the faces of Shelia and Mr. Rayller. They appeared to be as shocked as he was relieved.

Mr. Rayller was first out of the car, then Shelia. Mr. Rayller, with a concerned gait, carefully stepped over the debris and walked within five feet of Timmy. Shelia remained standing at the open car door, staring in Timmy's direction. She wasn't looking at Timmy, she was looking past him. Roger still remained where he had been stuck.

Mr. Rayller, not fully comprehending Timmy's jubilant state, asked, "Are you all right, son?"

The word "son" vanquished Timmy's smile. He thought about the word, "son."

My own father didn't even call me 'son,' so why is this old man doing it? I'm not his son. I'm nobody's son. Not anymore.

What he said was, "Yes, I'm okay. Just a little shaken up, is all."

With the smile gone, Timmy no longer appeared to be happy and pleased with the conditions he was now in.

Mr. Rayller studied Timmy for a moment. He had always known Timmy to be a little strange, but now he seemed to have become even more so. On every encounter with Timmy, he felt this. *Now he was screaming out, 'I'm really strange,' and he didn't seem to be upset about finding his father dead after the tornado. Only God knew where his mother was.* All this ran through Mr. Rayller's mind like a freight train. Not allowing himself to get caught up in his own thoughts, he asked Timmy, "Where's your mother?"

Timmy was struggling to restrain a smile, struggling to sound and act normal. With barely a trace of stress in his voice, he said, "I don't know. When the storm hit, she didn't make it to the storm cellar either. So, I don't know."

Mr. Rayller did not feel confusion coming from Timmy, but he detected joy just below the surface. He knew Timmy was happy and growing happier not seeing his mother. Remembering the promise he had made his wife and his best friend, he knew if they didn't find Timmy's mother alive, his trouble was just beginning.

"Timmy, come with me to the house while I call for help." Watching Timmy closely, he already knew what the answer was going to be.

"No, Mr. Rayller. I'm going to stay here and look for my mother."

Mr. Rayller sensed any discussion at this point would be a waste of time.

"Okay, but I'm leaving Shelia with you till I get back. You shouldn't be alone right now." He replied.

Timmy, not sure of what he was saying or even why, responded.

"I don't need a babysitter. I can find her on my own."

Mr. Rayller rocked back on his heels. The response was really too strong for the situation, but he refused to be dressed down by a teenager, especially this one.

"Timmy, you will wait for help to arrive, and Shelia will be here with you for a few minutes, whether you like it or not."

Timmy hated this. He'd just gotten rid of his parents, and now Mr. Rayller was stepping in and taking over. He was about to say something else but bit his tongue.

Mr. Rayller turned and called Shelia from the car. With the cast on her foot, she came from the car with a limp, all the while watching the body pinned on the tree. Nearing her grandfather, she said, "Grandpa, there's nothing I can do."

Mr. Rayller, now annoyed and confused by Timmy's reaction, knew he was running out of time if the mother had any chance of being found alive and in daylight. Shelia, now watching her grandpa, knew she was not going to like what he had to say.

"Stay here with Timmy while I go call for help."

This was not a request, it was an order. Shelia knew no matter how she felt, now was not the time to discuss it with him or to object. She simply nodded her head and kept silent. Mr. Rayller rushed back to his car and left in a hurry. Shelia and Timmy watched as he drove off in the direction of his home.

Shelia, feeling the sense of loss over her own parents, assumed the role of comforter when speaking to Timmy.

"I'm so sorry this happened to you. I hope we find your mom okay."

Timmy, still feeling intruded on, looked at Shelia for a long moment. He resented her presence, and now she was sounding like his babysitter.

"You don't know what kind of person she was, so don't feel too sorry yet."

Shelia felt as if she had just been kicked in the gut. She knew how much she missed her mother and father and could not imagine Timmy responding as he just had. She had avoided looking into Timmy's eyes, choosing instead to look at what was left of the house when he spoke. Now she looked at him.

"You are a self-serving, cold-hearted, gutless pile of dog crap. Your father is dead. Stuck to that tree behind you like a pin cushion, and your mother could be out there anywhere, hurt, or worse, dead. You're standing here acting like it's all just a big joke. You are the biggest piss-poor example of a man I have ever seen. I'm going to go look for your mother. With you for a son, she would be better off dead."

Having said her piece, she spun on her cast heel and hobbled away. Timmy's joy of being a new orphan turned to anger at Shelia. He imagined her suspended from the same tree, in the same manner as his dad and receiving the same treatment. Watching her walk away, his imagination soared.

Shelia hobbled toward the rear of the house, looking, but hoping she would not find a body. She could not stand the sight of Timmy for another second and wished her grandfather was already back, even though he had just left.

Timmy turned his attention back to his father's body on the tree. Looking past the tree in the lowcut lawn, he spotted the claw hammer. As if beckoning him, Timmy started walking toward it.

Standing above the hammer, Timmy looked down at the hammer and then up in the direction of Shelia.

It would be so easy to pick it up, walk over, and beat that thing to death. She thinks Mom is so great; she should go join her, dead.

Timmy bent at his waist, reached down, and gripped the handle of the hammer. With it firmly in hand, he made only two steps in Shelia's direction when he heard the siren of the sheriff's car approaching from a distance. He knew it would be here too quickly. Dropping the hammer, he turned toward the trees and began to walk.

Deputy Long's patrol car turned into the driveway, seconds behind Mr. Rayller's. Within minutes, five more people showed up to join in the search. Shelia put herself back in her grandfather's car to wait, and Timmy could be seen walking down the middle of the tornado-cut path.

Deputy Long took his field glasses from the car and began to search the area. When he turned in Timmy's direction, he said, "Oh my God, I think I see her."

He saw, with the aid of field glasses, what Timmy could now see with unaided eyes:the legs of Phyllis hanging out of the broken chimney at the old Breeker place.

Speaking to the other people present, he said, "We don't have to search far. She's stuck in the chimney at the Breeker place." This was greeted with comments and looks of surprise.

All got into their vehicles and drove down the road to the location of what had once been the Breeker house. Mr. Rayller, being the first to arrive, heard the laughter when he turned off the engine. It quickly stopped. He was not sure if Shelia had heard it. When he looked at her, the expression on her face showed she had. Mr. Rayller said nothing.

Two other cars parked beside him, one being Deputy Long's. Together the three men walked toward the chimney, all looking above the tall grass and through the young trees. All three could see Phyllis Scott's ripped and broken legs, spread and sticking out the chimney, one foot pointing east and the other pointing west.

Timmy stood at the base of the chimney. As Mr. Rayller neared where Timmy stood, it was clear tears ran down his face. To think they were tears of sadness would have been a mistake. Only Mr. Rayller knew the tears were from laughter. Deputy Long returned to his car to radio for the fire department. Removing Phyllis from the chimney was now the issue. To do that, they would need a ladder.

CHAPTER 47

Michelle lay on the sofa, taking an enjoyable afternoon nap. In her sleep, she heard the train whistle. At first, it began softly and continued to slowly build. Even in her sleep, she knew it was the whistle of the train from the station.

She knew the station well and knew the train was coming to pick up newly departed souls. She instinctively knew at least one passenger would be on board. That one, she should have warned. Someone she knew had run out of time. It pained her, even in sleep, to know she was not able to figure out who and warn them beforehand.

As if in the midst of a fog, Michelle began to see the spinning form. The whistle of the train grew louder while the spinning form grew clearer. When the fog cleared, Michelle could clearly see the spinning form was a tornado, but not just any tornado. This one was made of all things evil. As it passed her, she could see the demons twirling around and around in what could only be called great joy, then she saw why. The tornado had collected two victims: a man and a woman.

From the outside, she could clearly see the fear and terror on their faces along with the pain and agony. She knew their faces, she knew their names, and she knew Timmy no longer had parents.

She watched as demons wrapped Roger Scott in barbed wire and then pulled it with great force that caused him to spin like a child playing with a yo-yo, only to wrap him again and repeat the process, until death was his only possession. She watched helplessly as the demons did the same with Phyllis, but with one added touch: a fence post with barbwire attached was now her embracer, and her bondage.

To some death would have been quick, but for her it was slow and eternal. The tornado passed and faded away as the train whistle slowly decreased its announcements of new passengers.

A tear slipped silently from the corner of her eye. If she could have figured out who soon enough, she felt she could have warned them, and they would have had time to prepare. They wouldn't have been on the dark train.

Deep in the sphere of sleep, she listened to the whistle of the dark train. It was not really a whistle, but instead a collection of loud agonizing high-pitched screams, all weaved together to sound as one screeching, teeth-grinding, skin-crawling whistle. Feeling herself a failure, she quietly cried in her sleep.

Just when Michelle thought she could stand no more, a soft pleasant and familiar female voice came through.

"Michelle, be calm, child. You were not supposed to warn them. They had already made their choices. The knowledge of the consequences of their choices is your burden to bear, and there will be many others, but you will not always be allowed to give warning.

"Now, wake, child. Dry your eyes, and take us with you. The weight of the knowledge of future events is a burden of stone, and it is great, but we will help you carry it."

Off in the distance, Michelle could hear her name being called. She found herself turning around and around until she found the direction of the voice. Moving toward it, the voice grew clearer. It was her mother's voice telling her to wake up; it was just a bad dream. Over and over, she heard the same words, growing stronger each time. Very quickly, her mother's voice overpowered the sound of the train whistle as it faded away. Feeling someone cradling her head and rubbing her face, Michelle opened her eyes to see her mother's worried expression.

All the fear and concern for Michelle was clearly displayed on Kathryn's face. Holding her daughter and only child, she was painfully aware of the fragility of her family. Kathryn knew Michelle was far away, even though she held her in her arms. The words that escaped from her child's lips only served to build fear and dread in her heart. The questions of worry filled her mind.

When will she get so far away I can't reach her? Why did she have to be chosen? How do I fight what I can't see or hear? What do I do to protect her?

The questions continued, on and on.

Kathryn, looking down at her daughter, said, "Baby, why are you crying?"

Michelle looked back at her mother with dread. She knew what she was about to say would not please her mother, but her mother and father were her only place of safety and protection.

"Mom, is Dad home yet?"

"No, he's still at the paper."

"Could you call him and ask him to call the sheriff's office?" Kathryn's stomach, already in a knot, tightened even more.

"Michelle, why should I tell him that?"

The living room had taken on the dimness of nightfall, lit only by two lamps.

Michelle, looking into the shadows across the room, spoke clearly and carefully.

"Timmy Scott's parents just died, and I couldn't warn them."

The words hung in the air like a heavy mist. Kathryn's heart sank even farther, understanding another family had just been destroyed, and her child knew it. This knowledge was a burden she could not help her daughter carry. In her mind, heart, and soul, she prayed for God's protection.

Michael had just hung up the telephone and stood to his feet to fetch his hat, camera, and notebook. The sheriff's office had just called and said a tornado had set down close to the old Breeker place, and there were fatalities. When the telephone rang the second time in less than a minute, the hairs on the back of his neck stood erect. He answered the call.

"Hello, Michael Stone."

"Honey, Michelle just had a really nasty dream, and she wants you to call the sheriff's office. She thinks the parents in the Scott family are dead."

Now Michael knew the names of the fatalities. Gathering what he would need for the story, while talking to his wife, he moved about the office.

"The sheriff's department called me a minute ago to say a tornado had touched down in that area. Is Michelle sure it's the Scott family?"

He didn't dare confirm Kathryn's fears by saying Michelle was right, at least not just yet.

Kathryn, wiping tears from Michelle's eyes, said, "Michael, be careful and hurry home, we need to talk."

Michael, knowing the concern in her voice, said he would and disconnected. He also felt a building need to discuss things with his daughter, but first he had a story to write.

CHAPTER 48

Under any circumstances or conditions, victim recovery is shocking. The storm had passed, and the bodies had been recovered. The damage to them so extensive it caused some of the seasoned volunteer firemen to lose their meals.

Michael left the scene to write his story, and Deputy Long returned to the sheriff's department to write his reports. The firemen reported back to the station and then to their homes, and Timmy was able to maintain a grim, pitiful look the entire time.

Mr. Rayller and Shelia took Timmy to the home of their minister, Reverend Andrew Burns, who withdrew funds from a disaster account and paid for a week in the local motel for Timmy. To outsiders and onlookers, it appeared that all was being handled well; however, for Mr. Rayller, the truth was all too clear. No one in town or the county wanted anything at all to do with housing Timmy Scott, for any reason.

Even with the news of his parents' death, no doors opened. In fact, more than one good member of the church stated, death by tornado for Phyllis and Roger was by far too gentle for their deeds. Mr. Rayller had decided while at the remains of the Scott's house, Timmy would not be allowed to sleep under his roof. Watching Timmy throughout the evening, his dislike and distrust for the teen only grew stronger until getting away from him was his primary desire.

Shelia no longer offered any type of conversation. In her mind, whale waste could not sink lower than her loathing for Timmy. She didn't care where he slept, as long as it was not near her. Each time she looked in his direction, he gave her a hollow empty-eyed stare.

The good reverend gave the money to Mr. Rayller. With him an elder in the church and the minister not personally knowing Timmy, he was more comfortable letting Mr. Rayller handle the money.

What had been a cloudy starless night had become a clear moonlit panorama in the sky. In the car on the way to the motel, no one spoke outwardly, but inside of Timmy's head, the argument raged as it had all night long.

I want to jump, shout, and scream, I'm free.

You can't do that, not now. Do you want everyone to think you are crazy?

Timmy shifted in the back seat. He wasn't uncomfortable. He was having trouble keeping the conversation quiet.

Nats, I'm free. I don't have to get beat up anymore. They're both dead. No more using me for warm-up before the play.

Shelia turned her head to look at her grandfather. This did not go without the observation of Timmy. *Nats, I hate that girl.*

Easy, mighty warrior, she is what she is. Ignoring her would be best.

That was the last thing Nats said before arriving at the Night Light Motel. The motel owner had a monopoly, if you wanted to call it that, where Timmy would be staying was the only motel of any type for miles around. Situated on the edge of town along the main highway, it was positioned well for weary travelers along the U.S. highway. The building was a single level L-shaped brick structure with an office in front and twenty single units. Ten of those units could not be seen from the highway due to a tall hedgerow kept that way by the owner. It did not take much to figure out the owner knew some of his guests did not want their whereabouts known when they were there. Each room had a single door for entry and exit. Five of the rooms possessed double-size beds, ten with queen-size beds, and five with king-size. The motel's fixtures and furnishings were updated. The owner cared about his business, which was reflected in the care taken with the grounds and cleanliness of the rooms.

Mr. Rayller parked in front near the office, and then asked Timmy to come with him. Timmy, trying not to appear overly anxious, delayed getting out of the car a couple of seconds longer than Mr. Rayller. This was another irritation to Shelia, which she took advantage of. With Mr. Rayller already out of the car and the door closed, Shelia turned in her seat and said, "Get out of my car, you creep."

That was the strongest language she dared use, in the event she was overheard. Mr. Rayller's anger again began to rise, not at Timmy, but at Shelia. Mr. Rayller said nothing, but turned stiffly and walked to the office.

Timmy's mouth said nothing. His eyes relayed all he wanted to say. Inside his head, Nats screamed obscenities. Without saying a single word, Timmy exited the car and gently closed the door behind him.

At the registration desk, Timmy stood to the side of Mr. Rayller while he quickly explained the situation Timmy was in. The motel owner listened, and then gave Timmy a stern but concerned stare. He was familiar with the Scotts. Both Roger and Phyllis had frequented his establishment on more than one occasion, but never together. He clearly remembered having to call the sheriff because of a fight in a room Roger had rented. Phyllis, on the other hand, never registered, but was seen quite often in a waiting vehicle while the driver registered as John Doe. He'd never met Timmy, but concluded he could be trouble. He would not allow trouble.

"Timmy, I'm sorry to hear about your folks, and you can stay here, but any trouble at all, and I will personally kick you out of here so fast, your feet won't touch the ground till you are in the middle of the road out there. Do you understand me?"

Timmy, with the same dead-eyed stare, replied with a simple, "Yes."

"Good. Now, let's find you a room."

The motel owner was sorry to hear Phyllis and Roger were gone. They had paid him many dollars for the use of his rooms. The money he would miss; them he would not.

Timmy was put in a room two doors down from the office. The owner reasoned if Timmy were anything like his father, he would need to keep an eye on his activities. Two rooms down would be close enough.

With key in hand, Mr. Rayller escorted Timmy to his room. At the door, he turned and handed Timmy the key and the remainder of the money. It was clear to Timmy that Mr. Rayller wanted nothing more to do with him today. Mr. Rayller informed Timmy they would be paying the minister a visit tomorrow.

Timmy, curious, asked, "What do you have to talk to him about?"

Mr. Rayller, surprised by Timmy, said, "Your folks have to be buried."

He turned on his heels and walked away. He'd had enough of Timmy Scott for one day.

The ride home was neither quiet nor peaceful for Shelia. First, she received a stern lecture from her grandfather about having such a smart mouth, and secondly, for having a smart mouth with Timmy. Mr. Rayller now considered Timmy to be either evil to the core or a full-fledged nut. All the way home, Sheila said nothing.

Timmy waited until he saw the car pull away before closing his door. Securely housed in his room, he gave a shout of joy at being free of his parents and, for the most part, adults. He was seventeen years old and free. Now he could talk openly to Nats.

"I got no one telling me what to do. I ain't stuck in that stinking house anymore. I'm free of Dad and Mom, and they got it just the way I dreamed. This is great. It's greater than great."

Yes, it is delicious, isn't it?

Timmy carried on until nearly midnight. He played the TV too loud, soaked in the bathtub, ordered pizza, and simply enjoyed himself. Mourning for his parents was not anywhere close to his mind.

At eight o'clock in the morning, Timmy was awakened by the motel phone; it was Mr. Rayller. Blurry-eyed and barely awake, Mr. Rayller informed Timmy that he would be over to pick him up at ten o'clock to go see the reverend. Timmy answered with a sleepy, "Okay," and immediately hung up without saying goodbye.

At ten o'clock, Mr. Rayller was at Timmy's door, applying four firm knocks. Timmy was still asleep. The knocks increased to fist pounding until Timmy was awake enough to open the door ten minutes later.

Angry, sleepy-eyed Timmy wearing boxers opened the door to an angry, wide-awake Mr. Rayller. Without being invited to do so, Mr. Rayller entered the room. If Timmy had not had the good reflexes to step aside, he would have been shoved out of the way by Mr. Rayller.

With raw anger in his voice, Mr. Rayller said, "Get dressed. You got an appointment with the reverend."

Timmy, now standing with his back to the open door, was about to say something when a voice from behind him said, "Timmy, if you can't watch TV with the sound turned down, find someplace else to stay."

He turned around and came face to face with an angry motel owner. Finding himself between two angry men, Timmy was smart enough to know when to be agreeable.

"Yes, sir, I'm sorry for the noise. It won't happen again." In one smooth motion, he stepped around Mr. Rayller and moved in the direction of the bathroom. "I'll be ready in five minutes," then slammed the bathroom door, leaving the two men looking in his direction.

In the car en route to the minister's office, Timmy dared not say a single word. If he said the wrong thing or anything at all, he would likely be opening himself up for a full verbal attack from Mr. Rayller. Getting verbally beaten to death was not in his immediate plans.

Reverend Andrew Burns greeted them in the parking lot of the church and led them to his office. Seated in a comfortable office chair, Timmy had the reverend across the desk from him and Mr. Rayller, sitting in another chair, beside him. This particular pastoral office was well appointed, with theological certificates and degrees on the walls along with bible verses and dozens of books. The office and the men made Timmy extremely uncomfortable. His heart pounding, palms sweating, and every nerve in his body on edge, Timmy could barely sit still.

To Mr. Rayller, Timmy seemed to be holding up a little too well, not as giddy as the day before, but strange as if he was struggling to be calm.

Whatever is going on with him, it's got him tighter than Dick's hatband. He looks like he's ready to jump out of his skin.

Reverend Burns began the meeting with his condolences and regrets for the loss of Timmy's parents.

"Timmy, I understand neither your parents nor you were churchgoing people, but the elders of the church have authorized me to offer you the use of the church for your parents' funeral. Now, I know this may be a little unusual for you, but a church funeral service would be the best thing to do. Wouldn't you agree that the souls of us all must seek the forgiveness of God?"

Timmy just stared at him as if he had just spoken a mouthful of Greek. When he could finally speak, Timmy asked a devastating question.

"Why in the world should I give them a church funeral? The only time my mother ever attended church was for Mr. Breeker's funeral, and my father never did attend at all, as far as I know. But you want me to give them a church funeral like they were such good upstanding people. Did you know they used to beat up on me as a warm-up for their idea of fun? To tell you the truth, I don't care if you throw them out there in the grass and let the crows pick out their dead eyeballs. I will not agree to a church funeral for them. No sir, not at all."

Reverend Burns sat comfortably in his high-backed office chair and appeared rather relaxed; he should have, he was in his element. However, when Timmy finished his tirade, the reverend looked as if he had been hit in the face with a brick. His eyes bugged out in an abnormal fashion, and his mouth hung slack-jawed. He had just heard more than he had ever expected.

The room fell into silence. The only sound was the ticking of the wall clock opposite the reverend's desk and behind Timmy's head. The small office grew smaller with the passing of each second. Mr. Rayller, sensed a coming explosion between the two, spoke first, before the reverend could unleash an attack of verbal hellfire and brimstones onto Timmy.

"Timmy, your parents are dead and should, out of respect for the dead, be buried in a respectful manner. No matter how you feel, you should never disrespect the dead."

Timmy locked eyes with Mr. Rayller. The hatred Timmy had for his parents was unmistakable and impossible to hide. It could be seen by all present; it was as if evil had filled the room and was not ready to leave without a fight. Timmy didn't give an inch.

"No, I will not agree to a church funeral for them. Not when they did everything in the world they could think of to hurt me. I will not make it appear to anyone that they were nice people."

Having had a few minutes to cool, the reverend now rested both forearms on the desk with hands overlapping each other.

"Timmy, be careful. It is possible that the living can offend the dead, and if that happens, how do you say 'I'm sorry'? They may not be listening. Do the right thing, and give them a Christian burial."

Timmy felt no love for them or anyone else and was not about to give in when he was this close to showing what he really thought of them. Sitting on the edge of his chair, he said, "You people may think you're doing the right thing, but they didn't care about doing the right thing. They only cared about doing what they wanted and whoever they wanted. Well, now it's my turn, and they don't get no stinking funeral."

Mr. Rayller, seeing the impasse for what it was, and that it was a disaster about to happen, said, "Timmy, at least have a graveside service, and then they will be buried quickly."

Timmy's anger was clear, and so was the reverend's. As a last effort, Reverend Burns asked, "Timmy, if you don't allow at least a graveside service, you could be condemning them to hell—"

Timmy, not allowing the reverend to finish, shot to his feet and shouted, "Then let them go to hell."

He turned and stormed out of the office and the church. He was pacing beside Mr. Rayller's car and cursing under his breath when Mr. Rayller came out.

With more confusion in his voice than disgust, Mr. Rayller spoke. "Timmy, if I had known how much of a jackass you really were, I would have never promised your father I would watch out for you. You are the meanest and dumbest kid I have ever met in my life. Now get in the car. We're going to the funeral home."

In the car, Timmy stared straight ahead. He could not believe his father would ever ask Mr. Rayller to watch out for him. Not in a million years. So where did all that come from? These questions and more raced through Timmy's mind, but he said nothing.

At the funeral home, Mr. Rayller had a brief and detailed conversation with Timmy.

Mr. Rayller had parked to the side of the building, in the shade. This also allowed for some concealment from the passing public. He regretted his statement at the church. He should have waited until after the funeral to tell him, but he had lost his temper, and now it was too late. Besides, Timmy needed to know the truth, no matter how much it hurt.

"Timmy, it's time you knew the truth. Roger was not your real father."

Timmy's mind was spinning in all directions. He could no longer resist asking the obvious question. "Okay, so who do you say my real father was?"

Mr. Rayller cleared his throat and began, "Back before you were born, your father, Roger, went to prison for something stupid he did. I don't remember what it was, but he was gone for a few years. While he was up the river, your mother took on odd jobs to make ends meet and partied like there was no tomorrow."

Timmy's face had taken on a stiff, mean look. He didn't like what he was hearing. He wanted Mr. Rayller to get to the name and do it quickly, but Mr. Rayller ignored him and continued at his own pace.

Mr. Rayller's eyes took on a distant look as he looked through the windshield. He continued.

"One of the people she worked for was Bill Breeker. He used to own the newspaper. He sold that paper and then was killed by a tornado the day after the Stones, the new owners, got in town."

Timmy remembered the storm and finding his only living friend dead the next morning. His features softened, and all the pain he had felt then started returning. He didn't want to think about the man he had wished for years was his daddy.

Mr. Rayller spoke softly through his pain.

"Bill hired Phyllis to clean his house and cook his meals. His wife had died some years earlier. Well, along the way, things got personal between them, and before Bill knew what hit him, Phyllis quit and left town. Some nine or ten months later, she sent him a letter telling him she'd had his son. With that letter came a list of demands. Of course, Bill demanded proof, and when the proof came, he was in fact your father. You were made and born before Roger ever got out of prison.

Bill Breeker was your real father, and I know you were the one who found his body first, but he asked me to watch out for you in his last will and testament. The house you grew up in was given to Phyllis, by Bill, so you would always be near to him, but he died before he was able to tell you himself."

The pain in Timmy's heart finally tore through. His eyes filled with tears and overflowed down across his cheeks, dripping off his chin onto his shirt collar. Now he knew why Bill had always been kind to him, and why he loved that old man as much as he hated his parents.

Mr. Rayller, seeing his pain, said, "I'm going to ask you, for Bill's sake, to allow Roger and Phyllis to have a short graveside service before burial, because Bill cared enough for Phyllis to make you. Will you at least do it for Bill?"

The pain that sometimes came with clarity ripped through Timmy like a buzz saw. He easily remembered the casual comfort that had always accompanied Bill Breeker.

With new understanding, he recalled the day he stopped behind the barn at Breeker's place. A place selected by chance to hide and rest while he decided where he was going to run away to. The old man had sat and talked with him until he no longer felt he needed to run away. If he needed a place to hide, he could always go there. Now, it was all so clear why his father hated Bill Breeker. He had known he was not his father, and because of that, he inflicted pain and punishment on Timmy for years.

Through real sobs and deep sorrow, Timmy answered.

"Yes, I'll do it for Mr. Breeker. I will do it for my dad, but no one else."

After a few minutes to allow Timmy to regain his composure, they got out of the car and went inside the funeral home.

After attending to the matters at the funeral home, Mr. Rayller took Timmy shopping. The tornado had destroyed almost all of his clothes and personal belongings, so he basically had nothing. While shopping, Timmy questioned how he was supposed to pay for all this stuff. Mr. Rayller informed him that he, Timmy, had actually paid for everything he had bought.

Offering a general explanation, rather than a detailed one, Mr. Rayller said, "When Bill died, he left a will, and in that will, he left nearly everything he owned to you. He also arranged things so that I am in charge of your inheritance until you are twenty-one."

This answer only brought on more questions. The more questions Mr. Rayller answered, the more questions Timmy asked, until Mr. Rayller decided it would be better to arrange a meeting for him and Timmy with the attorney, after the funeral. This answer did not satisfy Timmy. When Mr. Rayller refused to discuss the issue any further, Timmy stopped asking questions.

For the next two days, Timmy was in his motel room alone. No one came to offer condolences, or even to check on his well-being, that is, with the exception of Mr. Rayller and Nats. Mr. Rayller met him two afternoons for dinner at the Lake Side Diner. At these dinner meetings, Mr. Rayller always kept the meeting short and his dinners light. He still didn't like Timmy's company.

Shelia so despised Timmy, she refused to attend. This did not upset Timmy at all. He felt he had enough trouble having to be around Mr. Rayller and certainly didn't want to have to deal with his "bitchy" granddaughter.

At eleven o'clock on the third day after the tornado, the funeral was held. Timmy arrived at the funeral home dressed in the only suit and tie he had ever owned. He felt like he was on his way to a party, rather than a funeral. The funeral was a closed casket service with no minister present; this was the way Timmy wanted it. By eleven fifteen in the morning, it was clear the fifteen people that showed were all that would be there.

Included in that number were Michael Stone, of the newspaper; Deputy Long, to make sure order was kept; Mr. Rayller, without Shelia, and none of their extended families. Timmy reasoned his relatives were as glad as he was that they were gone. He did not acknowledge Deputy Long as family. He never had and saw no reason to start now.

The purpose for gathering at the funeral home was not for a service, but rather a general meeting point, so everyone was together for the trip to the cemetery. The procession to the gravesite was small in number. The hearse, two of them, family car, carrying Timmy and Mr. Rayller, were followed by a few other cars. At the cemetery, the caskets were positioned over their graves as those in attendance took the few available chairs.

Timmy's chair was positioned at the head of the caskets, exactly in the middle, between the two. No honor guard had been arranged for Roger's funeral, so his being a veteran was not made clear with a flag. This was not an oversight. It was a deliberate decision made by Timmy. He wanted as little respect shown to his parents as possible. The absence of the American flag made Nats happy. To dishonor was his pleasure.

The funeral director gave the parting words over Roger and Phyllis. Near the end of the service, he plucked and crumbled one of the flower blossoms.

Dividing the petals evenly in each hand, he raised his hands above the coffins, saying, "Ashes to ashes and dust to dust …"

Timmy never heard him finish what he was saying, because Big Bobby Watson started crying loudly, directly behind him. This angered Timmy to the point that he stood to his feet and punched Big Bobby Watson in the mouth before yelling at him.

"Shut up! You hated them as much as anyone else."

This momentarily stunned and angered Big Bobby so much, he forgot he was at a funeral. He gave Timmy back as good as he had gotten, and a hundred pounds more, with a short jab to Timmy's jaw. The quick jab put Timmy on his back between the coffins. As if that was not enough, Big Bobby shoved his hand in his jacket pocket with the intentions of drawing his gun, but Deputy Long grabbed his arm while leaning toward him, whispering into his ear.

"What you pull out, you'd better be able to eat, or I will kill you where you stand."

Timmy got to his feet, screaming and cursing at everyone there, and tried to get at Big Bobby again but was restrained by two men from the burial crew. Big Bobby looked at Deputy Long before returning his attention to Timmy.

"You're as dumb as your daddy was and as mean as your whorish mama. Stay out of my face forever, boy."

He then turned and left the gravesite. The funeral service was now over.

Everyone else returned to their cars and left. The last at the gravesite was Timmy. He told Mr. Rayller he would walk back to the motel. He didn't need a ride. Without protest, Mr. Rayller drove away.

Timmy stood and watched as the coffins were lowered and then covered. When the graves were refilled and everyone was gone, Timmy made sure no one was watching.

As Nats had suggested, Timmy unzipped his pants, exposed himself, and urinated at the head position of both fresh graves. He listened, enjoying being left alone. "I hope that cools your thirst in hell."

Satisfied, he zipped himself up and walked away. Now he was happy, or so he thought.

Timmy had elected to ignore the reverend's warning, "Take care not to offend the dead."

CPSIA information can be obtained
at www.ICGtesting.com
Printed in the USA
LVHW081548190422
716634LV00016B/640